WHEN WE HAD SUMMER

WHEN WE HAD SUMMER

JENNIFER CASTLE

HYPERION
Los Angeles   New York

First Edition, April 2023
10 9 8 7 6 5 4 3 2 1
FAC-020093-23048
Printed in the United States of America

This book is set in Adobe Devanagari
Designed by Torborg Davern

Library of Congress Cataloging-in-Publication Data
Names: Castle, Jennifer, author.
Title: When we had summer / by Jennifer Castle.
Description: First edition. • Los Angeles : Hyperion, 2023. • Audience: Ages 12–18. • Audience: Grades 7–12. • Summary: When thirteen-year-old Summer Sisters Daniella, Alaina, and Penelope are about to be separated for the summer after the death of their friend Carly, they vow to complete the bucket list she wrote before she passed.
Identifiers: LCCN 2022009424 • ISBN 9781368081405 (hardcover) • ISBN 9781368081429 (paperback) • ISBN 9781368081542 (ebook)
Subjects: CYAC: Best friends—Fiction. • Friendship—Fiction. • Grief—Fiction.
Classification: LCC PZ7.C268732 Wi 2023 • DDC [Fic]—dc23
LC record available at https://lccn.loc.gov/2022009424
Reinforced binding

Visit www.HyperionTeens.com

SUSTAINABLE FORESTRY INITIATIVE — Certified Sourcing
www.sfiprogram.org
SFI-01681

Logo Applies to Text Stock Only

For Peggy Sweeney, my own Summer Sister
spring, fall, and winter, too

SUMMER SISTERS BUCKET LIST
(aka the SSBL)

<u>RULES</u>

1) All four of us have to agree on each SSBL item.

2) After a Bucket List is written up and signed by all of us, no changes allowed.

3) Not all of us have to do an item together, but it's a lot more fun that way.

4) Doing an item alone is okay, but much less awesome (see #3).

5) If an SSBL item is not checked off one summer, it automatically goes on the list for next summer.

6) SSBL items must be documented with pics or video (hopefully both) on FotoSlam.

7) The last item on an SSBL always has to be the same and we all know what that is, so we're not going to write it here.

8) The SSBL is summer, and summer happens every year forever, so we will do the SSBL every year FOREVER.

We do hereby agree to these rules, blah, blah, blah.

Signed, the Summer Sisters:

Carly McFadden

Daniella Franco

Alaina Calderon

Penelope Abrams

1

WHEN YOU STAY UP ALL NIGHT, THERE'S A POINT when you stop being tired and start feeling kind of indestructible.

Like you could do anything. Leap a tall building. Lift a truck off a little kid. Maybe even fly.

Or hop from one rock to another out toward the ocean without worrying about slipping. Without even looking back to see if your friends were right behind you.

Penny was in that zone. The no-sleep-totally-hyper phase in between being really tired at 4:00 a.m. and passing out at lunchtime, hopefully in the car way past the New Jersey Pine Barrens.

Every year, on the last night of summer, Penny and her friends Carly, Lainie, and Daniella had a sleepover on the screened porch of Lainie's grandparents' house. The house was right across from the beach. They'd drift off sometime after midnight, then wake up early to climb onto the longest jetty in Ocean Park Heights and watch the sunrise.

But this summer, they were thirteen. Officially teenagers. And they'd decided early on that they'd have to do something that fit better with how much older and cooler they were. So this year, *sleepover* meant they'd *sleep* when it was *over*.

"When there's only one day left of summer," Carly had said, "you should be awake for every minute of it, you know?"

Penny agreed completely. Summer was sliding away, like each wave at low tide after it hit the jetty and rushed back out to sea. She hopped onto another rock, breathing in the salty air, which already felt a little colder, a little more September.

"Hey, I can't go that fast!" Daniella called. "I'm carrying important cargo!"

Penny glanced back. Daniella was holding out one arm for balance. Her other arm hugged a giant bag filled with three colors of cotton candy: pink, blue, green.

"Ah, crap! My flip-flop just broke!" Lainie cried.

She stopped to pull it off her foot and held it up in front of her face, eyeing one piece of rubber that had come loose from another. "Really?" Lainie said to the useless sandal. "You made it all summer. You couldn't have held out for, like, another hour?"

"When you start talking to footwear, you know it's time to leave the shore and go back to real life," Carly said, laughing, her hands on her hips, her long auburn hair whipping around her face. Penny could see her freckles, even from seven rocks away. By late August, Carly always had twice as many as she started the summer with.

Penny could still remember the first time she met Carly, when they were six years old. She could actually *see* where it had happened: that stretch of sand down there, in front of Lifeguard Tower 9. Penny had

2

been digging in the sand for an hour, trying to find the little plastic lizard she'd buried the day before. When she finally gave up, she curled into one of her holes and stared glumly at the water.

Then a girl's feet had appeared in front of her, sand stuck to her skin halfway up her calves. "Hi," Carly had said. "What are you looking for?"

"Lost treasure," Penny had mumbled.

"Cool," Carly had replied, nodding her head. "Can I help? I'm good at finding stuff. My dad calls me Eagle-Eye Carly."

A few minutes later, Carly had pulled the lizard from the sand and Penny had tackled her in glee. From there, Penny's memories blurred into meeting Carly's cousin Daniella and then, later that summer, Lainie.

Now, the four of them were moving in a practiced zigzag across the stone shapes they'd all played on in the years since. At first, the jetty was a castle wall and they were princesses and witches and fairies and various flying animals. Then it was a ship, and they were all a crew of famous pirates . . . but nice pirates who stole stuff from other pirates so they could give it back to their owners. It all seemed so silly to Penny now. But in a good, we-were-so-cute kind of way. Once they all got big enough and brave enough, they started leaping across a series of smaller rocks to one huge, flat rock, which was a little separate from the jetty.

Rock Island, they named it. This was their place.

Once Penny stepped onto that rock, she looked out at the horizon, painted with a huge blue-gray stripe across the sky. They still had a few minutes, at least. Penny turned and reached her hand out to Daniella, pulling her (and the cotton candy) onto Rock Island. Then

Lainie scrambled on, the broken flip-flop tucked into the waistband of her sweatpants. Carly came last, gripping the strap of the purse that was strung diagonally across her body.

They arranged themselves facing the horizon, sitting with legs intertwined—a pretzel of limbs.

First, the light changed from blue-gray to gray-pink. The color of the smooth side of a seashell, or the perfect shade of frosted lip gloss.

Penny reached out and tapped the cotton candy bag. "Let's open that baby up!"

Daniella laughed as she ripped open the bag and put it in the center of the rock. They took turns reaching in and pulling out handfuls of fluff. This part of the tradition started four, maybe five years ago. One of them had grabbed a stash of leftover cotton candy on their way out to the jetty, and now the sunrise really wasn't the sunrise without it.

Carly mixed a tuft of pink with some blue and held it up, comparing its colors to the ones in the sky. "Yup," she said. "We got a match."

Penny let the candy turn to crystals in her mouth, sucking on the sweetness, hanging on to it as long as she could before it dissolved. Suddenly there it was: the brightest spot of the highest tip of the sun, glowing like a flame above the ocean.

"Look," Lainie said, and leaned her head against Daniella's shoulder.

That first fiery spark turned into a sliver, then a chunk, then a semicircle. Seagulls shrieked and a truck honked somewhere off in the distance, but the four of them were silent as the sun kept rising.

When Penny saw the lower curve clear the horizon, she whispered, "It always happens so fast."

"Now it's officially today and I totally don't want it to be," Carly added.

"Same," Daniella said, popping the last of the cotton candy into her mouth.

Today meant Penny and Carly and Lainie leaving Ocean Park Heights until next May, while Daniella stayed because she lived here year round.

It meant Daniella would be back in her youth orchestra's first chair oboe spot, and Lainie no longer skateboarding all over town. It returned Carly to the fabulous New York City life she shared online in artsy photographs and original fashion creations. And Penny would once again be "Pikachu," her nickname at school since third grade thanks to having yellow-blond hair and being overweight. She wasn't overweight anymore but the name had stuck, and she couldn't tell anyone how much she hated it.

Worst of all, *today* meant the four of them wouldn't be together again for months and months.

"Okay, down to business," Carly said, and lifted the purse off her shoulder. It was covered in seashells and made a half-pleasant, half-annoying *click-clack* sound when it moved. Carly had saved up prize tickets to get it at the boardwalk arcade five summers ago, the year they'd made their first Summer Sisters Bucket List. *Who the hell actually wins enough tickets to get a decent prize like that?* Penny thought as she looked at the purse. *Carly, of course.*

Now the purse had one purpose only: to hold the list. To keep it safe, folded in quarters on lavender-colored paper torn gently out of a journal. The purse traveled most places Carly did during the summer, and somehow, it always went perfectly with whatever she was wearing. Then again, everything Carly wore went perfectly with everything else she wore. Penny could never quite figure out how she did it.

Carly pulled the list, along with a purple pen, out of the purse. She unfolded the paper and laid it out carefully on the face of the rock. Penny let Lainie and Daniella wiggle in closer to see it.

*

SUMMER SISTERS BUCKET LIST
8th GRADE

✔ Go through the Village Pizza drive-thru on our bikes

✔ Get your ears pierced (or a third hole if ears already pierced)

✔ Make elephant toothpaste and post a video mash-up of it

✔ Watch the sunset from the lighthouse

✔ Ride the Delusion at FunLand and not puke

✔ Firecrackers on the beach

✔ Try waterskiing

✔ Cannonball off the Grove Street bridge (this year for real)

✓ Eat a whole Great White Sundae at Captain Cones

✓ Learn to read tarot cards and then do readings for people at the flea market

✓ Silly String fight on the boardwalk

✓ Trampoline sleepover

✓ Sing at Open Mike Night at the beach pavilion

✓ Go fishing on Lainie's grandpa's boat

✓ Hold hands with a boy

✓ Have a boy win something for you at a boardwalk game

___ See a humpback whale breach (this is the year!)

___ Labor Day cotton candy sunrise (stay up all night this time)

*

"I hate this part," Carly said, drawing a little sad face next to the humpback whale line.

Every single year, they tried and failed to see a whale breach. From Lainie's grandpa's boat or a sunset cruise, even one summer from an actual whale-watching trip. It was Carly's dream to see one. For them to see it all together. *That might be the one thing in the world Carly can't make happen,* Penny thought.

"Can't we just take it off the list?" she asked. "I mean, it's practically impossible to see one. I hate having that unchecked space."

Carly bit her lip. "I hate it, too, but giving up on a Bucket List item is like . . . I don't know, giving up on *us*."

Penny glanced at Lainie and Daniella. They shook their heads, so Penny shook hers, too. "No, you're right," she told Carly. "We can't give up."

"And now we get to do the best part," Carly said, her eyes brightening as she uncapped the purple pen. "Who wants this one?"

They were all silent. *Duh*, they all wanted it. Especially Carly, who, as usual, had come up with most of the list. But this was how they did things. It was the Summer Sisters way.

"Penny should go," Lainie said. "I don't think she's had a turn for a while."

Penny took the pen from Carly and put one hand on the SSBL. The paper felt warm from being in the purse and a little damp from the ocean mist. She reached out and made the check mark. Writing it once the normal way, bottom to top, then tracing it backward top to bottom to make it extra-thick. *Ahhh*, Penny thought. *So satisfying.*

Then Penny signed her name in the empty space below the list, and passed the pen to Lainie to do the same, who passed it to Daniella, who passed it to Carly.

"Selfie time," Carly said after they'd all signed it, her eyes sweeping over their handiwork.

They huddled in tight and Penny held up the SSBL just below her chin. Carly took out her phone and reached out her arm as they all pressed their cheeks, still cool from the chill, close together. Penny glimpsed the four smiling faces on the screen, each one so distinct: Lainie's dark brown skin and short hair. Carly's rusty-gold wisps, escaped from her high ponytail. Daniella's light-brown skin and curls. Penny's own paleness and sun-bleached highlights.

Somehow, though, on that screen they all fit together just right. Four parts of a whole.

Carly took a series of shots, then checked to see how they came out.

"Perfect," she said, then added, "Next year we'll have to crank it up. We'll officially be high schoolers and the SSBL has to be, you know, *worthy*." She got a devious look in her eye. "I might have to start brainstorming earlier than I usually do."

"Let me guess," Daniella said, elbowing her cousin. "You already have."

Carly gave a wicked little laugh. "Maybe."

"What do you have so far?" Lainie asked.

Carly wagged her finger at them. "Nuh-uh. No spoilers."

Penny felt her phone buzz in her pocket with a text message. Probably her mom, telling her to come home now. She had to finish packing, and they had to get on the road to Philadelphia soon.

She could ignore it for a few more minutes. As long as she was here, on Rock Island, at Ocean Park Heights, with her Summer Sisters and the Bucket List, nothing had to change yet.

Suddenly a laughing gull flew by them, low and squawking with its *haaaa* call. They all got quiet, staring at the ocean for what seemed to Penny like a super-long time. The sun was much higher in the sky now. This day had started for real.

Penny closed her eyes and took a deep breath.

"I need to go," she said, standing up.

Her friends rose with her, and they hugged. First one by one, then all together.

"See you later." Penny turned and started walking quickly back up the jetty. *Don't look back, don't look back, don't look back.*

She was stepping onto the sand when her phone dinged with a notification.

FotoSlam: One new post from your friend
CarlyRose212

It was the photo they'd just taken. The caption read:

Best one ever. Bucket List—over and out!
#SummerSisters

Penny laughed and clutched her phone to her chest as she kept walking up the beach. She didn't need to look back. Lainie, Daniella, Carly—and summer—were still with her, and they always would be.

⇒ **2** ⇐

Ten Months Later

LAINIE STARED AT HER GRANDPARENTS, WAITING for them to crack up laughing.

Just kidding! they were about to say.

Any second now.

That's messed up, she'd say. *You don't joke about stuff like that.*

Lainie glanced at Nana, then Papa. Their faces didn't change. Then Lainie turned to her mom, who looked even more sad and serious than she had a minute earlier.

"I know," Nana finally said. "It's big news."

"So this is for real?" Lainie asked, hearing her voice crack.

"Yes," Papa said.

"You can't," Lainie said, shaking her head. "You can't sell the house. And the bakery? I mean . . . No. Just . . . *no.*"

"We talked about this last year, remember?" Lainie's mother said softly. "Your grandparents have decided it's time."

"But nobody's mentioned it since then," Lainie replied. "I figured you'd changed your minds."

Nana looked pained. "We didn't mention it because . . . well, after Carly, we didn't want to upset you."

Lainie felt a jab in her stomach. It still surprised her when someone in her family brought up Carly, because she never did. She couldn't.

All she could say was "So *now* it's okay to upset me?"

Nana came toward Lainie and pulled her into a hug. That special Nana hug that was always just the right amount of squeezing and the perfect level of warmth.

"Oh, mija, we have all summer. We'll make the most of it."

"And we'll need your help getting the house ready to put on the market," Papa added. "There's fifty years of stuff here! It'll be like your own personal yard sale full of treasures."

Lainie shot her grandfather an irritated look, but he simply grinned back.

"Hey, Mami, Papi," Lainie's mom said. "Why don't we go over that paperwork for the bakery now? I think Lainie could use a few minutes to process everything."

They left Lainie alone on the screened porch, the door smacking closed with its signature squeal behind them. How was she supposed to start this "processing"? She stepped up to the screen and pressed her face against it. The little wire squares felt weirdly good on her skin, like scratching an itch she didn't know she had. Out at the beach, the waves swelled, spitting water against the rocks of the jetty.

Her eyes stung with tears at the sight of it.

Had it really been ten months since that morning? When Lainie and her friends stayed up all night and then marched out to Rock

Island, to sign the Bucket List as the sun rose? As if nothing would ever touch them and nothing would ever change?

Lainie watched as the waves kept doing the thing they'd always done. Back and forth, up and down. Did the ocean know about Carly? That she'd had a heart condition nobody knew about, and now she was never coming back to Ocean Park Heights? Or anywhere else, for that matter?

How could the waves keep acting like everything was the same? And what was the point of summer without Carly and the Bucket List, anyway?

"Maybe selling the house is a good idea," Lainie said aloud, even though nobody could hear her and she knew it wasn't true. Not for her, at least.

Suddenly her phone buzzed with a text message alert.

It was from Penny.

are you in OPH yet? meet us at 5:00 you know where

Lainie stared at the words on her screen. They were so . . . normal. She glanced back up at the waves and the jetty and the horizon behind them. Okay. She could do this. Maybe. If she forced herself.

Lainie went to find her skateboard. It was a brand-new one, a fourteenth birthday gift, the deck decorated with a hand-painted multicolored dolphin against a background of purple waves. Lainie's mom had suggested that she break it in on the boardwalk and streets of Ocean Park Heights.

If Penny and Daniella (and the ocean itself) could pretend this was just another summer, maybe she could, too.

★

The Sea Spray Café wasn't simply the big beachside restaurant with the glowing blue sign; it was the beginning of the "fun" part of the Ocean Park Heights boardwalk. Everything on the other side of the Sea Spray was colors and noises and, for Lainie, the heavenly smell of deep-fried Twinkies. The best part was, Daniella's family owned it.

Every year on the first Saturday of summer, Daniella would put a big reserved sign on the bright red picnic table with the yellow umbrella. Right on the corner of the Sea Spray's deck, with a perfect view of all the FunLand rides.

When Lainie got a new calendar each January, she put six dates in right away: her birthday, her grandparents' and parents' birthdays, and the Sea Spray meet-up. Lainie, Carly, Daniella, and Penny would squeal and hug when they saw one another, then order fries and talk about their last days of school. When the fries were gone and nobody wanted to talk about school ever again, Carly would pull out the shell purse and present her ideas for that summer's Bucket List.

As Lainie rode her skateboard down the boardwalk toward the Sea Spray, she could hear, in her head, the sound of Carly opening the shell purse. She could see Carly grinning like she had a huge secret to spill, and that secret was, *This is going to be the Best Summer Ever!*

She told them that every year. Somehow, every year it was true.

Lainie hopped off her deck and stepped onto the Sea Spray patio. Daniella and Penny were already at their table.

Penny glanced up, as if Summer Sisters telepathy had told her to. "Dude!" she exclaimed when she saw Lainie.

Daniella looked, too, and broke into a bright smile, eyes brimming with emotion.

When Lainie reached the table, she leaned in to hug each of her friends, then slid onto the bench next to Daniella. She hadn't seen either of them, in person or live on a screen, since their last group video chat back in January. Ten days before that morning Carly left for school and never came home. It was weird to be experiencing the 3-D versions after all this time.

"Is that the new one?" Daniella asked, admiring the skateboard as Lainie bent to stow it under the table. "It's gorgeous."

"Thanks," Lainie said, sitting back up, looking at Daniella, then Penny. "So . . . um . . . how are you guys?"

Is that okay to ask? she thought. There should be a rule book for these situations. *How to Act When the Coolest Person You've Ever Known Goes and Dies and Everyone Left Behind Has to Hang Out Together.*

"Done with middle school, for one thing!" Penny said, tossing a fry in her mouth. "Aren't you guys excited? Did you see the dress I wore to graduation? I posted some pics yesterday. You didn't put up anything from yours."

"I haven't been on FotoSlam much," Daniella admitted, shrugging.

"Me neither," Lainie added. She couldn't handle the emotional grab bag of FotoSlam lately. You never knew if something was going to make you laugh until you peed a little, or completely hate the human race. Lainie found it was safer to stay away.

"Here." Penny pulled up a photo on her phone and held it up for the other girls to see. "That's me and some of my school friends."

In the picture, Penny was wearing a lavender dress with spaghetti straps. *Whoa.* Penny had *grown.* She was taller and . . . bigger. As in, her dress was staying up and filling out, no problem.

"I know," Penny said, sighing. "I got boobs."

Lainie tried not to look at the evidence at point-blank range in front of her. "Congratulations?"

"I hate them," Penny muttered.

"Don't," Lainie said. "You look amazing in that picture. My class all had to wear a white dress and a big hideous floppy hat. Stupid private girls' school. Here, let me show you."

Lainie pulled her phone out of her hoodie pocket and opened up her photo app. See, she could do this. She was back with her Summer Sisters in Ocean Park Heights and . . .

She felt that jab in her stomach again. She dropped the phone onto the table and put her head in her hands.

"Lainie?" Penny said.

"You okay?" Daniella asked.

What was her problem? She'd waited months to see Daniella and Penny and now look, she was totally ruining it.

"Sorry," Lainie said. "It's just that . . ."

What was she going to say? That it seemed like they were all pretending at something? That Carly should be in that empty space across from her at the table and they should be writing out the new Summer Sisters Bucket List right now?

Okay, what about "Dye a streak in your hair?"

Ooh, I like that, Carly. I've always wanted to do that.

Me too. Any color?

I'm in as long as we all do it together.

Cool, so we all vote yes on this one?

They'd decided on purple, and even though the color faded after only three rides down a water slide, that wasn't the point. They'd always wanted to dye a streak in their hair and now they had.

Finally, Lainie murmured, "I'm sorry . . . I was thinking about—"

"Yeah, me too," Daniella said softly.

"Can we not talk about this right now?" Penny chimed in. "It's going to make us all sad and I can't take any more *sad*."

A new temporary language where *this* and *it* meant *Carly*.

"Same," Lainie agreed, feeling the extra heaviness of her grand-parents' news.

"*More* sad?" Daniella said. "Why? What's going on?"

Penny shook her head. "Nothing," she said. But Lainie could tell she was lying.

They all settled back into that awkwardness. *WTF, is this how it's going to be from now on?*

"You want to go for a walk?" Daniella finally suggested.

"Hell yes," Penny said.

Lainie pushed herself up from the table. Anywhere was definitely better than sitting here another second.

The girls left the Sea Spray Café and hung a left up toward the Anderson's Boardwalk area. Anderson's owned FunLand, the arcade, food and game booths, and a private beach. Lainie paused when they reached the frozen lemonade place that was shaped like a giant lemon. She needed to tell them about her grandparents. The longer she waited, the harder it would be.

Let's get this over with.

"So, guys," Lainie began. "I, uh, found out today that my grandparents are selling the bakery."

"What?" Daniella asked, stopping dead in her tracks.

"When?" Penny chimed in.

"As soon as they can find the right buyer. The house, too, probably

17

in the fall once it's cleaned out. They want to move to Florida. So I guess . . ."

Lainie cleared her throat. She wasn't sure the words would actually come out.

"This will be my last summer here."

Daniella's face. *Ugh, Daniella's face.* She looked like someone had just punched her in the chest. "Oh," she choked out. "That . . . uh . . . really . . ."

"I think the word you're looking for is *sucks*," Penny said.

"Yeah, that pretty much sums it up," Lainie agreed, fighting the urge to pound her fist on the giant lemon. There was a couple waiting in line for their drinks, and they were laughing about something, which made Lainie want to scream in their faces. Why should they get to be happy when her entire world was tumbling down?

"We'll just have to make this summer extra special," Penny suggested, then nudged Daniella. "Right, Dee?"

Daniella let out a long, deep breath, her expression still pained. "Uh, sure. But the thing is . . . " She glanced up toward the top of the Ferris wheel and inhaled, then exhaled again. "I kind of won't be here."

They were all quiet as a huge group of people—two sets of parents and what seemed like a dozen kids—jostled by them on either side.

Once they were gone, Penny asked, "What does *that* mean?"

"I'm doing this six-week music program in Manhattan," Daniella replied, still staring at the Ferris wheel, not looking them in the eyes. "My oboe teacher recommended me for it, and I got accepted."

"Daniella, that's amazing!" Lainie said, forcing a smile. But really, she was thinking: *Great, it's my last OPH summer and you're going to be in New York City instead?* Sure, Ocean Park Heights was Daniella's home and maybe she needed to get away sometimes, but why now? Why *this* year?

"Thanks," Daniella replied, and they all started walking again. "I'm actually going to be staying with Aunt Tina and Uncle Chris."

"Carly's parents?" Lainie asked.

Carly felt strange and clunky on her tongue, and Lainie realized she hadn't said her friend's name out loud in months.

"I know it's a little weird," Daniella said. "But if I stayed in a dorm at the school, it would cost a ton, so this was the only way I could do the program." Lainie could tell from the sound of Daniella's voice that her friend was way less than thrilled about these living arrangements. "Aunt Tina said Zoe's been having a really hard time," Daniella added, "so it'll be good to be there for her, you know?"

"For sure," Lainie agreed, because it felt like the right thing to say.

"Summer in the city!" Penny exclaimed, dramatically putting air quotes around it with her fingers. "Think of all the amazing FotoSlam posts you'll be able to make. You should put up one pic a day. I'm sure you'd get tons of new followers."

"Pen, I think she'll be busy playing the oboe with a bunch of other music geeks," Lainie said, officially annoyed now by Penny's rah-rah reactions. This was *not* something to get all psyched about. This news blew. Hard. And on top of her grandparents' announcement? Lainie felt like her head might explode right there in front of the Milk Bottle Knockdown booth.

"No offense," Lainie muttered.

"None taken," Daniella replied. "You know I embrace my music geek identity."

Lainie gave a wan smile at being forgiven so easily. But that was one of Daniella's specialties.

They'd reached the stretch of boardwalk that was lined with carnival games. Up ahead was the Goldfish Toss, where she'd won her beloved Nemo, then Nemo Jr., then Nemos the Third through Sixth over the years. Next to that, the water-gun race where everyone knew not to take the last spot on the left because the handle was messed up and never, ever won.

Then there was the balloon dart game. It was the hardest to win, but as Lainie and her friends grew taller over the years, had gotten easier. You could play a few games in a row and keep trading up for bigger prizes, like the giant stuffed rainbow llama with the words I ♥ OCEAN PARK HEIGHTS FOREVER embroidered onto its stomach. None of them had ever won the llama, but Lainie had always imagined bringing it home and knew exactly where she'd keep it.

Penny elbowed Lainie. "Maybe we could score jobs here this summer," she said. "That would be fun, right?"

"Yeah . . . but I already have a full-time job working with Nana at the bakery. And I have to help her and Papa purge a thousand years' worth of stuff to get the house ready."

"Well, that doesn't sound fun at all," Penny said, pushing out her bottom lip in a big pout. She was joking, but Lainie could tell she also kind of wasn't.

Daniella stepped between them. "Lainie, that's awesome. Haven't you been begging your grandma to let you officially work in the bakery?"

"For years," Lainie said, sighing. "She promised she'd finally teach me some of her secret recipes."

"Well, that's . . . something," Penny said.

"True. You can come by whenever you want and I'll hook you up," she told Penny, trying as best she could to sound positive, though it wasn't super convincing. "And I'll still have plenty of free time to hang out."

"Cool," Penny said half-heartedly. They'd reached the bumper car ride at the entrance to FunLand, where a guy and girl in uniforms were taking tickets and chatting with each other. "Maybe I'll get a job anyway," Penny added, watching the two employees.

The girls kept walking, and Lainie realized that none of them knew where they were headed, exactly.

"Psssst," Daniella suddenly whispered. "Grumpy Gus alert, two o'clock."

Lainie glanced over and there he was, coming the other way, reading a folded-up newspaper while he walked. All anyone knew about Grumpy Gus was that he'd lived in Ocean Park Heights his whole life. Every day, he strolled up and down the boardwalk with his newspaper, wearing mismatched outfits and barking at anyone who tried to talk to him. He sort of terrified Lainie, and she knew the others felt the same way.

A woman in Grumpy Gus's path was holding a plate of onion rings in one hand, talking on her cell phone with the other. As she gestured in her conversation, a ring fell off the plate and onto the ground, but she didn't notice.

But Gus did.

"Hey, lady!" he shouted at the woman. "The boardwalk's not your personal trash can!"

Before the woman could even turn around, a gull swooped in from nowhere, grabbed the onion ring, and flew away.

Grumpy Gus looked up and scowled. "That's not the point!" he yelled at the bird. "Littering is illegal!"

He shook his head, disgusted, and grumbled under his breath as he stalked away.

Lainie, Penny, and Daniella were all quiet as he passed. Once he was out of earshot, they looked at one another, then cracked up. Suddenly, things felt ever so slightly better.

Before long, the three girls had reached the end of the boardwalk. It stopped abruptly at the border between Ocean Park Heights and the next town over, Pearl Cove, which was famous for being boring.

Daniella took a deep, deep breath, then let it out as she leaned against the railing that divided the boardwalk from the sand. *She's been doing that freaky breathing thing a lot*, Lainie thought as she stepped up next to Daniella and grabbed the metal with both hands, like it was going to take her for a ride and she'd better hold on tight. Then she felt Penny flop against her and noticed how much taller Penny was now. *Also freaky.*

Before she could even think about what she was doing, she rested her head on Penny's shoulder.

Daniella put her arm around Lainie. Lainie put her hand over Daniella's on the railing.

They were quiet for a really long time. Lainie's mind was racing.

I'm angry and sad and this feels bizarre but also really nice, and who's going to talk first?

Without Carly there, they had nobody to say something like, "Get your hands off me, you creep!" And then they'd all giggle.

"So . . ." Lainie finally said, raising her head up off Penny's shoulder. "I guess we're not going to do a Bucket List this summer?"

Daniella got that kicked-in-the-chest look again. "I, uh, wouldn't even know what to put on it."

Penny nodded. "Me neither. And what would be the point? Dee won't be here, and you and I will be busy. We won't have time to run around trying to . . . I don't know . . . have a water balloon fight on the Ferris wheel."

"Right," Daniella said sadly.

Penny laughed quietly. "That was an epic day."

Lainie laughed, too. It was two summers ago. The four of them each got their own cars and tried to hit one another with the balloons. Carly had arranged with the ride operator to let them go on alone, the minute the boardwalk opened.

Just like that, the sadness screamed its way back in, drowning out everything good about that memory. Desperate to change the subject, Lainie asked Daniella, "When do you leave for the city?"

"Tomorrow afternoon."

"So we won't even get to say goodbye?" Penny asked.

"We can say goodbye now," Daniella said. Her voice broke down a bit, and she looked away. "I should probably get home and finish packing. But I'll be back the first weekend in August. And we can video chat all the time."

"We'd better," Penny said, then glanced around. "I think I'll stay for a bit and hang out. Maybe see who's hiring."

"I have to go, too," Lainie said, then scrambled for a good, solid fib. "Papa's bringing the boat in and I promised to meet him at the dock."

"Okay, then," Penny said. "Call me tomorrow."

"Text me whenever," Daniella suggested.

"Let's do a group chat ASAP," Lainie added.

They all nodded, staring at one another. Nobody needed to say it. It was so obvious and loud, Lainie could practically hear it shrieking in her ear.

EVERYTHING HAS CHANGED!

What if, when Carly had left them, she'd taken that strange and amazing magic of the Summer Sisters with her?

3

DANIELLA STARED UP THROUGH THE CAR WINDOW at the buildings, at how they glinted and gleamed in the sunlight.

That gleam was everything she loved about being in the city. It was energy and possibility and people-watching and Carly and—no. *Not Carly.*

Honnnnnnnnk.

Daniella jumped and turned around in her seat. The man driving the taxi behind them was pissed off and clearly not afraid to show it. He leaned on the horn again.

"Uh, Dad," Daniella said, "I don't think you can just stop here."

"It's Manhattan," Daniella's father said as he clutched the steering wheel. "You have to fight for your right to unload a car."

Honnnnnnnnk. The cabdriver was now banging on his own steering wheel and shouting something in a language Daniella didn't recognize, but it was definitely not friendly. Daniella felt her heart start to flutter and her throat tighten.

She took a deep breath and closed her eyes, remembering what Dr. Richards had taught her. *Picture the forest. Deep and thick and green. Birds chirping. The breeze—*

Honnnnnnnk.

"Why don't you hop out here?" Daniella's dad suggested. "I'll park in a garage and bring your bag up."

Daniella grabbed her oboe case and threw open the car door, launching herself at the sidewalk. She kept her head down as she ran, convinced the angry cabdriver was going to start screaming at her. When she reached the paved courtyard of the apartment building, she paused for a moment, half expecting Carly to come running through the set of glass doors from the lobby. Grabbing Daniella into a hug so tight it would hurt, but in a good way.

Reality: That was not going to happen again, today or ever. The thought of it made Daniella nearly double over, clutching her oboe case. She might have started sobbing right there if someone hadn't called out "Daniella!" in a bright, familiar voice.

It was the doorman, stepping into the courtyard to greet her.

"Hi, Joe," Daniella replied, swallowing hard.

Joe had worked in Carly's building since before the girls were born. He'd watched Carly grow up and she called him Uncle Joe as a joke, but also not as a joke. He was the one who waited with her for the school bus every day and taught her how to Rollerblade in the basement. When they were six, Daniella was so jealous that Carly had a Joe, she decided she needed one, too. She still remembered the fit she threw when her mom refused to hire a doorman for their house.

"It's great to see you," Joe said. He paused, his cheerful expression flickering into something darker and sadder. Daniella recognized it from watching him at Carly's funeral. It was like one of those lenticular pictures that change when you tilt it, but now Joe was smiling again.

"You too," Daniella murmured.

"The McFaddens said to send you right on up when you got here."

Joe pressed the elevator button for Daniella, and she found herself waiting for the doors to slide open so Carly could pop out.

Dear Brain: You'd better stop this crap right now.

She stepped into the elevator and glanced at herself in the one mirrored wall. At the outfit she'd carefully picked out, trying to find the most "city-ish" look she could (denim miniskirt, floral boho blouse). Every Thanksgiving, Daniella and her parents would visit overnight to spend the holiday with Carly and her family. Daniella's dad was Carly's mom's brother. They'd all get up early to find a spot to watch the Macy's Thanksgiving Day parade. The next morning, they'd go ice skating at Rockefeller Center and see the windows at Saks Fifth Avenue.

Carly loved to style Daniella in some of her clothes and use her tricked-out camera to take photos of their day doing touristy things, pretending she was a fashion photographer. Riding down this elevator, they'd check themselves out in that mirrored wall.

"Look at us," Carly would say. "We're awesome."

And Daniella always knew that in that moment, with Carly, she was.

As the elevator approached the sixth floor, Daniella's eyes swept over the empty, Carly-less space next to her in the reflection and felt her throat closing up again. She couldn't do this. There was no way she could spend the summer here. Not where everything around her was a place Carly used to be and wasn't anymore. Why had she ever thought this would work? What had she been thinking? She could just drop out of the music program. She could—

Ding!

The elevator stopped and the doors opened.

Aunt Tina, Uncle Chris, and her cousin Zoe were waiting on the other side. A family missing a piece. Daniella felt her throat grow tight.

"There she is!" Aunt Tina cried, taking Daniella's hand and pulling her out of the elevator. "Ready for her NYC adventure!"

Aunt Tina hugged her first, then Uncle Chris.

"Where's your dad?" Tina asked.

"He should be here any minute with my giant suitcase," Daniella said, surprised that her voice didn't crack. She glanced over at Zoe, who was leaning against the wall and staring at her. Zoe was only two years younger than Daniella and Carly, but she always seemed like a totally different species from her sister. The only thing Carly and Zoe had in common was that auburn hair, although Zoe kept hers short.

"Zoe, aren't you going to say hi to your cousin?" Uncle Chris asked.

Zoe stayed frozen for a few long moments, that laser gaze trained at Daniella. Then, suddenly, she threw herself forward, wrapping her arms tightly around Daniella's waist. Maybe a little too tightly.

"Come on," Zoe finally said as she drew away. "I'll show you my new bed."

Daniella followed her cousin into the apartment, her aunt and uncle trailing behind. Through the living room and down the hallway, and then before Daniella could prepare herself, they were passing the door to Carly's room. It was closed, even though a red sign on the door read COME IN! WE'RE OPEN! in big white letters. Carly had bought it at a flea market in Ocean Park Heights two, or maybe three, summers ago. Daniella looked the other way and kept going until Zoe opened the door to her own room.

"Voilà!" Zoe said.

The tiny space was almost completely taken up with a bunk bed.

"I'm on the top," Zoe said. "Obviously."

"Obviously," Daniella echoed.

"Mom said, this way I can have sleepovers all the time. Starting with you. This will be like a sleepover that lasts all summer!"

A sleepover that lasts all summer. Aunt Tina had said the same thing to Carly and Daniella, the first year Carly came to stay at the shore on her own for most of July and August. But it had been more than a marathon sleepover. It had given Daniella an almost-twin—five months older than her, but sometimes they pretended it was only five minutes. A taste of what it was like not to be an only child. Even when they got on each other's nerves and argued over stupid things like forgetting to flush the toilet or borrowing a barrette without permission, Daniella secretly loved it.

Zoe showed Daniella the drawers she'd emptied out for her, the chair she'd set up for Daniella to practice her oboe. Her eyes brimmed with excitement.

Daniella suddenly got it. Why she needed to spend most of the summer in New York. Carly would want her to be there for Zoe, even if staying with her family was going to be hard and strange and sad. Zoe had lost her sibling and Daniella had lost the person she most thought of as one.

They both needed the same thing. *I'm not sure Zoe will ever feel like a sister*, Daniella thought, *but I can totally try to be one for her.*

✳

It was midnight, and Zoe was snoring like a sputtery boat engine.

Outside, a siren screeched. Cars honked, probably by more pissed-off drivers shouting in every possible language. Nighttime city sounds were so different from the crickets, cicadas, and distant waves she listened to at home every night, during the hours it took her to fall asleep.

Earlier, after Daniella's dad arrived with her suitcase, they'd all had a big Chinese takeout dinner together. Then he kissed Daniella on the top of her head and headed home to Ocean Park Heights.

Now she was huddled into Zoe's bottom bunk. Wide-awake. Trying to do the breathing Dr. Richards had taught her.

In for four. Hold for seven. Out for eight.

Four-seven-eight. Four-seven-eight. Toss, turn, repeat.

Usually, at this point, Daniella would prop her phone next to her pillow, dial up the dumbest online video she could find, and hate-watch it until she drifted off. But she didn't want to wake Zoe, and she couldn't sleep with earbuds in.

Great. And now she was kind of hungry.

Daniella swished out of bed as quietly as she could, then opened the door just wide enough for her to slip through. Carly's voice was in the back of her head as she padded to the kitchen: *Come on, I know there's half a pie in here somewhere.*

That was another one of their traditions. The night after Thanksgiving, she and Carly would raid the fridge for desserts.

There was no pie, but there was a carton of milk and some fortune cookies left over from dinner. Daniella ate and drank standing at the counter, reading the fortunes.

A cynic is only a frustrated optimist.

You will know it when you see it. It will know you when it sees you.

"Oh, bite me," she said to the little slips of paper, tossing them in the trash. She cleaned up the crumbs and put away the milk, making sure to destroy all of her snack-scarfing evidence.

She started tiptoeing back down the hallway, but her feet stopped halfway to Zoe's room. In front of that closed door.

COME IN! WE'RE OPEN!

She wanted to go in so badly, it hurt. Also, she never wanted to go in, ever.

Then Daniella heard footsteps and she froze, heart racing again. A shadowy, bathrobed figure stood at the end of the hallway: Aunt Tina. She shuffled closer and Daniella could see her face. A crease straight down the middle of her forehead. Eyes red from crying. Dark circles beneath them—circles her aunt had never had before.

Now they were both standing outside Carly's door. Tina smiled slightly, glanced at the sign, then reached out and grabbed the doorknob. She turned it, pushed the door open, then nodded toward the room before continuing on to the kitchen.

Daniella hesitated for a brief moment. Then she stepped inside and closed the door behind her, switching on the light.

It almost took her breath away, how nothing had changed. Like no time had passed since Thanksgiving. Carly could be in the bathroom right then. She could pop in any second, wearing her dad's old college jersey as a nightshirt, and say, "It's only twelve? Bruh, the night's just getting started."

Carly's bed was made, but the pillows were too perfectly arranged. Daniella knew her cousin would never have set them up that way. She liked to throw them and let them land wherever. Several strings of fairy lights hung on one wall, with miniature clothespins that each held a photo. Daniella spotted the one from that morning last summer, all of them celebrating the Bucket List.

Her heart pounded faster and her throat started to close again. She couldn't draw in a deep enough breath.

Don't start hyperventilating now, she warned herself. *Aunt Tina will hear. Also, Carly would freaking hate it.*

She crawled onto Carly's bed, closed her eyes, and started doing her deep breathing. *Four-seven-eight. Four-seven-eight.* She pictured her forest. Then she pictured a knight holding a sword, dressed head-to-toe in black armor, hiding behind a tree. That was Anxiety Man.

This is my forest! Daniella yelled at him (in her mind). *I'm in control and you don't belong here, so get the hell out!*

Amazingly, after she repeated that a few more times, he did.

The whole forest scene with Anxiety Man was embarrassing. It made her feel childish and silly, but it usually worked. She could control her panic attacks now, unlike when they'd first started a month after Carly died. Dr. Richards had really helped her.

Daniella kept breathing, staring at the ceiling, her eyes searching out patterns of shadows against filtered light from outside. Wondering if they were the same ones Carly had seen when she went to bed each night.

Once her heart felt like a normal beating heart, instead of a thing on the verge of exploding, Daniella got up and walked over to Carly's desk. All her school textbooks and binders were arranged in a definitely non-Carly way. Carly always lined up her binders in rainbow order. Daniella knew this because she'd thought it was so cool, she'd started doing it, too.

A giant bulletin board above the desk was covered in pages torn gently from fashion magazines. Designs that Carly liked and would re-create with her own spin, either from store finds or sewing her own clothes. She had an old dress form that she used for putting together those outfits. Where was it? Daniella scanned the rest of the room, then spotted it half-hidden in the corner, draped with fabrics and vintage clothing.

Daniella went over and touched the edge of the faded black velvet jacket that was hanging on the dress form's shoulders. She remembered Carly texting a photo of herself wearing the jacket, on the day she discovered it, with the message *Thrift store score!*

Then Daniella saw the purse.

The shell purse.

Strung diagonally across the dress form the same way Carly always wore it.

Daniella reached for the purse and as it moved, it made that familiar clinking noise, and she drew her hand back. The purse was only halfway zipped. Daniella could see a folded sheet of paper inside. *Last summer's Bucket List,* she thought. *Last summer when everything was still okay.*

She turned away from it, her eyes stinging. Her throat tightening again.

A car honked loudly outside and Daniella froze, that morning last September reaching out, pulling her close.

The four of them on the jetty. Cotton candy and the waves and someone's broken flip-flop. The Summer Sisters signing their names and watching the sun come up. If someone told Daniella she could live inside one moment for eternity, that's what she'd pick.

She turned and went back to the shell purse. Slid the zipper all the way open. Pulled out the paper, and unfolded it as carefully as possible, like it was an ancient artifact.

Daniella scanned the page, excited to see Carly's handwriting.

Wait. No.

This wasn't what she thought it was.

★

SUMMER SISTERS BUCKET LIST
9th GRADE (!!!)

____ Finally see a humpback whale breach (come on, universe)

____ Watch the sunset from a rooftop with a cute guy

____ Perform in public until we've collected enough money to buy lunch

____ Kiss a boy

____ Win the giant rainbow llama at the balloon dart booth

____ Go parasailing

____ Take a photo booth pic with Grumpy Gus

____ Finish a Titanic sundae at Captain Cones

____ Chalk art a whole driveway

___   Late night 80s movie marathon

___   Create our own hashtag and make it go viral

___   Make a music video

___   Go to Candy Universe and buy one piece of candy from EVERY SINGLE barrel, then slowly eat them during the rest of the summer and give each a rating.

___

___

*

A new Bucket List. Carly really *had* started one.

Daniella put the paper on the desk and stared at it. Then she glanced up at the photo of the Summer Sisters from last Labor Day.

She didn't know what to do with this thing. But she *did* know whom she had to share it with.

Daniella took out her phone and snapped a photo.

⪢ 4 ⪡

FOR PENNY, PUBERTY HAD ONLY ONE UPSIDE SO FAR: it meant she got her own room at her family's beach house.

Okay, it wasn't a room, exactly. Most people would call it half an attic, maybe a loft if they were being fancy, with a futon tucked into one corner and a small dresser in the other. A musty space up a narrow staircase, where the ceiling was only a few inches from your head and the dormer window didn't even open all the way.

But Penny called it heaven. No more sharing a room with her brothers, no more locking the door and frantically changing clothes before someone started banging to come in. Penny's older brother, Nicholas, was sixteen and everything he did, everything he owned, everything he touched actually, smelled disgusting. Her younger brother, Jack, who'd just turned twelve, always stayed up late gaming on his laptop, muttering "Bro!" or "Dude!" into his headpiece microphone every few minutes.

Penny would have slept in the bathtub this summer if it meant having some privacy.

The best thing about the low, slanted attic ceiling: It was great for posters. Or rather, *a* poster, and Penny had bought the one she knew would make her new space perfect. It was the main art from her favorite animated series, *Tomcat Vigilante*.

On day three at the shore, with everything else in the house unpacked, Penny was ready to add that finishing touch. She sat on her futon and pulled the poster out of its cardboard tube, then unrolled it slowly, careful not to make a single nick in the paper. With one hand on the top and one holding the bottom, Penny took a moment to admire its awesomeness.

She gasped out loud when she saw it.

There was Tomcat, in all his half-boy, half-feline glory. And there was Tomcat's sidekick, a striped kitten-girl hybrid named, well, Kitten Girl, known for her curvy figure and airhead personality. But someone had taped *Penny's face* on Kitten Girl's body. Cut out from a copy of her yearbook photo, which on top of everything was the worst picture taken of her *ever*.

Penny knew what it meant to feel your blood boil. She knew about volcanoes erupting in the pit of her stomach and her brain imploding into fireballs. Every metaphor for feeling rage—as the sister of two brothers, she'd been there. She'd learned how to handle it. But this was different.

This, she felt throughout her whole body at once as a combination of hatred and hurt. They'd gone too far, messing with the one special thing she'd brought to the beach house that summer, her connection to a show that had helped her through her grief over Carly. And then . . . that body. The huge chest and the big butt. Was that how her brothers saw her? Was that how *everyone* saw her?

Penny stormed downstairs to the living room, where Nick and Jack were swallowed up in beanbag chairs in front of the TV. They took one look at her and turned to each other, smirking.

"Been decorating your new room?" Nick asked Penny, raising one eyebrow, straight out of the evil supervillain handbook.

Penny opened her mouth to let out the string of creative curse words she had ready, but something stopped her. She knew they were waiting for her to do this. That it was part of the fun. She also knew there was nothing she could say or do that would make them understand or even feel bad for a single second. Besides, Penny had already peeled off the photo—carefully, so carefully—and the poster was now in its place on the wall, looking exactly how she'd imagined it.

"Yup," Penny replied to Nick. "And it looks *amazing.*"

This was where, in the past, she'd text Carly to slam her brothers, and Carly would shoot back with some venting about her little sister, Zoe. Daniella and Lainie didn't have siblings, so Carly was the one who understood.

Now Penny could only offer Nick her best smile, then go find her mom. No way was she going to give him and Jack what they wanted. Also, there was a definite possibility that she'd open her mouth and instead of yelling at them, she'd burst out crying.

Penny heard her mom's voice from outside and hovered at the screen door in the kitchen. "I don't buy it . . ." her mother was saying. "Why can't you come early Saturday morning?"

Mom was sitting at the picnic table in their backyard, hunched over her phone.

"Lisa," Penny's dad said through the phone speaker. "I told you, if they call a weekend meeting, I have to be there. This is just going to be one of those summers where work is more important than going to the beach."

"Don't be an ass, Adam. It's not *going to the beach*. It's spending time with your kids. And me."

"Oh, please. You're the one who said you wanted space!"

"Not if you're going to use it as an excuse to check out of our family!" Penny's mom snapped.

Penny stepped away from the screen door. A few months ago, she would have interrupted this conversation. She hated it when her parents fought. But they'd been doing it so much lately, and Penny was tired of trying to stop it. Maybe if she let them finish each time, they'd finally get all argued out. Then their family would be okay again.

She backed herself into a corner where the kitchen counters made an L shape, then slid down to the floor and hugged her knees. Maybe getting a job was a bad idea; her mom might need her around. For a few long minutes, she listened to her brothers talking to their gaming characters ("Don't do it, man! Don't open that door!") and her mother's voice getting higher and sharper on the phone ("I am so tired of this!").

This is not how it's supposed to be, Penny thought. *The Summer Sisters should all be here. My dad should be here. I should be at the beach by now or eating a deep-fried Oreo on the boardwalk.*

But even if she had the energy to get up off the kitchen floor, the beach or the Oreo wouldn't be the same. Nothing would be the same, so why bother?

Ding!

Penny's phone was in her pocket, so the vibrating message alert made her leg and foot rattle. She pulled out the phone and saw that Daniella had texted a picture to both Penny and Lainie.

She opened it and zoomed in. It was a photo of a Bucket List she'd never seen before, scribbled in very familiar handwriting.

Carly, Penny thought, then had to blink a few times. *No, that's not possible.*

Another text from Daniella: Found this in Carly's room

Then, in a separate bubble: I know we said we wouldn't do an SSBL this year but I keep thinking she'd want us to do this one. Am I crazy?

Penny read through the Bucket List, picturing Carly starting it in the dead of winter. Always keeping an eye on summer and the Summer Sisters. Looking at it now was like feeling Carly's hand grabbing hers. Yanking her away from the hard, cold tiles beneath her.

Come on, Carly was saying. *Get UP! You and I had special secret plans for this summer, remember?*

Penny remembered.

So she got up.

Then she typed a reply to Daniella's message: No you're not crazy

Daniella: So are you in?

WAY in. Penny added an excited-face emoji. Then about thirteen exclamation points, just to be clear.

Lainie's reply zipped in right after Penny's. OMG me too, can't believe you found this

Daniella wrote, Who can talk tonight so we can make a plan?

After a handful of texts back and forth, Penny, Daniella, and Lainie had set a time for a group video chat. Penny navigated back to the photo of Carly's new Bucket List. She scanned the items and could almost hear Carly reading them out loud at their Sea Spray Café table. Every item whispered *yes* and *let's go* and *summer summer summer*.

Penny followed the whispers. Out of the kitchen, into the backyard, past her mom, who was still arguing with her dad. She opened the garage and there was her aqua-blue beach cruiser bike, coated with a thin layer of dust from a winter of waiting.

She wiped a cobweb away from the seat and threw her phone into the coconut-shaped cup holder on the handlebars. Penny hopped on, riding slowly at first, then fast and confidently, toward Anderson's Boardwalk.

⋆

"How many years has your family been coming to Ocean Park Heights?"

Keri, the woman who did all the hiring for Anderson's, clicked her pen as she looked over Penny's job application. They were sitting across from each other in peach-colored chairs in a peach-colored office.

"Ten years, I think," Penny said. "My parents bought our beach house when I was little. I honestly don't remember any other kind of summer."

"*Is* there any other kind of summer?" Keri asked, smiling as she put down Penny's application. "You seem like an excellent candidate, and I'd be happy to have you join our team. Let me see what we still have available."

Penny watched as Keri turned to her computer, fingers tapping the keyboard and eyes darting back and forth across the screen.

"Hmm," Keri said. "We do most of our hiring in late May and early June, so at this point in the summer, we don't have much to offer . . . Oh, wait. I do see something, but it's only part-time. Is that okay?"

"Part-time is perfect," Penny said, sitting up straighter. *This job thing is actually happening!*

"I can offer you a position as a beach attendant . . ."

"Oh—" Penny felt herself deflate.

Keri smiled knowingly. "Not what you had in mind?"

"Well, since I don't really have any work experience, I figured I'd be filling arcade games with prizes or, like, putting sticks into hot dogs in a back room somewhere. Beach attendant is . . . uh . . ."

Keri laughed. "You can say it. Intense, right? I know that job has a reputation for being very, very hard," she said. "Let me tell you, I've done it . . . and it *is* hard. It's like waiting tables in that you have a lot of interaction with people." She glanced at Penny's application again. "I see you've done some volunteer work at a retirement home. So you're actually better qualified than most."

Penny thought of the uniforms the beach attendants wore. White, formfitting polo shirts that showed every curve, and red shorts that needed to be much longer. At least on her.

Maybe there were other jobs in Ocean Park Heights. She could keep looking. How could she turn down the offer without sounding like a spoiled brat and ruining her chances of getting hired next year? Penny started putting together an excuse-apology combo in her mind.

There was a sudden knock at the door. "Yes?" Keri called out.

The door opened and a boy poked his head in.

Black hair with shaggy, dyed-bleach-blond bangs. Intense eyes. And now, a dazzling smile.

"Ah," the boy said. "Sorry, Keri, I didn't know you were in a meeting."

"No, it's fine, come on in," Keri said, waving the boy toward her. Penny saw that he was wearing the exact uniform she'd been picturing. But it looked good on him. Better than good.

"Penny, this is Dex Nakashima," Keri continued. "You'd actually be working with him. He's a beach attendant, too."

Dex turned to Penny and flashed another luminescent smile as he extended his hand. "Hey, Penny. Welcome to the team."

"She hasn't accepted the job yet," Keri told him.

"I'll take it," Penny heard herself say. A little too fast. A little too enthusiastically.

Dex's smile widened.

Oh crap, Penny thought. *What did I just do?*

WHEN DANIELLA'S PHOTO OF THE BUCKET LIST landed on Lainie's phone, Lainie was lost in 1984.

May 14, 1984, to be exact. The day her grandmother officially opened Dulcie's Bake Shop in a corner storefront three blocks from the beach.

The photo was faded and a little blurry, but Lainie could see how brightly Nana was beaming as she stood next to the display case full of pastries. She was holding up a five-dollar bill from Dulcie's very first customer (aka their next-door neighbor Fred, but he still counted).

Lainie was supposed to be cleaning fingerprints off the glass cookie jars, but it was more interesting to examine the collage of photos on the wall above the cash register. There was a shot of Nana in front of the bakery oven, holding a baby that, unbelievably, was Lainie's mom. Then one of her mom as a little girl mixing up a bowl of batter, and another as a teenager in an apron working the counter. Pictures of friends and neighbors and decades of a life in Ocean Park Heights.

How can they just say goodbye to all this? Lainie thought.

"Hey, you! Don't get distracted." It was Nana's voice, over her shoulder. "There's a possible buyer coming in today and everything needs to be clean."

Lainie raised her eyebrows and glanced at the cookie jar, fantasizing about smearing it with chocolate-covered fingers. "What, so if the place isn't spotless, they won't want to buy it?"

Nana shook her head and wagged a finger. "I see where that brain of yours is going and . . . nuh-uh. Don't even think about it."

Damn it, she's good. "You really believe I'd try to sabotage you selling the bakery?"

"Okay," Nana replied, softening into a smile. "Maybe you wouldn't try. But you'd fantasize about it."

Lainie snorted a laugh. "And what would happen if I found a way to pull it off, and nobody buys the bakery? Would you have to stay through next summer, and maybe even the summer after that? And then, you know, forever?"

Nana searched Lainie's face. "Or until you can run it yourself? Is that what you want, mija?"

How was her grandmother so creepy-good at reading her mind?

Lainie just shrugged, thinking, *Yes. No. Maybe?* She returned to that opening-day photo and poured herself into it.

"Do you ever wish you could go back in time to that moment?" she asked Nana, pointing to younger-Nana in the picture.

Nana peered at her old self. "I don't need to. Those days are always right here." She put her hand over her heart.

Lainie rolled her eyes. "Easy for you to say. You and your heart will be living it up in Florida. I'll be stuck in boring upstate New York with Mom and Dad." *And the friends I only know from online,* Lainie added in her head. She ran a Discord server for skater kids, and sometimes

45

they were the only people her age she could really talk to. Except in Ocean Park Heights, where Daniella, Penny, and Carly made friendship feel easy . . . and for two months a year, she didn't feel so alone.

"You can stay with us in Vero Beach for as long as you want each summer," Nana said. "And I'm sure your friends will invite you down the shore for a visit."

"That's one hundred and ten percent not the same."

Nana stared at Lainie, then ruffled her hair. "I know. But things change, and you have to change with them."

Lainie scoffed, then dropped the rag she was using to clean the cookie jars and started walking toward the door to the back room. She didn't want advice or words of wisdom. She just wanted her family to understand how hard and truly horrible all of this was for her.

Suddenly Lainie's phone dinged. She stopped outside the kitchen door to check it and saw the message from Daniella with the photo of Carly's Bucket List. That unmistakable handwriting in the legendary purple pen.

so are you in? Daniella had texted. For Lainie, there had never been an easier question to answer.

"Everything okay?" Nana asked.

Lainie looked over at her grandmother, tears welling in her eyes. She nodded.

That Dulcie's opening day photo was the past, a dead end. This photo on her phone, though. The Bucket List. It was the past and also, somehow, the present and the future. Or at least, the next two months. That was enough future for now.

Lainie had just finished texting with Daniella and Penny when the bakery door jingled open. There was a wave of high-pitched voices, and the lower, musical tones of Nana greeting them. She sighed and braced herself for the morning rush.

The next two hours were a blur of customers. Lainie could tell who was a vacationer, who was "summer people," and who was a year-round local. The locals were the ones she'd seen playing cards on her grandparents' screened porch and other faces she knew from the boardwalk and shops and restaurants. Did they know her, too? Next summer, would they notice she wasn't here anymore?

It was busy and loud and exhausting, but she loved working side by side with Nana. Nana took the orders and used her own shorthand language, sometimes with colorful hand motions (jazz hands plus peace sign fingers = one dozen) to let Lainie know what to pull from the display case or refrigerator. This way, Nana could sit when she needed to and Lainie did all the bending, lifting, and twisting.

They'd just served their way through a line of customers and finally—at least for a few minutes—had a break. Nana went into the back to take something out of the oven. The bakery was empty except for two people sitting at the table in the far corner. Lainie tried to scan them without being obvious. A woman in a business suit and spiky high heels. A guy in a leather jacket and expensive-looking sneakers. She didn't remember handling their orders.

"Hi, folks," Lainie called to them. "Can I get you anything?"

"We're looking for Dulcie," the woman said. "I'm Christina Hamady? We have an appointment, but we're a bit early."

Heat flushed through Lainie's body as she realized who these people must be. Could she tell them Nana wasn't there? Could she say Nana had changed her mind about selling and they needed to please go away and never come back?

"She's in the kitchen. I'll get her for you."

Lainie found Nana resting in a chair, her head against the wall.

"Nana," she whispered. "That buyer person is here. Although he looks more like a movie star than someone who wants to run a bakery."

"Oh my!" Nana exclaimed, standing up and smoothing her skirt. She bounced up and out of the kitchen so fast, she let the door swing into Lainie's face.

Lainie watched from the small round window in the door as Nana shook hands with the man. He flashed her a smile that was too white and bright. Then he peered at the walls and ceiling, and moved his face close to the huge glass windows to examine those, too. He ran one finger along the counter and touched all five of the tiny tables in the seating area.

Jeez, dude, Lainie thought. *Where are your white gloves?*

When Nana led her guests toward the kitchen, Lainie backed up and grabbed a rag, pretending to be wiping down the front of an oven.

"Mr. Mason, this is my granddaughter, Alaina," Nana said when they came in the door.

Lainie knew she should offer her hand or at least put on a friendly smile. She wasn't going to.

"Hello," she said stiffly. In her head, she added, *FYI, jerk, you are NOT going to turn Dulcie's Bake Shop into a place that charges five dollars for a plain old cup of coffee or sells only one very specific thing, like macarons. I will* not *let you.*

"Honey," Nana said to Lainie, "Mr. Mason owns two cafés in Chicago. They're very well known!"

"He's a key player in the restaurant world out there," the Realtor added. "We're lucky that he's relocating to OPH."

Mr. Mason smiled as he glanced around the kitchen. "*I'm* the lucky one. This place is a treasure. I was just telling your grandmother that if I bought Dulcie's, I'd want to keep everything on the menu. Maybe add some gourmet grab-and-go sandwiches and salads, easy things for people to bring to the beach. A few craft drinks, too. And I would paint. Probably bring in some new tables and chairs."

"Oh, we've needed new tables and chairs for years," Nana said. "And the last time we painted, Lainie was a baby."

As Mr. Mason did a slow lap around the kitchen and Nana's office, taking in every inch of the space, Nana came over and put her arm around Lainie's shoulders. Lainie wanted to relax into her, knew she needed to, but she kept her back squared and stiff.

Finally, Mr. Mason shot the Realtor a meaningful look and pointed to the door.

She nodded and turned to Nana. "Mrs. Muñoz, do you mind if we go out front so we can talk in private?"

Nana gestured for them to go ahead. While they were out of the room, Lainie repeated a little prayer in her head. *Please make them walk away and never come back. Please make them walk away and never come back.*

But a few minutes later, Mr. Mason burst through the door with a bright smile on his face.

Hey, higher power, Lainie thought. *You suck!*

"Mrs. Muñoz," he began, "I can tell you right now that I'd like to buy your bakery. But I have a few conditions."

"Oh?" Nana asked, raising her eyebrows.

"First, would you let me keep the Dulcie's name?"

Nana let out a relieved laugh. "Of course."

"And would you let me work with you on the transition?"

Nana stopped laughing, bemused.

"I don't see why not. That would make sense, yes?"

"A lot of sense," Mr. Mason said. "And finally . . ."

He turned and opened the door. A teenage girl stepped through it. She appeared to be a couple years older than Lainie, with short brown hair in a pixie cut. Heavy black eyeliner, nose ring, pierced septum. A half-bored, half-resentful expression to complete the look. She looked Lainie up and down then rolled her eyes, discreetly enough that the adults didn't see it. But Lainie definitely did.

"This is my daughter, Sasha," Mr. Mason said. "If I buy the bakery, I'd like her to have a job here this summer as part of the transition."

Lainie shot Nana a desperate, panicked glance that said, *No. Freaking. Way.*

Nana didn't see it. She gazed at Sasha, then broke into a friendly smile and reached out to take the girl's hand.

⋛ 6 ⋚

DANIELLA LISTENED TO THE WAIL OF A SIREN through the tiny bathroom window, super loud, very close, catching her breath as the noise started fading into the distance.

"Daniella?" Dr. Richards asked on the other end of her cell phone. "Are you still there?"

She shook herself back to the here and now. "Yes, sorry."

"I was asking, how do you feel about the skills we just went over? Can you realistically use them today, if you need to?"

"I think so," Daniella replied, taking three slow steps toward the bathroom door, turning around, then taking three steps toward the tub. She'd been pacing like this for the whole call.

"Good. I'll look forward to hearing about it when we have our video session next week. Until then, you can text me anytime."

Daniella sank down onto the closed toilet seat. "Thanks for being able to talk to me this morning," she told Dr. Richards, even though she knew her mom had arranged this weeks ago.

After she and Dr. Richards said goodbye and hung up, Daniella crept back into her and Zoe's bedroom, then flopped onto her bottom bunk. During the call, she'd been asked to mentally walk through her first day of the music program, dealing with different situations and triggers that might come up. She'd done an incredible job, in her imaginary day. Really rocked it.

"Yo!" Zoe's head appeared over the edge of the top bunk, her hair hanging straight down so she looked like a Troll doll. "You excited for camp?"

"It's not camp," Daniella murmured. "It's the Future Forward Music Academy. And yeah, can't wait."

That was true. Probably. Maybe?

"Me too." Zoe was starting theater camp that day, too. "Let's do this!"

"Are you girls up and getting dressed?" Aunt Tina called. "We have to leave in half an hour!"

Bam. Reality. This was actually happening—not just in her mind, and not with Dr. Richards's calming voice in her ear. Daniella sat up, but did it too fast. She felt dizzy right away, and then a wave of nausea crashed through her.

Zoe scrambled down from her bed and saw Daniella bent over, taking deep breaths. "Mom!" Zoe shouted. "Daniella's sick!"

"Shhhh!" Daniella snapped, then whispered: "Don't get your mom worried. I'm fine. Just tired and really needing some food."

Aunt Tina popped her head in the door, frowning with concern. "Daniella, how's your anxiety level? I have that medication if you need it."

"I'm okay, thanks," Daniella told her aunt. "I don't like taking it if I don't have to. It makes me really sleepy."

"All right," Tina said. "How did your phone check-in go this morning?"

"Good, I guess."

Tina smiled, but it was a heavy smile. Daniella hated that her stupid anxiety gave Tina one more thing to deal with. She needed to be better at keeping it under control . . . or at least, pretending it was.

"What time does your camp end?" Zoe asked, hopping down from the top bunk. "I want to show you the new bubble tea place around the corner. It has sixty-eight different drinks! I counted them."

Daniella glanced at the door, then got an idea. "That sounds fun," she said to Zoe. "I'll make a deal with you. If you see me like that again, looking sick or something, don't tell your mom or dad. Okay? Keep that stuff a secret and we can get bubble tea whenever you want."

Zoe beamed at her. *Secret* and *bubble tea* were clearly the magic words. "Okay, deal."

"Thanks."

"I'm gonna go make us some cereal. It's my specialty."

As Zoe zoomed out of the room, Daniella laughed, then remembered how Carly was always so annoyed by her little sister. But Daniella thought she was hilarious . . . and she really, really needed *hilarious* today.

$\star$

Uncle Chris had escorted Daniella on the Q train downtown, and now it was a five-block walk from the subway stop to the academy. For the first four blocks, Daniella felt fine. Possibly even excited.

But while they were waiting at a stop signal to cross onto the last block, something heated and jittery started to rise up in her. Daniella's fingers trembled. She squeezed the handle of her oboe case, felt with her thumb for the familiar bumps and ridges.

Then she closed her eyes and imagined walking on the beach at Ocean Park Heights, smelling the salty air, the breeze cooling her skin. The water was just getting warm enough to swim at this point. If she were home, she'd probably have plans to meet up with Penny and Lainie that afternoon. Ice cream on the boardwalk and a quick dip in the waves. Shopping at the jewelry store they all liked. They'd get bracelets with matching crystals and then each lose them before summer was over, because that's what always happened.

Breathe in for four, hold for seven, out for eight. Again. Then again.

The signal changed, started counting down the amount of time they had to cross. Uncle Chris started walking again, and Daniella put one foot in front of the other to follow him. The sidewalk on that last block was full of other kids, all carrying instruments, but she didn't look anyone in the eye. Finally, they were entering the courtyard of the private school that was hosting the summer program. A huge banner above the ornate front door read WELCOME YOUNG MUSICIANS!

"Looks like we're over here," Uncle Chris said, pointing at the L-Z check-in table. As they stepped up to the line, Daniella passed a student with short turquoise hair, a kitty-ear headband, shorts, fishnet stockings, and platform sneakers. The kid's eyes swept over Daniella's button-down blouse and flowered skirt, her white flat sandals, and then looked away.

That's right, Daniella said to the kid in her head. *There's nothing to see here. Move along to the interesting people.*

At the check-in table, a woman handed Daniella a thick black binder full of sheet music, her schedule, and other information, along with a blank name tag. She noticed that other kids had added personal pronouns under their name on the tags, so she did the same. After she stuck the tag on her shirt, Uncle Chris clapped her on the back.

"Looks like you're good to go," he said. "I'll be back at four to pick you up and ride with you, so you know the route both ways for tomorrow. In case you want to go alone from now on, without your dorky uncle. But it's okay if you don't feel ready. We'll figure it out."

Daniella glanced around to make sure nobody had heard. Was she ready to ride the subway alone? Walk those five blocks by herself, with nobody there to help if she got lost or some random creeper started following her?

She had no idea, so all she muttered was "You're not dorky."

Uncle Chris patted her on the back again and gave her a friendly little shove forward into the dark, cool air of the auditorium where everyone was headed.

"Have the best day ever, Daniella," he called after her, then disappeared into the crowd.

✲

Five minutes into Daniella's first session with her chamber music group, the teacher was already pissed off at her. Her sheet music was in the wrong order, but when she tried to explain to Mr. Novikoff that it had come that way in the binder, he didn't want to hear it.

"Excuses are infinitely useless," he said, dismissively waving a hand in her direction. "Just fix it."

As Daniella fumbled to rearrange the papers, she glanced over at the chamber group's violin player, a tall girl with a tight ponytail that tugged at the edges of her face. The girl frowned at her and flicked her eyes away. *Yeah*, Daniella thought. *I wouldn't associate with me, either.*

Daniella, the violinist, the cellist (a younger boy who'd sat next to her in orientation, playing *Minecraft* on his phone), and the violist (a painfully enthusiastic girl who mentioned, at every opportunity, that this was her fifth year at the academy), all stumbled through the first piece of music. Daniella didn't think it was that bad, considering none of them had played together before.

After the last note faded, everyone paused, waiting for Mr. Novikoff's reaction. Which he appeared to be thinking really, really hard about.

Finally, he said, with a kind of wicked smile, "Well, that was atrocious."

"It was?" Ponytail asked, surprised.

"Yes!" he replied. "But that's the way I like it. It means we have work to do, and we won't be bored this summer. If I can't give you a hard time about how badly you're playing, it's no fun for me."

Minecraft Boy laughed nervously, then glanced at Daniella and the two other girls. *Was this guy for real?*

"I want you all to take a ten-minute break to really think about why you're here and what you plan to do this summer," Mr. Novikoff continued. "When you come back into this room, pretend it's the first time you're seeing my face."

Everyone glanced uncomfortably at one another, then got up and swept out the door. The three other kids started a whispering huddle in the hallway. Daniella started to walk toward them but felt her heart rate speeding up. Her breath caught before she could fully inhale.

Before the others noticed her, Daniella headed the other way, out the front door and into the courtyard. There was a nook between two bushes that looked especially cozy. She tucked herself into it, pulled out her phone, and dialed her mom.

The call went straight to voicemail.

"Mom?" Daniella was surprised to hear how high and thin her voice sounded. She cleared her throat. "Mom, it's Daniella. I'm . . . um . . . I need to talk to you because I think I . . . made a mistake. Coming here. I've had a bunch of panic attacks already and I'm up half the night and Mr. Novikoff hates me and Aunt Tina seems so sad and worried and . . ."

She felt her eyes begin to sting. *Pull it together, Daniella.* No way was she going back to Mr. Novikoff's classroom with tears streaking down her face.

"Everyone is super-talented and confident and serious and nobody's talking to me and I don't think I belong here," Daniella continued. It was so easy to say all this to a voicemail box instead of her real, live mom. "Plus I just really, really miss being home and being with my friends this summer. Dad needs to come and get me and bring me back. So call me as soon as you can. Okay? Bye."

Daniella hung up and stared at the phone. She had no idea what she was hoping it would do.

"I had almost the same conversation with *my* mom last night," a voice behind her said.

Startled, Daniella turned around. It was the kid with the turquoise hair, wearing a name tag that said: JULES (THEY/THEM).

"I swear I wasn't eavesdropping," Jules added. "I came out for some air and . . . well, you were being pretty loud."

"Sorry," Daniella said.

Jules sat down on the low wall dividing the sidewalk and the courtyard.

"Don't be," they said. "I'm sorry you feel like you don't belong here. I'm pretty sure I don't, either."

Daniella glanced at Jules, amazed at how quickly and comfortably this stranger was sharing personal stuff. She was overcome with a sudden urge to vent.

"My oboe teacher and my parents thought the academy would be good for me," Daniella began, letting the thoughts spill quickly out of her. "So I could, you know, become a more well-rounded musician and figure out how serious I was. But this whole place—the academy, the city—it's . . ."

"A lot." Jules nodded. "Believe me, I get it. I had my freak-out two days before the program even started, so how much of a loser am *I*?"

Daniella bit her lip. "Are you going to drop out, too?"

"Nope," Jules replied. "My mom wouldn't let me. Then I woke up this morning and remembered that I applied because I wanted to spend the summer playing music. Because it makes me happy and makes me feel like *me*. So it doesn't matter if I'm not as serious or experienced or talented as some of the other kids here. I'll just do my thing. You should stay and do your thing, too."

Jules was so confident and honest. Daniella wondered, *Could we possibly have anything in common?* Maybe it was worth sticking around long enough to find out.

"Okay," she said. "I'll stay and do my thing."

Jules smiled, standing up and offering a hand to Daniella. "Let's go back in," they said. "I told my chamber group teacher I was going to the bathroom, and I've been out here for a while. I don't want her to think of me as Diarrhea Kid for the next six weeks."

★

By the time Daniella limped into the apartment behind Uncle Chris, all she wanted to do was crawl onto her bunk and curl into a ball.

She'd barely hit the bed when her phone dinged with a message alert from Lainie. HOW WAS IT?

Daniella sighed. There were a lot of ways she could answer that question:

For icebreakers, we played two truths and a lie, and I couldn't think of two truths about myself that were even the tiniest bit interesting.

I think I was the only person in my West African drumming class who couldn't manage to keep a beat, and I can't decide if that's more ironic or embarrassing.

I started to have a panic attack before I even got there. So that was fantastic.

Oh, and I did meet one cool person so far, named Jules, who will probably ditch me as soon as they find nonpathetic people to hang out with.

Instead, she typed out the only other honest thing she could think of:

It was hard. I miss you and OPH

Lainie's reply: miss you too

Then Lainie added: have you started working on any of the bucket list? Penny and I are going to Candy Universe tomorrow

Daniella stared at the message, feeling the gut punch of it. Lainie and Penny were doing a Bucket List item. Without her. Sure, yeah, they'd agreed on this plan. They were going to have to do some items separately, in separate places. But now that it was actually happening, Daniella couldn't block the crappiness of being left out. She burrowed her head underneath the pillow.

"Yo, bestie!" Zoe was suddenly standing over Daniella's bed. Arms crossed, foot tapping. "Time for bubble tea."

"Can we do it tomorrow?" Daniella asked. "I'm just . . ." *Really wanting to be alone. Too tired to be around anything but dark, empty space right now.*

"That's what you said yesterday when you were too busy unpacking."

"I know, I know," Daniella said. "I'm really sorry, Zoe."

"Seriously," Zoe muttered. "You're worse than Carly. She never wanted to hang out with me, either, but at least she wouldn't *pretend* she did and then bail."

Daniella flinched. She was doing that, wasn't she? It was strange to hear someone talking trash about Carly, even though it was Zoe, who'd been talking trash about Carly for years. Were you allowed to trash-talk someone who died?

"I'm not pretending . . . ." Daniella started to explain. She sat up so she could look Zoe in the eye. And when she did, she saw a kid who was having a crappy day, too.

"When you're feeling unsure of yourself," Dr. Richards had told her during their phone session, "reach out and connect with someone. Give them your time, your energy, even just an ear for listening. I promise it will help."

Daniella took a deep breath and sat up. "Bubble tea will give me some energy, right?"

Zoe broke into a huge smile. "Uh, *yeah*! It's basically caffeine and sugar that you drink with a giant straw."

"Sold," Daniella said. "Let's go."

Once they were in the hallway waiting for the elevator, Zoe turned to her. "After bubble tea," she said excitedly, "we can go to the craft store a few blocks away. Mom gave me money to get some stuff to do inside on rainy days. You know, like making jewelry and slime."

The elevator dinged, the doors opened, and the girls stepped in.

"That sounds fun," Daniella said, remembering one winter day during a snowstorm. Carly had called her, complaining about how she was stuck baking cupcakes with Zoe when all she wanted to do was get in bed and have a marathon video chat with Daniella.

Daniella caught a quick glimpse of herself and Zoe, framed together in the mirrored wall. It was a picture she'd never seen before, but she liked it.

⋛ 7 ⋚

CANDY UNIVERSE STOOD TALL ABOVE THE BOARD-
walk, a mint-green, glass-fronted building sandwiched between a
T-shirt store and the place where you could take fake old-time photos.
It always reminded Lainie of Emerald City from *The Wizard of Oz*.

As Lainie rode her skateboard toward the store, she spotted a lone
figure sitting out front in the chair shaped like a giant ice cream cone.
The person was also *eating* an ice cream cone.

"Hey," Penny said as Lainie came up to her.

"Hey," Lainie answered, hopping off her skateboard and flopping
into the other chair, which was a huge plastic cupcake.

They were quiet for a few moments, as if they were expecting
Daniella and Carly to show up any second now. Then it hit Lainie—
she wasn't sure whether she and Penny had ever hung out together,
alone. She couldn't think of a single time. She and *Daniella*, yes. Constantly. And Carly was always going over to Penny's house.

It felt like Lainie and Penny, by doing this first Bucket List item as a team, were drawing the last line in a connect-the-dots square. And it was awkward as hell.

Not sure how to deal with it, Lainie took out her phone. No messages. With nothing else to do, she snapped a photo of Penny.

"Eating an ice cream cone, sitting in an ice cream cone, at ten a.m.," Lainie said, examining the picture on her screen. "This is a great look for you."

Penny smiled mischievously. "I'm trying to make myself feel sick so I won't want to eat any of the candy before we get a picture of the full haul."

Lainie laughed. "Is it working?"

Penny examined the remains of her cone and stood up. "Yep. I might puke, but I'm ready."

"Ugh!" A voice growled from behind Lainie. She turned to see Grumpy Gus with his folded newspaper, glaring at them. "Are you leaving? Or are you just going to stand there so nobody else can use these chairs?"

Lainie shot Penny a look, expecting her to be the one to answer him. But Penny only shook her head, eyes wide. Everyone knew you didn't want to talk to Grumpy Gus. It never ended well.

"Sorry," Lainie muttered, head down.

"Yeah, sorry." Penny threw out the rest of her cone and bolted for the Candy Universe entrance. Lainie quickly followed her inside.

As soon as they walked into the store, the icy blast of air-conditioning made the hair on Lainie's arms stand on end. She and Penny watched Grumpy Gus through the window. He took a moment to decide which chair he wanted, then settled into the cupcake, unfolded his newspaper, and started to read.

"I can't believe Carly expected us to get him into a photo booth," Lainie said.

"Knowing Carly, she probably had a plan," Penny replied.

"Too bad she didn't write *that* down."

With a sigh, Lainie turned to face the spectacle that was Candy Universe. The outside of the store had Emerald City vibes, but the inside was all Willy Wonka. She took a deep breath and closed her eyes.

"Ah, smell that sugar."

"Let's do this," Penny said.

Together they made a beeline for the back wall of the store, where all the bulk candy was laid out in three rows of round bins. Penny grabbed a plastic bag from the dispenser.

"Get a bunch," Lainie told her.

"Right," Penny said, pulling out another. Then she just yanked out a handful and handed half to Lainie.

Lainie scanned the bins, which were arranged by type. "So what do you think Carly's plan would be right now?"

Penny pursed her lips and narrowed her eyes. "Let's start on opposite ends and meet in the middle."

"That makes sense," Lainie said. "I'll take that side, with the gummies first?"

Penny nodded. "I can start on this side. Chocolate city, baby!" She got a wicked gleam in her eye. "Wanna race?"

"Pen, that's not part of the Bucket List."

"Come on, we can add stuff to an item. We always have."

This was true. Carly and Penny were experts at coming up with ways to make the Bucket List even more challenging, more crazy, more embarrassing, or extra fun.

"Fine," Lainie said, then darted over to the far side of the candy wall. Penny rushed to the other side, then took out a pair of black plastic tongs and clapped them together like they were the mouth of a hungry beast.

"Okay, candy," Penny growled. "We're coming for ya!"

Lainie took out her phone and snapped a photo of Penny and the Tong Monster, then shook open her first plastic bag. *Let's do this.*

Swedish Fish and strawberry laces and cherry licorice. Red gummy bears. Multicolored gummy bears. Gummy worms. Sour gummy worms. Sour gummy *kids.*

SweeTarts. Candy Legos. Starburst. Taffy. Pixy Stix.

As Lainie added one of each, her bag grew heavier and thicker. She glanced over at Penny, who was still working her way through the chocolates.

Someone tapped her on the shoulder, making her jump a little.

"Here," the store cashier guy said, holding up more bags. "If you're gonna do every bin, you'll need these."

✳

It was a close finish, but Lainie reached the middle of the candy wall first.

Now she and Penny had taken over a picnic table by the boardwalk, trying to arrange all the candy bags for a good picture.

"Can't we do this later?" Penny asked.

"Nope. We need to get a photo before we eat a single one," Lainie explained matter-of-factly. "Okay, wait . . . That's good!"

Lainie stepped away from the table. Penny stood on the bench so she could fit all the candy in the shot—not easy—then snapped a few with her cell phone.

"What should I put as the caption?" Penny asked.

Lainie stared out at the ocean for a moment. *What do you say about $50.32 worth of sugar?*

"Say, 'We came, we saw, we candied. Stay tuned for our favorites.'"

Penny chuckled as she typed. "I'll tag Daniella."

Lainie heard the *whoosh* sound from Penny's phone that meant the post had been launched into the world. Penny put her phone down on the table and dug into one of the bags, pulling out two chocolate-covered somethings.

"The ice cream's worn off. I think I can handle some candy now," she said as she handed one to Lainie.

Lainie popped the chocolate into her mouth. "Are you excited for work?"

"Excited to be out of the house," Penny said. "Not so excited about the uniform I have to wear. It's like, 'Hi, I'm Penny. I know you can see my bra through this tight white shirt, but how can I help you today?'"

Lainie started laughing, almost choking on her candy. "I'm glad we wear aprons at the bakery. Not that I have anything worth staring at."

"You should be glad about that, too," Penny said. "Trust me. So what are you doing today, since the bakery's closed?"

"Today is *ugh*. The guy who wants to buy it is coming over with his Realtor, and probably his creepy daughter, so they can talk about details or whatever. Nana's making all this food to serve them."

"Why? Is it, like, a party?" Penny asked.

"No. I think she's going to see if he's worthy of Dulcie's by how he reacts to her cooking. My mom said Nana put several of her boyfriends through the same test."

"Do you want him to pass?" Penny asked, brushing her hair out of her face as the wind picked up from the water.

"No." Lainie fished out a gummy bear and bit off its head. "Maybe. I don't know. I mean, he seems nice enough. He says he wants to keep the name and most of the menu, so that's good. But if Nana decides he's not the right person to buy the bakery, nothing has to change yet. It could take a while to find another buyer."

"And that's better?"

"Way better," Lainie said.

Penny nodded. "I get it."

Do you really? Lainie thought as they both fell silent. Penny's situation in OPH was completely different than hers. She'd probably be coming to her family's beach house for years and years into the future. How could she truly understand what Lainie was losing?

Penny checked the time on her phone and sighed. "I guess I should go home and change into the world's shortest shorts."

"Yeah, Nana should be done with her meeting by now. I think it's safe for me to head back."

"Hey," Penny said, reaching out to swipe away a fleck of chocolate from Lainie's cheek. "Let's do the next Bucket List thing together, too."

Lainie smiled. "Deal. But which one? I think we should wait and do some of them when Daniella comes back. Like the music video and parasailing. And I can't even begin to think about Grumpy Gus."

"Ugh, yeah," Penny agreed, shuddering. "That one could take all summer."

All summer.

As she said goodbye to Penny and started riding her skateboard toward Nana's house, Lainie thought of how those two little words swelled with promises and possibilities. Days that could be counted but also felt endless, too big for the squares on a calendar.

Today, Lainie sensed something else in those words. A good kind of newness. *Fresh.*

She and Penny had just spent a morning with each other for maybe the first time ever, and it was the most fun Lainie had had in months.

✶

The fastest way into Nana's house from the beach was through the backyard, which had a gate on the alley. Lainie stepped through it, skate deck under one arm, and took a deep breath.

The yard was tiny, but decades of Sunday afternoons had given Nana and Papa time to turn it into their own little paradise, with dozens of different types of plants and flowers growing around an ancient iron patio set. Nana loved gnomes and Papa collected old fishing gear, which made for some freaky decorations. One gnome stood smiling in the middle of a rusted lobster trap. Another hung from an old net strung across the fence.

Lainie opened the back door and stepped into the kitchen.

The sounds of laughter. Her grandmother's high-pitched giggle, which was where Lainie got her own high-pitched giggle. Then a deeper voice chuckling in a satisfied way.

Crap. The meeting was still going on and everyone sounded happy. Not a good sign.

Lainie took off her Converse high-tops, tiptoed down the hall toward her room, and opened the door.

"What the—"

It was a girl. That Sasha person, standing by the window.

"Oops, sorry," Lainie heard herself say. *Wait, why the hell are you apologizing and what is she doing in your room?*

"I was exploring," Sasha said matter-of-factly. She took in Lainie's baggy T-shirt, jean shorts, and bucket hat. The mammoth bag of candy. "Did you know your lips are blue? That must be really toxic stuff you're eating."

Lainie put down her skateboard, then wiped her mouth as she spun around and marched into the living room. Nana, Mr. Mason, and Christina the Realtor were drinking coffee, the trays of food mostly eaten.

Nana turned to Lainie, her eyes bright . . . and Lainie knew. Mr. Mason had passed the test. It was all going to happen right away. She wanted to scream and pound a fist into the wall, then run off and stay out long enough for everyone to get worried about her.

"Ah, here she is!" her grandmother exclaimed. "My fabulosa Alaina. We can't do any of this without her help. Come join us, mija."

With that, Lainie's urge to yell or hit or disappear vanished, swept away by a wave of guilt. She forced her (blue) lips into a smile and sat down.

≳ 8 ≲

THIS IS TOTALLY NOT WHAT I SIGNED UP FOR.

Well, okay, it is. But apparently I am an idiot.

Daniella tried to catch her breath in the corner of the dance studio, waiting her turn to move diagonally across the hardwood floor. According to the academy brochure, mandatory dance classes were a way to "get out of your comfort zone, expand your horizons, and grow as a complete artist."

What they'd left out: When you take a bunch of kids used to sitting and playing music, then put them in a mirrored room and force them to learn jazz choreography, the result is not pretty.

"Today, your body is your instrument!" the teacher called out. She wanted everyone to call her Gem and appeared to be wearing three different-length skirts at once. "Feel the rhythm in every limb and organ!"

Daniella glanced across the room at Jules, who'd already taken their turn. Jules gave a huge eye roll, then imitated the way Gem wiggled her hands and fingers. Daniella had to fight back a snort-laugh by clapping her hand over her mouth.

Then it was her turn, and she tried to remember the combination. She counted to herself as she willed her feet to do the steps they'd just learned.

"Don't forget your arms!" Gem called to her. "They're an extension of the music! They're another instrument you're playing right now!"

Daniella waved her arms in an attempt to copy what the other kids did. She purposely did *not* look in the mirror as she neared the opposite corner. If she caught even a tiny glimpse of how ridiculous she looked, she'd never be able to un-see it.

Once Daniella had finished and Gem moved on to the next victim, Jules grabbed her hand and leaned in to whisper: "After we're done, meet me in the courtyard."

"We have lunch next," Daniella reminded them.

"Exactly."

Daniella frowned, confused. "What does that—"

"Okay!" Gem shouted to the class. "Now we're going to do the combination *backward*!"

✶

Three minutes into their lunch break, Jules was leading Daniella out of the academy courtyard and down the street. Her new friend was so confident, so sure of where they were going, that Daniella decided not to ask any questions.

One block down on the opposite corner, there was a small park—a handful of benches, a play structure, some swings, and a basketball court inside an iron fence. A falafel cart was stationed at the entrance, covered in giant photos of the food it sold.

Jules stepped up to the cart and pointed to an enormous picture of a falafel sandwich. "I've seen this three mornings in a row now, and I can't stop thinking about it. Want one?"

"I have my own lunch and didn't bring any cash," Daniella said.

"My treat," Jules said. "You can cover me next time."

Daniella glanced at the giant falafel. It did look amazing, and she'd been too chicken to remind Aunt Tina that she didn't like peanut butter. Plus, she didn't want to be rude to Jules. "Okay," she said. "Thanks. I wonder how it compares to the falafel we have at our restaurant."

"You have a restaurant," Jules echoed, amused.

"Well, my parents do."

"Dimitri's falafel is much better than your parents' falafel," the man at the cart said in a dead-serious voice. "I am Dimitri, and I know."

"Oh yeah?" Jules asked, raising one eyebrow. "I guess we'll see."

"Yes, you'll see," the man said, and started to make their sandwiches.

As they waited, Daniella took in the way Jules was standing, with hands on hips and chin up. Tall in black platform boots with tiny bat wings on them. It was only a matter of time before Jules discovered just how un-special and completely *blah* Daniella was. Tomorrow, for sure, they would find someone else to eat lunch at the park with, but today, Daniella would make the most of it.

After they got their sandwiches and sodas, Jules led Daniella to the play structure. "Let's sit up there," they said, then climbed a short ladder to a platform. Daniella followed.

"This is so much better than the academy cafeteria," Jules added once they got settled. "I don't want that school-jungle vibe in the summer. Know what I mean?"

"Totally," Daniella said, wondering if she could keep coming here after Jules ditched her. She took a bite of her sandwich. "Oh. That guy was right. This is way better than the one they make at our restaurant."

"Never doubt Dimitri," Jules said in Dimitri's monotone.

Daniella laughed and did her own version of the monotone. "Dimitri has a secret falafel recipe that he will protect with his life."

Jules cracked up, and Daniella felt a surge of pride.

"Hey, look," said a voice from somewhere below them. "It's the oboist from my chamber group."

Daniella glanced down and saw two kids peering up at them. One was the tight-ponytail girl. The other was a blond boy she also recognized from the academy. She didn't know either of their names.

"I'm Margot, remember?" the girl said, as if she could read Daniella's mind. "Violin. But you knew that. And this is Adrian."

"Percussion," Adrian said.

"You guys discovered our lunch spot," Margot added. "We ate here yesterday."

Daniella started to wrap up her sandwich, expecting to be asked to leave. Then Jules said, "There's room for all four of us. Climb on up."

Adrian and Margot exchanged a look, then Adrian hoisted himself onto the platform. "By 'spot' we meant the park in general," he said. "But you're right, *this* right here is the place to be."

Margot climbed up, too.

"I'm Jules," Jules said.

"Daniella," Daniella added. "Hi." She waved, then inwardly cringed. *They're sitting three inches from you, why the hell would you wave?* It was like she couldn't *not* be awkward.

"So, Daniella," Margot said as she began unpacking her lunch from a brown paper shopping bag. "What are you?"

Daniella coughed on her piece of falafel. Thanks to her caramel skin tone and curly hair that tended to frizz in the slightest humidity, she'd gotten this question countless times in her life, but wasn't expecting it just then. Lately, after her mom suggested it, she'd started answering with another question: "Do you mean, what's my ethnicity?"

Usually people got squirmy and embarrassed at that point, but when Daniella said that to Margot, Margot lit up.

"Sort of! I'm really interested in people's ancestry. Which means your ethnic *descent*. I'm half-Irish on my mom's side and one-quarter French and one-quarter Lebanese on my dad's side. Also, I'm autistic." Margot paused. "We're not sure what side that's from."

"Oh, cool," Daniella said, then scrambled for a better follow-up. "My, uh, dad's Italian and my mom is . . . well, she did some ancestry stuff, too, and found out her family is originally from West Africa."

"Like the drumming we're doing?" Adrian asked.

"Yeah, I guess. But I've never really tried it before. We don't have a lot of African music opportunities where I live in New Jersey." Daniella paused as something occurred to her. "Maybe that's one of the reasons why my mom wanted me to do the academy. Too bad I suck at it."

"Eh, we're all bad at it right now," Adrian said. "Give it a few days. I hear people catch on quickly."

"What about you, Jules?" Margot asked. "Ancestry?"

"Well, according to my grandma, we're 'European mutts,'" they replied. "German, Austrian, English, it's all in there. But I don't know the exact breakdown, sorry."

"It's okay," Margot said. "Most people don't. I still like to know as much as I can about the countries where their families came from." She paused. "Obviously, I'm the least popular kid in my school."

Everyone cracked up. To Daniella, it felt like a bubble of awkwardness had just popped, and they could all be themselves now.

"I play *percussion* in the band," Adrian said. "Nobody has a lower social ranking than me."

"Oh yeah?" Jules said. "What happens if you're such a weirdo, you don't even *have* a social ranking?"

"Then you're a true oddball," Adrian replied, "and I salute you."

He held up his energy drink, and Jules clinked it with a seltzer.

"To us oddballs!" Jules said.

They all laughed again, taking turns clinking their cans and drinking. Soon they were sharing more information about where they lived (Jules lived in the West Village, Margot was from Brooklyn, Adrian from Long Island), why they decided to try the academy, what they liked about it so far, and how much Gem scared them.

At one point, Jules turned to Daniella and casually asked, "How are you doing, by the way? Better than that first day, I hope."

Margot frowned. "What happened on the first day?"

Daniella hesitated for half a second, wondering whether she should throw her personal mess at these kids she just met. She took a breath and said, "I had a freak-out about feeling like I didn't belong here. But now . . . maybe I kind of do? Because there are so many different kinds of people here, compared to where I live. At the academy *and* in the city. Not only racially but personality and style-wise, you know? It's like, everybody belongs because belonging isn't even a thing."

She paused, about to ask Margot what Brooklyn was like, but then her phone dinged. She looked down to see a FotoSlam notification.

Your friend LuckyPennyA777 has a new post.

The others started talking again, but Daniella couldn't resist peeking at FotoSlam. She opened the app and saw Penny's post about the Candy Universe trip. The colorful bags of candy against the beige metal of the picnic table. Penny and Lainie grinning. Being goofy.

"Oh my gosh," she muttered. "They actually did it."

She felt a pang, heavy and hard, like she'd been gut-punched.

They actually did it.

Without me.

On their Bucket List planning chat, Daniella, Penny, and Lainie had agreed to wait on some items until everyone was together again. They'd also agreed that until then, they'd each have to do one or two, otherwise they wouldn't have time to get to them all. Daniella thought that meant they'd each do them alone. She hadn't imagined that Lainie and Penny would do one together and post about it, like it meant absolutely nothing that Daniella—or Carly—wasn't there.

"What's up?" Margot asked, scooting over to look at Daniella's phone. "Ew. That's a lot of candy. I don't eat sugar."

"Let me see," Adrian said, leaning in.

Daniella took a deep breath and tried to shake off this feeling of . . . what? Being betrayed? Being pissed? Both?

"It's part of a thing I'm doing with my friends who are at the shore this summer," Daniella explained. "A bucket list."

"What kind of bucket list?" Margot asked.

Daniella found her photo of the SSBL and read it out loud to them.

"Carly came up with the list," Daniella said. "She always does."

The present tense just slipped out.

"So which one are you going to do first?" Jules asked, leaning in to see the list again.

"If you want to kiss a boy, you can kiss *me*," Adrian said.

"I bet you don't like girls," Jules teased.

"And you'd win that bet," Adrian said matter-of-factly. "But I like to be helpful."

Daniella giggled and shook her head. "Thanks, but the list doesn't work that way. It has to be *real*, you know?"

Adrian sighed. "I sure do."

Daniella laughed again. Then that image of Penny and Lainie—huddling for a selfie with their epic haul from Candy Universe—slid back into her brain. Were they trying to hurt her on purpose? Didn't they know how she'd feel, looking at the post?

Screw them. The thought came suddenly, poking at her, sharp at the tip.

"Hey, can you guys do me a favor?" Daniella asked, a bit nervously. "Would you take a selfie with me? So I can, you know, introduce you all to my friends at the shore?"

"Duh," Jules said.

"Of course," Adrian echoed.

They gathered in close to Daniella. She stretched out her arm as far as she could to get them all in the shot, took the picture, then showed it to everyone.

"We really are glorious oddballs," Adrian said, smiling and shaking his head.

Daniella laughed. She loved the sound of that. *Glorious oddballs.* And she loved that these kids were actually proud of it.

"Oh my gosh," she said. "That's the hashtag."

"Say what?" Jules asked.

"*Create our own hashtag and make it go viral*. It's on the list."

Margot nodded. "Glorious oddballs."

"My brain is already exploding with photo ideas," Adrian said.

"I love it," Jules added. "Run with that."

"Really?" Daniella looked at the three of them and wondered . . . If Lainie and Penny didn't have to do Bucket List items alone, why should *she*? "Would you all want to help me with this?" she asked.

Adrian excitedly grabbed Daniella's shoulder. "Yes, please!"

"Of course," Jules added, smiling wide.

Margot glanced up at a tree for a pondering moment, then nodded. "I agree. That sounds fun."

"Let's do another selfie," Jules suggested. "A super-ridiculous one, to launch the hashtag."

They all huddled together again, making crazy faces for the photo. It took Daniella a bit of typing, deleting, then typing again to come up with just the right caption:

> Me and my Future Forward Music Academy
> peeps. We are weird and we are proud!
> #GloriousOddballs

Then she clicked *share*.

Jules put their arm around Daniella and squeezed. "Can't wait to see what your friend Carly thinks!"

As Jules got up to throw their lunch garbage in the trash, Daniella felt a mix of panic and guilt rush through her. She hadn't meant for them to think Carly was still —

Should she say something? But then she'd have to explain. And everyone would feel sorry for her.

Besides, it felt like a little bubble of freedom, Jules, Margot, and Adrian not knowing about Carly. And with them, in a twisted secret way, Daniella could keep Carly alive. Daniella watched the three of them walk over to the swings. Adrian sat in one, and Margot and Jules started pushing him. The three of them laughed, like they didn't have one single thing in the world to worry about.

Carly would have liked these guys so much. She'd approve, I'm sure of it.

It was going to be okay. Right?

⋛ 9 ⋚

IN OCEAN PARK HEIGHTS THERE WAS THE TOWN beach, which was mostly everywhere, and then there was Anderson's Beach, which existed only between Captain Cones Ice Cream and the Jumping Fish Grill.

It was a private beach, across the boardwalk from Anderson's Arcade and Anderson's FunLand amusement park. Every year, they installed thatched tiki umbrellas and planted palm trees, pots and all, in the sand, to make it look like the Caribbean instead of the Jersey Shore.

Penny knew the unspoken rule: If you were a local or a summer regular, you didn't go to Anderson's. You got a seasonal badge for the public beach, and you called each part of that beach by the name of its closest major street. Anderson's was for the weekly or weekend renters, or people visiting for the day. So when Penny stepped onto that clean, silky stretch of sand for her first-ever work shift, wearing her white shirt and red shorts and wishing she could drape herself in a towel to cover them up, it was also her first time there.

She paused to snap a photo of the palm trees and tiki umbrellas, blue-green ocean behind them and blue-purple sky above. Then she typed out a caption.

> Starting the summer job! If I squint, I can pretend
> I'm in the Bahamas.

"I was you last year," said a voice behind her.

Startled, Penny whirled around . . . and there he was. Dex, of the adorable messy bangs. Dex, with a smile that somehow made dimples out of dimples.

"What?" she mumbled.

"I started as an attendant, too," Dex said. "Now I'm the beach supervisor. Hopefully next year, when I'm sixteen, I'll be up there."

He pointed toward the lifeguard chair, which was occupied by a girl in a red swimsuit with long, tan legs. She twirled her whistle around one finger and looked out over the ocean like she owned it.

"*That's* the raddest job in OPH," Dex added.

Penny watched as the lifeguard blew her whistle and waved at some swimmers to come closer to the shore.

"Yeah, unless someone drowns on your watch," Penny said. Then she saw the frown on Dex's face. Ugh. Why did she always get snarky when she was nervous?

I managed to insult my supervisor in the first five minutes of my job. Fantastic.

"Sorry," Penny added. "I can't believe I said that . . ."

But then Dex nodded thoughtfully. "No worries. I've been thinking about that, and whether I could handle the guilt. There are definitely other cool jobs out there, but with less pressure."

Penny breathed a sigh of relief but still felt nervous. Which meant, still snarky.

"For instance," she offered, "the person who plays the scary pirate at the eighteenth hole of the mini golf course."

Dex broke out another star-powered smile. "Or the guys who test each slide before the water park opens, to make sure the flow is just right."

"Wait, that's a job?" Penny asked, raising her eyebrows.

"Yeah, but I'd rather do this. I get to be on the beach all day and when the waves look good, I can take a break with Kiani."

Penny's heart sank. *Kiani.* Of course a guy like Dex would have a girlfriend. Dex was staring lovingly at someone over Penny's shoulder. *Oh, even better, she's here.* Penny turned around, expecting to see a supermodel. But Dex was gazing at a big yellow surfboard resting against the wall of the beach rental hut.

Relief whooshed through Penny. Then she made the connection. "You named your board after the character in *North Shore*?"

"Yes!" Dex looked pleasantly surprised. "You're, like, only the third not-old person who's ever gotten that."

Penny shrugged. "It's my dad's favorite movie from the eighties. He used to make us watch it at the beginning of every summer."

But not this one, so far.

Dex tilted his head, as if trying to see Penny from a new angle. "That's cool. *You're* cool. I think this is going to be good. Let me open up the rental shack and we'll go over the routine." He checked his watch. "Gate opens in ten minutes. You ready?"

"Totally ready," Penny said. She added a quick salute, then instantly regretted it. *Don't be such a nerd. Being a nerd is worse than being snarky.*

As Dex headed for the rental shack, Penny's phone buzzed in her hand; Lainie and Daniella had both liked her post.

You'll rock it! Lainie had written.

Daniella hadn't made a comment, and Penny realized she hadn't seen any posts from her since she'd left for New York. When she clicked on Daniella's profile name, one new photo popped up. Wait, who were these people with Daniella? She read the caption twice, confused, thinking they'd all formed a band and Glorious Oddballs was the name. Daniella's mad skills in music always gave Penny an itchy, uncomfortable feeling. A little intimidated, a little wistful, a touch jealous. Daniella had a "thing." Lainie, too, with her skating and Discord crowd. And Carly, of course, had had her photography and fashion obsession. Penny was still on the lookout for her thing.

who are the Glorious Oddballs? Penny texted to Lainie, fully aware that she should be messaging Daniella with that question.

her new friends in the city i guess, Lainie replied. i think maybe she's doing the hashtag item from the Bucket List

Penny started to type: Without us? But she stopped halfway through and deleted the message. Of course without them. She was in a different city. Instead, she wrote, Is it weird that she didn't ask us or even tell us first?

Lainie's answer came back quickly: Yup.

"Gate's open!" Dex called suddenly.

Penny slid her phone into her back pocket and hurried to the door of the rental shack.

✳

With Dex's help, Penny picked up the beach attendant routine on the fly as the day got busier. When a guest rented a lounge chair or umbrella (or usually both), Penny carried it across the sand, then helped set things up. Sometimes the umbrella had to be moved so it blocked the sun better, or pushed deeper into the sand.

Then she had to remind guests if they were breaking the rules. If their cooler was too big or their music playing too loud. If they had glass bottles or were smoking. If the baby stroller they brought didn't actually have a baby in it but a very small dog, because dogs weren't allowed even if they *were* quieter than any baby.

Penny tensed up every time. When her brothers did something wrong, she loved calling them out. Relished every part of it. But these were strangers and she never knew if they were going to react with an "Oh, sorry, my bad!" or a "Thanks for killing the fun, asshole." She watched Dex handle the tougher situations with a friendly, chilled-out attitude. That smile was his secret weapon that worked on everyone. Penny couldn't tell if he knew that. Was it a calculated thing, or was Dex just naturally . . . amazing?

"Not *there*," a woman with three little kids said when Penny was moving her umbrella for the fourth time. "Closer to the water, see where I'm pointing?" She wore a big floppy hat and flowy dress, like she'd shown up for a photo shoot instead of a day chasing toddlers who kept peeing in the sand.

"Yeah, but the tide's coming in," Penny said.

"I know. My kids want their sandcastle moat to fill up with water."

"Okay, but as soon as the water comes up high enough, you'll have to move again."

The woman lifted the front of her hat brim to look Penny squarely in the eye. "So?"

Grrrrr, Penny thought. That I'm-better-than-you expression, the snotty edge to her voice. Exactly like all the girls Penny hated at school. It had taken her years, but she'd finally learned how to deal with their kind.

"Look, lady," she shot back at the woman. "You're not the only person on this beach. I have other people to help."

The woman fixed Penny with a death-stare. Instantly, she knew she'd crossed a line.

"Excuse me?"

"Sorry," Penny babbled. "It's . . . it's my first day." She quickly wriggled the umbrella into the sand, exactly where the woman wanted it, muttered *Letmeknowifyouneedanythingelse* and ran back to the shack.

It was almost time to do her hourly sweeping of the beach entrance ramp and outdoor shower platforms, then pick up garbage and recycling. Which was a huge relief. Sand was annoying and trash was gross, but at least she didn't have to be polite to them.

Halfway through her shift, Penny walked into the rental shack to find Dex staring wistfully out at the water. The waves had picked up.

"I'm going to take my lunch," he said to Penny. "Can you cover the shack on your own for a bit?"

"Sure," Penny said, then wondered if that was actually true.

Dex flashed her a thumbs-up and left. A few seconds later, he was running, shirtless, toward the water's edge with Kiani tucked under one arm. Penny watched him go, feeling like the big-hearts-for-eyes emoji.

Stop being so obvious! It's pathetic.

She took out her phone and saw a new message from Lainie.

how's it going so far?

Penny glanced up to see Dex paddling out to a wave. She typed back: Haven't gotten fired yet, so I guess okay. She paused, then added, My supervisor is really cool and cute.

Ew! Lainie wrote.

Penny sighed. Typical Lainie. He's only a year older than us, she replied.

She was going to write more, but then decided, why bother? Lainie wasn't going to get it. Daniella wouldn't, either. Only Carly would have answered the right way, with a More deets please! or Need a pic ASAP.

All Penny had to do was close her eyes, and she was back on Lainie's grandparents' screened porch, at that final sleepless sleepover last year (or was it a century ago?). Sometime close to midnight, Daniella and Lainie had gone inside to the kitchen for more snacks. Carly plopped herself on Penny's air mattress and leaned in to whisper.

"Pen, I need to tell you something. I'm going to burst if I have to keep it a secret another second."

"Don't burst," Penny had replied.

Carly had glanced up to make sure the others weren't on their way back yet. "That guy who worked the rides at FunLand? You know, Blond Shawn Mendes?"

"Uh-huh . . ."

"I kissed him. Or he kissed me. I think it happened at the same time, actually."

"Carly!"

"I know, right?" Carly had wiggled her eyebrows up and down. "We spent the whole afternoon together, just goofing around in stores on the boardwalk. It was so fun."

"Lucky," Penny had muttered, remembering how many times she'd seen other girls hanging out with boys that summer, wishing she could do it, too. Then she felt a swell of pride, of being chosen. Carly had handed her a secret, something she didn't want to share with anyone else.

"It'll happen for you next summer," Carly had said, as if she were reading Penny's mind. "We'll both get boyfriends. Let's totally plan on that."

They'd heard Daniella and Lainie coming back toward the porch.

"Okay, but can we not tell them?" Penny had whispered frantically. "I feel like they'll be weird about it."

Carly had nodded, all serious. "Agreed."

Then they'd quickly, silently, locked pinkies before the two other Summer Sisters burst through the door.

Penny kept her eyes shut for a moment longer, letting that dark, desperate feeling flush through her. Then out of her.

She opened her eyes and stared up toward the water again, where a huge wave was approaching Dex. He got into position, stood up on his board, let the wave catch him, and . . . wiped out. Penny saw his head finally appear. Okay, so he wasn't a perfect surfboarding god.

Unfortunately, that only made her like him more.

$\star$

By three in the afternoon, people started to gather their belongings and leave the beach. The sun had moved into the western part of the sky, and the wind was picking up.

Dex was in the middle of showing Penny how to process rental returns when a guest appeared in the window of the beach shack. "I need help," the woman said.

Penny glanced up, then thought *Oh no.* It was the floppy-hat, flowy-dress mom.

"What can we do for you?" Dex asked.

"I've tried and tried, but I can't get my umbrella closed. Or out of the sand."

"No problem, let me—"

"I'll handle it," Penny jumped in.

Dex raised an eyebrow at her. "You sure? It can be tricky when the wind's whipping like this."

Penny shrugged. "I have to learn these things, right?"

Translation: *You don't know it, but I screwed up earlier and I need to redeem myself.*

Alternate translation: *I want to impress you.*

Dex gave her a sideways smile and waved his arm toward the beach. "Go for it."

Penny followed the woman to her umbrella, which was now turned inside out from the breeze. She bent down and tried to pull it closed, but it wouldn't give. She glanced up at the shack, where Dex was making a motion with his hand, pointing to the ground. What was he trying to tell her?

Ah, she thought, then knelt on the sand so she could pull the umbrella closed from below. It still wouldn't move, so she pulled harder, then harder again. Finally, it snapped shut . . .

And Penny was trapped inside the umbrella. With a bleeding finger, because somehow she'd pinched it so badly it broke the skin. She started to wiggle her way out, which caused the whole umbrella base to come free of the sand. Which then made the whole umbrella topple over, Penny and all.

She took a deep breath. *That didn't happen. You're actually still at the shack and you're just having a hallucination from being out in the sun all day.*

Then she heard pounding footsteps, and a shadow fell over her.

"You okay?" It was Dex's voice.

"Yup!" Penny chirped, trying to sound casual.

"Stay still. I'm going to slide this thing off of you."

Dex slowly pulled the umbrella away from Penny's body. Now there was sun and sky and air again. She sat up, but didn't want to look at Dex. He'd see that her face was flushed so red, it matched her shorts.

"I hope the umbrella's not damaged or anything," she mumbled as she scrambled to her feet.

"It's fine," Dex said. Penny heard him close the umbrella. "I was trying to tell you, pull it out of the sand first, *then* try to close it."

"Ah," she said, dusting off her legs and arms. "That makes sense."

Dex checked his watch. "It's a few minutes to five, but you can take off now. Nice job on your first day, Penny."

"Thanks," Penny said, still not able to look at him. "I'll try not to mess up like that again."

Dex laughed. He probably couldn't wait to meet up with his friends so he could tell them about this and howl as loud as he wanted. She started marching up the beach toward the gate.

"See you tomorrow morning," he called after her. "And, Penny?"

Uh, she thought. *The way he says my name. Also, Uh, I have to look at him now.*

Penny turned around. Dex was leaning against the folded-up umbrella, his head tilted to one side as if he was trying to see her in a new way.

"If something like this happens again, please don't worry about it," he said, with that easy smile. "It was pretty fun coming to your rescue."

Penny felt herself blush. She didn't like it.

"Really?" she said. "Well, maybe I can return the favor someday."

Then she spun back around and left as quickly as she could, wondering if Dex was watching her go.

⋛ 10 ⋚

"I'D TELL YOU TO BE NICE TO SASHA," NANA SAID as she unlocked the front door of the bakery. "But I don't need to. You're always nice to everyone."

Lainie scowled at her grandmother as she followed her inside. "I know what you're doing."

Nana smiled. "And is it working?"

"I have a right to be annoyed by this whole thing."

"Yes, you do," Nana said. "But I need you to try to be friendly. That girl has been through a lot."

Lainie raised her eyebrows, intrigued. "Like what?"

"Her father asked me not to share the details."

"What? You can't ask me to be friendly to someone who's totally rude and then not tell me why!"

Nana sighed, exasperated. "Okay. How about, you need to do it for my sake."

Damn it, Lainie thought. She couldn't say no to that.

Nana turned on the lights. "I have a lot of baking today, with the holiday weekend coming up. Sasha can help you handle things out here. You're in charge, okay?"

As her grandmother vanished into the kitchen, Lainie walked to her spot behind the counter. She felt a little smile coming on as she got to work prepping the register. Nana was giving her permission to boss this girl around. And she was going to make the most of it.

Fifteen minutes later, Sasha appeared in the front window and Lainie braced herself for whatever cringe-worthy thing was going to happen when she came inside. Instead, Sasha popped in a set of earbuds, fiddled with her phone, then closed her eyes and leaned against the side of the building.

Lainie checked her watch. Dulcie's opened in one minute. Sasha should have already washed her hands, put on an apron, and asked Lainie to go over the specials. *Nice job, dude*, she thought. *The work day hasn't even started and I'm already pissed off.*

Another minute later, Sasha still hadn't moved. Lainie unlocked the door and turned on the open sign, glaring at Sasha as she remained still.

Then a customer hurried in, brushing past Sasha on the way. Sasha didn't budge or even react. After Lainie served the customer and he left, coffee and muffin in hand, she approached the window, imagining how it would feel to bang on it right where Sasha's head was.

She was about to raise her hand to pound (okay, maybe just tap) on the glass when Sasha's eyes fluttered open and looked directly at Lainie. Sasha drew in a sudden breath, checked her watch, then rushed into the bakery.

"Sorry," Sasha mumbled as she removed her earbuds. "I was listening to something and lost track of time."

She paused and took a long look around, then sighed.

Yeah, I don't want you here, either, Lainie wanted to say. "We're about to get super busy," she mentioned instead. "I'll show you how to make the coffee."

"God, yes, coffee!" Sasha said, lighting up. "Can I have first dibs? I'll be, like, a taste tester."

Lainie bit her lip, wondering how much free food and drink this girl was going to mooch. "Sure, but you have to keep your cup out of the way. Things can be a little crazy if there's a line. You'll see what I mean."

Sasha watched as Lainie made a fresh pot. Nana popped out of the kitchen to say hello, then lingered a bit. Time to be fake-friendly.

"So, Sasha," Lainie asked. "Where did your family move from?"

"It's not my family," Sasha replied curtly. "It's just me and my dad. My mom lives in California."

"Oh. Where are you and your dad from, then?"

"Outside Chicago."

"What do you think of Ocean Park Heights?"

"It's lame as hell. I'm not really a beach person."

"Well, there's more to OPH than the beach. There's a lot of cool stuff in town."

"You mean that two-block stretch of Main Street? I wouldn't call that a town."

Alrighty, then. Lainie had officially tried. She shot Nana a glance, but Nana shrugged and went back into the kitchen. Lainie followed.

"Alaina," Nana said sternly once the door swung closed. "You need to be out front."

"I'm not sure I can do this," Lainie whispered. "Sasha doesn't even want to be in OPH and she clearly doesn't care about working at the bakery."

"Oh, mija," Nana said. "That's not on purpose. Think about it from her point of view. Everything in her life has just changed."

Um, hello? My life is changing, too, but you don't see me acting like I hate everyone and everything on the planet.

"Well, I can't act all nice to someone who's basically awful."

Nana paused. "It's usually people who seem 'awful' who need kindness more than anyone else. But I'll go work with her for a while. Can you finish these cookies?"

"Absolutely," Lainie said, relieved. Dulcie's famous almond cookie recipe was one of the few she knew by heart. After Nana left the kitchen, Lainie grabbed a spoon, dipped it into the batter, and licked it off. It was the taste of late-afternoon treats on the screened porch, of rainy summer mornings spent cooking with Nana. Would this taste always make her sad from now on?

Sad opened the door for Lainie to think about Carly. How would Carly handle Sasha? Lainie could picture Carly walking into the bakery and starting a conversation with her. It would probably have taken her two minutes to find something they both had in common. Carly would have come up with a way to handle this person, to make everything better. She always did.

That was how Lainie had met them all, at Anderson's Arcade, eight summers earlier. Lainie had wandered away from Papa and spilled her cup of game tokens. A group of bigger kids found this hilarious and encircled her, laughing and shouting "Arcade Fail! Arcade Fail!" Carly had stepped right past them, kneeling down to help Lainie pick up the tokens. "Get lost, Nick!" she'd yelled up at one of the boys. "You smell like hot-dog water!"

The weird insult made Lainie crack up, which made Carly crack up, and before she knew it, she was playing pinball with Carly and these two other girls—Daniella and Penny.

Carly's not going to come in and deal with this Sasha situation for you, Lainie thought. *Call someone else.* Daniella would understand what she was feeling, but was probably busy with her music program at the moment. . . . Maybe Penny was around? Lainie called.

"Hey!" Penny said when she answered. "What's up? I'm leaving for work in a few. Gah, that sounds so weird."

"I'm just so annoyed," Lainie said. "This girl Sasha whose dad is buying Dulcie's? I have to work with her all summer and she's literally the worst. She says OPH is lame."

"Well, she did just move here, right? She probably needs time to get used to everything."

"But I'd switch places with her in a second. She gets to live here year-round, and her dad will own Dulcie's! She has everything and she doesn't even know it."

"Sorry, Lainie," Penny said. "That sucks."

Lainie took a deep breath. Penny couldn't completely understand, but it had felt good, kind of, to rant a little. "So how was your first day at Anderson's?"

"Oh my God," Penny said. "Remember I told you about my supervisor, Dex? He's super sweet and really, really hot. Like, an unfair level of hot."

Lainie rolled her eyes, glad this wasn't a video call. She had bigger problems than super-hot coworkers. "Yep, I remember," she said tonelessly.

"I did this embarrassing, horrifying thing where I got caught in an umbrella—"

"What? How?"

"That's not important. What's important is that he thought the whole thing was adorable! We really clicked, too."

"That's great," Lainie told Penny, knowing that was what she was supposed to say.

Penny paused. "It sounds like you're not interested in hearing about this."

"What? No, I totally am," Lainie said defensively. "It's just hard for me to get all excited about this stuff with everything else going on."

"Wow," Penny shot back. "I didn't think it took that much brain power to be, like, happy for me."

"Penny! I *am* happy for you!" Lainie tapped the spoon against the mixing bowl. "But, I mean . . . what am I happy for? The fact that this guy Dex is hot and thinks you did something adorable?"

Lainie could hear Penny huff into the phone. "Arrrrgh, you're hopeless."

"Alaina!" Nana suddenly called from out front. "Can you bring out some buns?"

"I have to go," Lainie told Penny. Then, not wanting to end the call on this awkward note, asked, "Hey, what candy do you have with you today?"

Penny made a huffing sound that was almost a laugh. "Gummy penguins and chocolate malt balls."

"I've got lime taffy and sugar-free chocolate caramels," Lainie replied. "I can already tell they're disgusting."

"I like lime," Penny said. "Next time we meet up, we can do some trades."

At least it was something.

*

For the rest of the morning, Lainie went back and forth between helping Nana in the kitchen to serving customers out front. Sasha took a break every hour. She didn't even ask. She simply announced, "I'm going to get some air," or "I need a breather." Then she would go sit in the alley behind the bakery, drawing in a little black sketchbook.

Lainie kept sneaking glances at Sasha when she was on these breaks. She expected to see Sasha lighting up a cigarette, or smoking something worse. She almost hoped it would happen, so she could point it out to Nana. Then, Nana might understand why Sasha made Lainie want to scream.

But Nana smiled at Sasha as if Sasha didn't scowl at the customers when they ordered more than one or two things, or at those three boys who paid for their cookies with nickels and dimes.

"Ew!" she heard Sasha say at one point, when Nana and Lainie were packing up a large phone order. Lainie turned around to see Sasha eating a doughnut-shaped pan de queso, one of the Colombian specialties Dulcie's was best known for.

Sasha shook her head and scrunched up her face, spitting the bread into a napkin. "What is *in* this stuff?"

"Feta cheese," Lainie replied.

"Ugh, I can't stand feta. It tastes like spoiled food." Sasha dragged the back of her hand across her mouth, as if she'd eaten something truly vile.

Lainie's nostrils flared. "Well, maybe you should ask before sampling food that's meant for customers."

Sasha glanced at Nana as she tossed the napkin in a trash can. "Sorry, Dulcie."

Nana nodded at her. "It's fine. It's important that you know what's in everything on the menu, because people will ask about ingredients. Tomorrow, I'll talk you through every item. Okay?"

Sasha shrugged. "Okay." Then she went over to the coffee station to pour herself a cup.

Lainie shot her grandmother a baffled look. *This dreadful person completely disrespected your baking . . . and you just took it?*

But Nana simply smiled at Lainie, then went back to her work as if nothing had happened.

≳ 11 ≲

"I NEED A LATTE AS TALL AS THAT BUILDING OVER there," Jules said.

"Or a Dragon energy drink," Margot added. "Maybe three."

Adrian closed his eyes, drew in a deep breath. "I'd be happy with a Twix."

Daniella and the rest of the Glorious Oddballs shuffled out of the academy courtyard and onto the sidewalk, weighed down by their instruments and a long day of learning music, playing music, drumming, and dancing.

"What about you, Daniella?" Margot asked. "Wanna come with us?"

Daniella checked her phone. She'd made a plan with Zoe to go to the park as soon as she got back to the apartment. That bubble-tea-and-craft-store outing had been really fun, and the best time they'd ever had on their own (there had only ever been a few, but still). Zoe had come up with a whole picnic idea for them next.

"I should get going," Daniella said.

"Hang out for a few minutes," Jules said. "I'll ride with you to your subway stop."

"Isn't that completely out of your way?"

Jules shrugged. "I have a friend who lives on the Upper East Side. I can drop in and say hi."

Daniella was a little in awe of how Jules, Adrian, and Margot navigated the city on their own. One ticket on public transportation or a few clicks on a ridesharing app, and they could go wherever they wanted, to do (mostly) whatever they wanted.

Meanwhile, as a New York noob, Daniella still hated riding to and from the academy alone. She worried about someone harassing her, or the train getting stuck for hours, or losing track of time and missing her stop. Or a derailing accident. A fistfight in front of her. The list was getting longer.

Having Jules with her, even for just one trip, would make a big difference.

"Fine," she agreed. Zoe could wait a bit.

"There's a great deli a few blocks down that way," Adrian said. "Follow me."

$\star$

The deli was on a corner, with a smattering of tables outside.

Daniella, Jules, Adrian, and Margot plunked their purchases onto the biggest table and started digging in. Daniella had opted for a pineapple-flavored Italian ice. It wasn't the same as grabbing a pineapple whip from one of the boardwalk shops, but if she closed her eyes, it was a similar sensation.

Cold. Sweet. Summer.

When Daniella finally returned to reality, she noticed a little boy at the next table staring at them. Daniella waved at him, and he waved back.

Three seconds later, the boy was standing at their table. Jules, who was mid-swig on that giant coffee drink, froze. "Hi," they said, swallowing.

"What's in your suitcases?" the boy asked.

Jules looked over at their instrument cases, stacked against the wall, and turned back to the boy with a mischievous expression.

"Do you want to see?" they asked the boy, who nodded excitedly.

Daniella glanced at the boy's mom to see if she minded her kid talking to strangers, but the mom only looked up once before turning back to her phone.

Jules opened their saxophone case and took out the instrument to show the boy, then attached the mouthpiece.

"How do you play it?" the boy asked. Jules raised one eyebrow at him, then put the saxophone around their neck and started to slowly play. Daniella instantly recognized the beginning of the song "Señorita."

The boy started laughing with delight and clapped. "Cool!" he exclaimed.

Jules kept playing.

"I guess the coffee kicked in," Adrian muttered to Daniella.

The boy's mom got up and came over to listen, putting her hands affectionately on her son's shoulders. An elderly couple who had just crossed the street stopped in front of the table.

"Hey," Adrian said. "I have a brilliant idea. Isn't there something on that Bucket List about performing in public and earning money to buy a meal?"

"Yeah," Daniella said. "Carly's always trying to get us to do something at the boardwalk bandshell where I live. There are usually a ton of musicians out there, playing for donations. But we've never had the guts. I guess she figured the only way to get us to do it was to put it on the list."

"Well, forget the bandshell," Adrian said. "Let's do it here."

"Like *here* here?" Daniella asked, gesturing at the street corner around them. "Is that allowed?"

"Are you kidding? This is New York City. Busking is legal. Actually, they might arrest you if you're a musician and you *don't* play on the street."

Adrian unzipped his backpack and grabbed the pair of drumsticks that were always poking out of the top. He drummed them against the side of the table, then two empty chairs at the table next to him, then dinged one on the empty energy drink can. "Okay. This will work."

He watched and listened to Jules for a few beats, then started drumming a rhythm to match.

Without a word, Margot stood up and opened her violin case. She took out her violin, put the open case on the sidewalk in front of them, and started playing the same "Señorita" melody as Jules.

Jules stopped long enough to flash them a wicked smile before getting right back into the song.

Plink.

The elderly man tossed two quarters into the case, winked at Daniella, and continued down the street with his companion.

Oh my God, this is happening! Daniella thought. This crazy idea that had been a joke for the Summer Sisters was currently a right-in-front-of-her reality. She frantically dug out her phone and shot a bunch of photos, then some video, of her friends playing.

The song ended and everyone clapped—a few more people had stopped to listen. Now all those people were tossing coins and bills into Margot's violin case.

It won't count if you're not part of it, Daniella thought, the voice in her head sounding a lot like Carly. She knew, suddenly, that if she didn't join in, she'd always regret it. Always feel that she missed her chance to do something Carly had wanted her to.

Daniella picked up her oboe case and popped it open.

"Yes!" Adrian shouted as they finished up the song.

She assembled her instrument as quickly as she could, then stepped in between Jules and Margot.

"What do we play next?" Jules asked her.

The answer came to her, crystal clear. Carly's favorite song: "Riptide."

Looking at Jules, Daniella started to play the song. Jules recognized it almost immediately and began to play along. It took Margot a few bars before being able to jump in with her violin. For a really painful minute, they didn't sound so great. Fortunately, Adrian was drumming so loudly on the chairs, it was hard to notice anything else.

Then, suddenly, they weren't bad anymore. They sounded okay. Maybe even . . . great. Or at least, good enough for random people on the sidewalk to keep throwing money into Margot's case.

Jules led them from "Riptide" into some Lady Gaga, then Fall Out Boy, and then Taylor Swift.

These strangers, their audience, didn't know who Daniella was. She could be anybody. From anywhere, with any one of a thousand stories. In between songs, she pulled the oboe away from her face and took a deep breath of muggy summer city air. To her, it felt like the first true oxygen she'd had in a long time.

After five songs, Margot did a quick count of the money.

"We have eighteen dollars and seventy-five cents," she said. "Is that enough for dinner?"

"Depends on how hungry we are," Adrian said.

Daniella didn't feel that hungry; maybe because her stomach was full of happy butterflies. *I love, love, love this.* The music, her new friends, the joyful looks on strangers' faces. She wanted to keep going. "Let's play for a little longer," she suggested. "And then let's go to the first pizza place we find."

*

Three more songs and ten dollars later, Daniella, Jules, Margot, and Adrian packed up their instruments and began walking downtown.

Daniella felt her phone vibrate and checked it; she had three missed calls from Zoe.

UGH.

Zoe picked up on the first ring when Daniella called her back. "Where *are* you?" Zoe asked breathlessly.

"I'm so sorry," Daniella said as she walked. "I had to stay late and practice some music with a few other kids."

Margot, who was walking in front of Daniella, glanced back over her shoulder with a questioning expression. Daniella shrugged at her. So it wasn't the complete truth, but not a complete lie, either.

"Mom picked up some food for us to eat at the park," Zoe said. "Are you on your way back?"

Daniella stopped walking and held the phone against her chest for a moment. She knew the right answer to that question.

Yup, I'm headed to the subway now. Can't wait!

But the honest answer was something else. It sounded like *I'm having a really great time with my friends and somehow I don't feel so sad with them and sorry I want to stay.*

Daniella took a deep breath and brought the phone back up to her ear.

"Zoe, can we do the park tomorrow? I'm in the middle of something with these guys."

Adrian realized Daniella wasn't right behind them and motioned for everyone to wait. Daniella heard Zoe breathe out heavily, then pause before speaking. Her voice shaky.

"But you promised . . ."

Daniella winced. "I know. It's just that we can have a picnic at the park any day and today I really have to work on this assignment for my music program. I'll make it up to you, okay?"

"Sure," Zoe said, sounding half-furious, half-disappointed. Then she ended the call.

Daniella had lied. In her mind, she scooped up that lie with both hands, then put it down on the sidewalk in front of her to get a good look. As lies went, it wasn't too bad. She'd leave it right there by the fire hydrant and move on.

She hurried to catch up with the others.

A block later, Adrian spotted a place called Giacomo's New York Pie across the street.

"Are you Giacomo?" Margot asked the guy behind the counter as they all poured in through the door.

"I'm Ted," the guy replied. "Giacomo is my boss's great-grandfather. He died like a million years ago."

"Condolences," Margot said. "We'd like to order a New York pie and some sodas." She held out all the crumpled bills and started dropping quarters and dimes on the counter. "Do we have enough to get a basket of garlic bread, too?"

Ted began to count, but after a minute, he gave up. "Let's assume you do," he said. "Grab your drinks from the fridge and we'll get that food started."

Margot grinned and turned to Daniella. "Glorious Oddballs play for pizza!"

Daniella laughed. She took a quick photo of all the money on the counter, then she and Margot chose their drinks and sat down with Adrian and Jules at a table in the window.

"So, what did your friends think of the Glorious Oddballs hashtag?" Jules asked.

"Not sure," Daniella said. "They 'liked' the post but haven't said anything else yet. We haven't really had time to talk." What Daniella left out: She was afraid to ask Penny and Lainie directly.

"If it's going to go viral, we need to post more," Adrian said. "Maybe we could take pics of random weirdos we see in the city and post those."

"That feels mean," Daniella said, shaking her head. "We can't just decide someone's an oddball *for* them."

"And I think it's probably wrong to post people's pictures online without telling them," added Jules.

"What if we ask their permission?" Margot suggested.

Before Daniella could respond, Margot jumped up, went over to Ted behind the counter, and held up her phone.

"Hey," she said to him. "We're doing a social media project on people who are weird and proud. Can we take your picture for it?"

Daniella cringed. Margot really had a talent for being . . . direct.

Ted stared at Margot for a moment, and Daniella braced herself for whatever string of curse words was about to come. *Great, we're going to get kicked out before our food comes and I really wanted some garlic bread.*

Then Ted burst out laughing. "I do consider myself weird. I never thought about whether or not I'm proud of it but yeah, maybe I am. Normal is boring. Weird is . . ."

"Glorious!" Jules exclaimed.

Ted laughed again. "Yeah, glorious. Why not?"

Daniella couldn't believe it.

"So we can take your picture and post it on FotoSlam?" Margot asked. "We won't put in names or anything."

Ted shrugged. "Okay."

Margot turned to Daniella and pointed at her with a dramatic *You're up!* gesture.

Daniella went up to the counter to snap some photos of Ted. First, he simply leaned against the cash register and flashed a cheesy grin.

"Wait," he said after a few shots. "Let me try something else."

He picked up an empty pizza box, opened it, and put it on his head like a pointy hat. Instead of smiling, he took on a dead-serious expression and crossed his arms over his chest. Daniella laughed.

"Oddball enough?" Ted asked. Daniella nodded and took a few more pictures.

"That was perfect," she told him, amazed she'd just made that happen. "Thank you."

When Daniella sat back down at the table, Adrian high-fived her.

"Two Bucket List things going at once," he said. "You're killing this. Is it like, a contest? How are your other friends doing?"

"Not a contest," Daniella said, trying to find the right way to explain it. "We're simply, um, dividing up the work."

"So what have the others done so far?" Jules asked.

Daniella paused to think for a moment. "Well, Penny and Lainie did the candy thing together. That's about it so far."

"What about your other friend? There are four of you, right?" Jules looked at Daniella with an innocent, questioning expression. They had no idea that those words, *there are four of you*, caused Daniella physical pain.

"Carly," Daniella heard herself say. "I'm not sure. I hope she's working on something."

It didn't feel like a lie. Not here, in New York with the Glorious Oddballs. Completely by accident, Daniella had made a world where Carly wasn't gone, but simply . . . somewhere else. And she had only one thought about that world:

I don't want to leave yet.

⋛ 12 ⋚

A TOUGH-LOOKING GUY WITH A PIZZA BOX ON HIS HEAD.

Two older women wearing purple-sequined baseball hats, sitting on a park bench.

A toddler in a stroller, sticking out his tongue at the camera.

Each post had the same caption:

> Are you one of us #GloriousOddballs? Show us,
> tag us, and be proud.

Penny scrolled through the photos on Daniella's feed, making sure she'd "hearted" all of them. It still felt strange, and really not okay, that Daniella had (a) tackled two Bucket List items before checking with her and Lainie first, and (b) done them with random people she'd just met. WTF?

But still. She couldn't *not* like the photos. That would be plain wrong.

She thought about taking a selfie of her best crazy face to post and boost the hashtag, but a petty something held her back. *If Daniella wants to take over this part of the Bucket List, it's on her to make it go viral.* As for the post with Daniella and her friends playing music on a street corner and using the money to buy pizza . . . Penny would never have believed it without photo proof. She'd never known Daniella to do something so brave, which only made her more annoyed that she wasn't there to be part of it.

Then she glanced up from her spot at the rental hut counter.

There was Dex on the beach, pushing an elderly man in a special sand-friendly wheelchair, laughing as they made small talk.

Actually, no. She'd rather be right here.

"Are you ready for the invasion?" a voice behind her said.

It was Zohar, another beach attendant. He was fifteen, like Dex, but spent most of his time training in the Junior Lifeguard Program.

"You mean, Fourth of July?" Penny asked. "I think so. Are you?"

"I'm preparing for the worst. If we survive, we're going to need to celebrate, so I'm having a party tomorrow after the beach closes. Lots of Anderson's peeps will be there."

"Oh," Penny said. "Nice."

She glanced back at Dex, who was now setting the elderly man up with an umbrella.

"Hey. Hello?" Zohar said. Penny looked over again. "I'm *inviting* you to aforementioned party."

Penny laughed, surprised. Something told her this was going to be a *party* party. Not a bunch of kids playing video games in someone's basement, downing cupcakes and juice boxes. A party like the ones her brother Nick went to and described with words like *epic* and *insane*.

"That's . . . um . . . cool," Penny stammered, trying and failing to hide her excitement. "Thanks."

"No problem. Feel free to bring friends if you want."

Zohar grabbed a Beach Gear Rental Agreement from the clipboard on the counter, flipped it over, and wrote an address on the back. Penny began mentally browsing her closet, wondering if anything she owned would be good enough for this older-kids-and-probably-alcohol situation.

Dex returned to the hut and smiled at Penny, which had the effect of making her legs feel suddenly boneless. She leaned against the counter for support.

"That guy was really interesting," Dex said, pointing with his thumb at the man he'd just wheeled across the sand. "He's been coming here for decades and used to surf here in the sixties."

"Wow," Penny said.

"That's old-school, dude," Zohar added.

"He said he even met his wife here, right on this beach. She passed away a few years ago, but he still makes the trip on their anniversary every year. I know this sounds corny, but that could be the most romantic thing I've ever heard."

Dex had said the word *romantic* so naturally, so comfortably. The boys at Penny's school would rather get pantsed in public than talk about *romance*. Last year, Penny had seen one of them pretend to throw up when a girl gave him a red carnation on Valentine's Day.

But Dex was different, and he knew it, and he was more than okay with it.

Maybe if I got to spend more time with him, Penny thought, *some of that confidence would rub off on me.*

★

"Come onnnnnnn, Lainie!" Penny took a bite of a Dulcie's red velvet cupcake and didn't even swallow before adding, "It'll be fun." It came out as *Ilbefuh*.

Lainie wiped crumbs off the Dulcie's counter and bit her lip. "I'm not going to a party with a bunch of people I don't know."

"That's the point of going to parties," Penny said with a sigh. "So you meet people. Then after you meet them, you *know* them. Also, there'll be boys there. Older ones."

Sasha, who was sitting at a corner table and decorating bakery boxes with Sharpie drawings of dolphins, suddenly glanced up. "Those are the best kind," she said.

Lainie rolled her eyes at Sasha. "Thanks for sharing."

Sasha glared back at Lainie and returned to her drawing.

"Lainie, please," Penny urged. "We've had almost no time to hang out this summer. Also, I don't want to go alone." She paused. "If Carly were coming with us, you'd say yes."

Lainie looked at Penny like she'd just been slapped. "That's not fair."

"Maybe not fair," Penny said, shrugging, "but totally true."

They were both silent for a few moments, until Penny wished she could un-say that thing about Carly.

Finally, Lainie sighed and said, "It's the Fourth of July, Pen. We go out on Papa's boat to eat sandwiches and watch the fireworks from the water. You know that." Lainie looked down at her hands, and Penny noticed the nails bitten to shreds. "Actually, I was, uh, hoping you'd come with me this year. Since, you know, it's the last—"

Lainie's voice choked up and she bit her lip again. Penny could tell she was on the verge of tears.

"I get it," Penny said. "I'm sorry I pushed. You should do the boat."

Lainie nodded, trying to pull it together. "And you should, you know, have a good time with that guy Dex."

"Eh, I don't even know if he'll be there," Penny said. "And that's not why I want to go."

"You keep telling yourself that!" Sasha piped up from the corner.

Lainie glanced at Sasha, and Penny could almost see death rays coming out of her friend's eyes. Suddenly she understood just how sad and angry Lainie was.

"Let's get together on Sunday, okay?" Penny suggested. "And bring your candy."

Lainie managed a small smile. "Okay."

As Penny left the bakery, she tried not to think about Lainie's about-to-cry face. Why did she have to be so emotional and serious all the time? *Things change for everyone. Deal with it.* It was probably a good thing, Lainie not coming to the party. She probably would have ruined it for Penny.

But did she have the guts to go on her own?

$$\star$$

Penny rode her bike home and walked in the door to find her little brother, Jack, vacuuming the living room. Nick was doing dishes in the kitchen. Her brothers only did chores when their mom was desperate to clean and offered them cash, so something was up.

"Oh good, you're back," Penny's mom said as she popped her head out of the bathroom. "They'll be here soon."

Penny rolled her eyes closed. She'd totally forgotten that her mom's best and oldest friend, Kathy, was coming to stay for a week. Along with her daughter, Jamie, who was sixteen. She and Penny saw each other several times a year and for as long as Penny could remember, Jamie had the life Penny wanted. First, it was simply *bigger*, with more privileges because she was two years older. Then, Jamie was . . . *Jamie*. She had tons of friends, the best clothing style, listened to new music before anyone else discovered it, and was able to rock any hairstyle or makeup look she saw online.

Unfortunately, Jamie was also one of the nicest people Penny had ever met, making it impossible to hate her for any of it.

Penny went to join her mom in the bathroom. "What else do you need help with?" she asked. "I'll do anything except set up a beach umbrella or chairs."

"Can you finish up in here?" Mom said. "Also, I would like it on record that if either of your brothers ever manages to clean their own hair out of the shower drain, I will die of shock."

"I'll make sure to tell that to the police when they're investigating your death," Penny said.

This made Mom laugh, a laugh that always lit up a place, even if was the bathroom. Penny realized she hadn't heard it in a while.

An hour later, Penny was in her attic room when she heard the screen door slam and a lot of high-pitched shrieking. She followed the noise outside, where her mom and Kathy were hugging and somehow also jumping up and down. Would she be that way with Lainie and Daniella, when they were older? With Carly, she would have. No question. But Daniella and Lainie? She wasn't so sure.

Penny felt a quiet, desperate sadness creep along a frayed edge somewhere inside her. She mentally flicked it away, focusing on the person emerging from the driver's side of Kathy's car.

Now the person was walking toward Penny and it took her a moment before she realized, *OMG, it's Jamie.*

And she's hella gorgeous.

In the six months since they'd seen each other, Jamie must have finished whatever process morphed you from a pretty teen into an adult-level beautiful *young woman.* Even the way Jamie was moving up the driveway was more like gliding than anything you could do with your feet.

Plus, she drives now. Jealousy thrummed through Penny's veins, just imagining the freedom Jamie had.

"Penny!" Jamie exclaimed, folding Penny into a hug. "It's so great to see you."

"You too," Penny said, hugging back, realizing with horror that Jamie's chest was now smaller than hers.

"I'm all creaky from being in the car," Jamie said. "I'm going to go for a quick run, and then we need to catch up."

Penny felt a brainstorm hit.

"For real," she began. "And then, you wanna come to a party with me tomorrow night?"

✶

Zohar wasn't kidding about the invasion thing. The next day, July 4, was 100 percent the busiest day of the year, the busiest day Penny ever wanted to imagine, at Anderson's Beach. She was the most exhausted version of exhausted she'd been in her life. So tired, she didn't even notice when her brothers made rude comments about her windblown hair and sweat-soaked definitely-see-through shirt when she got home.

Now she was clean, her hair was untangled (mostly), and she was wearing the only dress she could find that didn't feel like it was going to fall down any second in a traumatic wardrobe malfunction.

"Whoa!" Jamie said when Penny stepped out onto the porch. "My little girl is all grown up."

"Stop," Penny replied, rolling her eyes. "Let's get out of here before my brothers see us."

As they started walking, Penny sneaked a thorough look at Jamie. Her long, straight brown hair was pulled back into a loose braid. She wore a simple lace-trimmed tank, denim miniskirt, and leather flip-flops. Some pretty handmade jewelry and not much makeup. *Great,* Penny thought. *Next to her, I look like I'm trying way too hard.* But there wasn't time to change now.

"How's life at the shore?" Jamie asked.

Penny wasn't sure where to even start with that. Drama with her parents, her brothers, Lainie and Daniella. Maybe Jamie could be the person she shared it all with. Soon, maybe. But not yet.

"It's okay," Penny finally said. "I have a job at Anderson's Beach."

"I heard! Congrats."

Penny remembered that her mom told Jamie's mom everything, and Jamie's mom usually turned around and told Jamie. The result: Jamie always knew tons about Penny, but not vice versa.

"And how are you doing?" Jamie continued. "You know . . . without Carly here."

Penny stumbled for a half second, tripped up by the question. Jamie had met Carly a handful of times over the years, but nobody else had asked her that since the summer began.

"It sucks," Penny said.

"I get it," Jamie told her. "I've been there. Let me know if you ever want to talk."

Jamie's dad had died of cancer when Jamie was little. Jamie could probably answer some of the questions Penny kept in a secret drawer in her head. *When does it get better? Are you able to feel happy when you think of your dad now?* Jamie had given her helpful advice in the past, on everything from using a wet toothbrush to comb your doll's hair to how to put in a tampon in less than five seconds.

But Penny didn't want to feel the feels those questions would bring her, even if Jamie's answers were helpful. Plus, there was a good chance whatever she said would get back to her mom, and her mom had enough to deal with.

Finally, Penny just said, "Thanks," and they walked the final block to Zohar's house in silence.

As they got close, Penny could see light and movement through the screen door. As she climbed the steps to the porch, she turned to Jamie.

"Can you go first?" Penny asked.

Jamie chuckled. "Sure."

Inside, Penny spotted Zohar standing with a group of people. He waved Penny and Jamie over, and everyone started introducing themselves. The other kids seemed happy to meet them. One of Penny's favorite songs played through hidden speakers. "I love your dress!" one girl told her. "I wish I could wear this kind of thing."

Penny felt a woosh of relief and accomplishment. She was now, officially, at her first real OPH teen party. *If Carly had finished the Bucket List, I bet this would have been on it.*

Suddenly Penny heard several people roaring with laughter, and glanced over to see Jamie with a bunch of guys clustered around her. The girl who'd just been talking to Penny now edged toward Jamie's group. Zohar was doing the same. It was like watching magnetism happen in slow motion.

"I'm obsessed with this bracelet," the girl was saying to Jamie, touching her wrist.

"Thanks," Jamie said, smiling brightly at her like they'd been lifelong friends. "I actually made it."

"No!"

Penny watched Jamie for a moment, trying to figure out how, exactly, she pulled this off. She didn't seem to be trying at all. Simply being herself. Her beautiful but approachable, down-to-earth but stylish, confident but easygoing self.

I'd do anything to be like her, Penny thought.

All the boys in the room had moved into Jamie's orbit. By the looks on their faces, they wanted to stay there as long as they could. Then came the sensation of intense, almost painful, regret.

Oh God. I've made a terrible mistake.

What boy is going to want to talk to me if she's here? What GIRL, for that matter?

Penny's next instinct was to get far, far away from Jamie.

"I'll get us more drinks," Penny heard one girl say to another. As the girl started walking through the house, Penny followed, trying not to be creepy about it. Down a hallway, through a kitchen, and then out another door to the backyard . . . where there were even more people.

The yard was lit with strings of red, white, and blue lights. A big table full of snacks and drinks stretched along one side, near a small swimming pool. Penny scanned the scene but didn't see anyone who looked familiar.

"Don't be a loser," Penny muttered to herself. "Just go up to someone and say hi."

"Or you could experiment with 'Hi, I'm a loser' and see what happens."

Penny flinched, mortified. It was Dex. With his constant companion, The Smile.

"Hey!" she said. *Crap, did I sound excited enough to see him? TOO excited? What's the right amount of excited to seem when you secretly want to jump up and down squealing with happiness that he's here?*

"Nice work out there on Cray-Cray Day," Dex said.

Penny laughed. "I like that. Zohar called it the Invasion."

"It does feel like we survived some kind of battle." Dex was holding a beer, and he paused to take a sip. Penny took a micro-glance at the bottle, trying to be blasé about it. "My feet are killing me," Dex added. "Wanna go sit over there and dip them in the pool?"

"Yeah, sure." *Are you serious, of course!*

"Do you need something to drink?" he asked, pointing to the table.

Penny checked out the other kids in the backyard. Most had beer or hard seltzers. Should she? Did she even want to?

"I'll start with a soda, thanks," she said, listening to her gut. Simply being at this party felt like a big enough deal.

Sitting next to Dex on the edge of a swimming pool, surrounded by colors and American flags, felt very different from standing next to him in the beach rental hut. Suddenly he wasn't her supervisor. She wasn't sure what to say to him if it didn't involve lounge chairs or annoying beach guests.

"So," Dex said, nodding toward a nearby table with an open umbrella in the middle. "I don't know about you, but I have the urge to go close that. You'll see. After a few more weeks as a beach attendant, open umbrellas just sitting there after hours, without anyone under them, will totally drive you insane."

Penny smiled. "Well, I'd go close it for you. But you know me. I might get stuck in the process."

Dex laughed and Penny's smile widened until it hurt.

"Honestly, that was nothing," Dex said. "I've seen some weird stuff. Last year, I helped this couple set up a big fancy picnic on the beach. The second we finished placing everything in the perfect spot, two seagulls came by. One stole all the smoked salmon and the other pooped on the salad. Then a stray cat who was living under the boardwalk smelled everything and started stalking the food."

"Maybe it was Tomcat Vigilante," Penny said.

Dex frowned, confused. "What?"

Oh God. What did I just do? "Sorry, he's from this cartoon—"

"I know who he is," Dex said, his face lighting up. The dimples emerging. "I *love* that show. You watch it?"

"Yeah. My mom got me into it. That's sort of our thing, watching wacky cartoons together."

"I discovered it one day when I was flipping channels," Dex said. "And I cracked up at every single line. It's so . . . different from anything else I've seen on TV. Everyone I know thinks it's too weird."

Dex stared at her, and Penny found herself staring back. Was she supposed to say something now? What should she say? Was it okay that they were looking at each other for three, now four, now five seconds?

A guy came up behind Dex—Penny had seen him surf with Dex a few times—and put his hand on Dex's shoulder.

"Dude," the guy said. "The sun's going down. Should we head out to . . . you know?"

Dex checked his watch. "Yeah, totally." He stood up, and beads of water from the pool spritzed Penny's arm, making the hairs stand on end. "Penny, do you want to come with us? We're going to watch the fireworks from a top secret location."

"Um . . ." Penny stood up, too, feeling the cool air on her wet feet.

"If I tell you where it is, you may not be able to say no," Dex said. "Brady here, he works at the batting cages. He can sneak us in. The view from there is perfect, and there's no crowds."

The batting cages. It wasn't a place she went. Under the word *klutz* in the dictionary, there should be a picture of her playing softball in gym class. But she'd been there once to pick up her brother. It was above the arcade, and the view was probably perfect like Dex said . . .

Wait. The cages were on a *rooftop*.

And Dex was a *cute boy*. (Well, way more than cute, but that was beside the point.)

Penny felt a nervous flutter in the tips of her fingers. This situation sounded amazing. Also terrifying. She heard the sound of more people spilling into the yard; it was Jamie and her instant entourage. Penny knew, instinctively, that she needed to keep Jamie from meeting Dex. There was no way she could compete.

What would Carly do in this situation?

Hell, Carly would go to the batting cages. Carly would be super-pissed if Penny didn't.

"Okay, sure," Penny said.

The words had just come out of her mouth. But Dex was smiling again, so she was glad.

Penny glanced up at the sky. *Hope you're satisfied. Now, can you send me a little of your courage?*

$\star$

There were six of them. Brady had a key card and after the *beep* of the lock opening, they shuffled silently up the stairs and into the batting cages. A couple of guys carried six-packs of beer. Brady led them to the chain-link fence that faced the water. Dex sat down on the ground and motioned for Penny to join him.

The fireworks would be starting soon, and while they waited, Penny and Dex talked. Penny admitted she was nervous about high school, and Dex offered his best advice: "Remember, all those movies and TV shows and books that make you think high school is going to be the best years of your life—they're all wrong. If you can keep that in mind, that's like half the battle right there."

Out of the corner of her eye, Penny could see that the four other kids—two boys and two girls—had paired off and were making out in different shadowy corners of the batting cages. A tingling heat crept up the back of her neck.

Dex glanced over at one of the couples, then down at his hands.

Penny could hear what her brother Nick called "mixing tuna-and-mayo sounds." *GAH.*

"So . . ." Penny began, trying to think of some conversation starter. "What happened to make you so anti–high school?"

Dex laughed softly, and Penny could hear relief in there somewhere. "I'm not anti–high school. At least I don't think I am. I guess I'm more of a realist. You can't expect something to magically be the way you pictured it. You have to just, like, make the best of what it actually is. You know?"

Penny watched Dex's eyes flick over to another one of the couples, then back to her.

"Not really," she admitted.

"All right. Here's an example." He started telling Penny some hilarious stories about his freshman year, and he was in the middle of a sad tale about going to the wrong English class for a full week when the first firework shot into the sky and exploded above them.

Penny let out a sigh. One of her secrets was that she super-loved fireworks. And right now she loved them even more because they were rescuing her from this awkwardness of *everyone's making out and we're not*.

The Ocean Park Heights July Fourth Spectacular was set to a soundtrack, and Penny got lost in the combination of music, lights, and patterns against the backdrop of a star-speckled night. It gave her chills, and she shivered a bit.

"Are you cold?" Dex asked, taking his sweatshirt from around his waist and draping it across Penny's shoulders.

No way was she going to correct him.

After the big fireworks finale accompanied by "Party in the U.S.A.," everyone clapped softly and tiptoed out of the batting cages. On the way down the stairs, Dex put his hand on Penny's arm. Chills again.

"Which way are you headed?" he asked.

"My house is, like, three blocks that way," Penny replied, pointing.

"I'll walk you back."

They were quiet for the first block.

In the middle of the second block, Dex suddenly spoke. "Hey, would you want to hang out some night next week? We could get food on the boardwalk and hit the arcade. Or whatever."

Penny kept putting one foot in front of the other, moving her body as if this were a normal moment.

But it wasn't. Inside her, there was a whole new set of fireworks launching. She hoped Dex couldn't tell when she turned to him, smiled casually, and said, "That sounds fun. I'm in."

After Penny waved goodbye to Dex and headed up the front steps of her house, she started mentally typing a message to Carly. Then she remembered, and it stopped her in her tracks.

You could cry, she thought. *Or you can text Lainie and Daniella about this.*

It wouldn't be the same as telling Carly, but it was what she had, and maybe that was enough.

⪢ 13 ⪡

LAINIE REACHED INTO HER CANDY BAG AND PULLED out the first thing her fingers touched: a huge green gummy frog.

Yessssss.

She popped it into her mouth, knowing it was strange to stress-eat candy when you worked in a bakery. But the candy made her feel closer to Penny and Daniella. And Carly. Which was also strange, but whatever. This gummy frog was delicious.

Lainie opened up a notes app on her phone where she'd been keeping track of her candy and their ratings. Green gummy frog, she typed. 8.5

It made her forget, for a few seconds, how annoyed she was, and how her annoyance had one source: Sasha.

Sasha came late every day. She had to be reminded to take out her earbuds when working behind the counter. She kept calling pastries by the wrong names on purpose. She grabbed every opportunity to step outside for a break or go to the bathroom. The only time Sasha appeared to be enjoying herself was when her dad came in to work with Nana in the kitchen. Then she put on a big, fake smile and acted like everything was fine.

The thing that drove Lainie the craziest, made Lainie hate Sasha extra-intensely, was how rude she was about customers. Especially the regulars, most of whom Lainie had known her whole life. People who were a big part of Ocean Park Heights and the reason it was such a magical place.

"Oh my God, I wish I could *burn* that dude's hat," Sasha had said that morning after they waved goodbye to Wes. Wes ran the fishing supply shop at the dock where Papa kept his boat. Without him, there would be no shrimp, crab, or lobster in Ocean Park Heights and even beyond. He wore a fishing hat with homemade lures sewn onto it. It was a famous hat. Everyone knew the hat. Everyone loved the hat.

"Don't trash-talk stuff you know nothing about," Lainie snapped at her. "I mean, I know your life goal is to hate on everyone and everything, but it might be good to take a break sometimes."

Sasha rolled her eyes, then retreated to her corner table with that sketchbook. Her doodles had begun showing up here and there throughout Dulcie's. First on the bakery boxes—which, unfortunately, customers loved—then on the corners of the memo board, and just that morning, two of the display case signs. Now that Sasha was focused on something else, Lainie reached into the case, took those signs out, crumpled them up, and threw them in the garbage. Then she made two new ones. Only words. No stupid drawings.

Afterward, Lainie dipped into her candy bag again. One more, and she'd go back to wiping down the espresso machine. What would it be this time? She was hoping for something crunchy now, but she'd made a rule for herself that she'd pull the pieces out randomly and eat whatever fate gave her. That's the way Penny said she was doing it. That's the way Carly would have insisted on.

SweeTarts. Not naturally crunchy, but if she bit into one instead of sucking on it . . .

"More sugar to poison your brain?" Sasha asked.

Lainie slammed her hand on the counter. "Why don't you work on getting a life instead of picking apart mine?"

Sasha simply stared at Lainie until Lainie had to look away. She grabbed a rag and started wiping the counter with a vengeance.

"I see you with that bag every day," Sasha said then, shrugging casually, like nothing had happened. "What's the deal?"

Lainie kept wiping. Should she explain? Did Sasha deserve to know about the Summer Sisters and the Bucket List? Some small, possibly masochistic part of her was curious to hear what Sasha would say.

"It's from Candy Universe," Lainie began, just waiting for Sasha to start bad-mouthing the place. "My friend Penny and I had to take one piece of bulk candy from every single barrel. Then we have to taste each one and rate it."

Sasha frowned and tilted her head. "Like, on a dare?"

"Kind of," Lainie said. "We have a summer bucket list of fun things to do."

"Well, *that* figures," Sasha muttered.

"What the hell does that mean?" Lainie asked.

"You're all about *doing stuff*. Accomplishing. Checking items off an actual list of fun! That's the most pathetic thing I've ever heard."

Lainie felt her nostrils flare and heat creep up her neck. "And there you go again, talking trash about something you'll never understand."

Lainie turned around, hoping that would end the argument. She had to try harder to get along, for Nana's sake. She grabbed a broom and started sweeping. If she stayed busy when there were no customers, she wouldn't have to talk. No talking equaled no fighting.

"Then again . . ." Sasha said after a few moments. "Being stuck in this dumb little town all summer, I'd probably need something dorky like a bucket list to survive."

Dumb little town. Stuck. Dorky.

Carly would have lost it if she'd heard this.

Lainie stormed over to Sasha and pointed the brush end of the broom at her, jabbing at the air.

"Shut. The. Hell. Up. If being here is some kind of punishment, then leave! Run away! Hitchhike to Chicago. Or wait. Maybe you can't go back there. Maybe everyone in that whole city freaking *hates* you!"

Sasha's eyes went wide, like dark, round pools. That were now filling with tears.

Oh God, Lainie thought. *She's not going to—*

A sob escaped from Sasha's throat, a cry like she'd stepped on something sharp and painful. She burst out of her chair and out the bakery door.

Nana came running in from the kitchen. "What just happened?"

Lainie felt dazed. What *did* just happen? She turned to her grandmother. "We had a fight."

"Alaina, what did you say?"

She swallowed hard. "Uh . . . a few things. But she started it!"

The second the words were out of her mouth, Lainie realized how childish they sounded. Nana shook her head, glaring at her. "I told you, mija. There's a lot going on there. You don't know what Sasha's been dealing with."

Lainie threw up her hands. "Do you know what *I've* been dealing with? First Carly, now losing the bakery and the house and everything?"

"Yes, I do know," Nana said, softening, taking Lainie's hand. "It's a lot to carry, and you haven't been yourself lately. So maybe you can understand why Sasha hasn't been herself, either."

They both fell quiet as Nana stroked Lainie's thumb. It felt so good, so comforting. Suddenly all Lainie wanted to do was crawl into bed and take a three-day nap.

"I'll call Mr. Mason and he'll talk to her," Nana said finally. "Do you know where she went?"

"No," Lainie replied. "But she left her phone and earbuds here, so I'm sure she didn't go far."

Nana nodded and moved over to the register to pick up the bakery phone. Lainie retreated through the door to the kitchen and put her face down sideways on a counter. Ever since she was little, that feeling of cool, clean metal on her cheek helped her calm down.

A few minutes later, Nana came in and, without a word, pulled her into a big hug.

"I'm sorry," Lainie murmured, resting her chin on her grandmother's shoulder. "She just made me so mad."

"I know. It hasn't been easy having her here. But it's better, yes? Knowing who'll be running the bakery? It's better for *me*."

"Yeah," Lainie said, squeezing her grandmother. "It's better for me, too."

Nana sighed heavily. "I can tell you about Sasha now. Mr. Mason said it was okay. It'll help you understand."

Lainie frowned and pulled out of the hug. "Okay. . . ."

"It's been a rough few years for that girl. Her father says she has depression and anxiety. She used to . . . hurt herself. She's been in and out of hospitals and other programs. Part of the reason they're moving here from Chicago is to start fresh, to give Sasha a new environment. But when she's anxious, she gets angry."

Lainie was silent, taking all that in. "So . . . she must be anxious all the time, then?"

Nana shrugged. "Mr. Mason said she's really struggling with the changes. She's acting mad, but really, she's sad. Hopefully, she'll feel more settled soon."

But really, she's sad. This struck Lainie in a deep, raw, too-familiar spot.

Lainie remembered the way Sasha leaned against the window that first morning, with her eyes closed. Sasha taking lots of breaks to get fresh air. Maybe she wasn't doing that because she was lazy, but because she *needed* to.

"I feel like a giant jerk," Lainie said.

"Don't. You had no way of knowing. And she *is* difficult to be with. Believe me, I get frustrated by that, too."

"But you're so nice to her."

Nana smiled, then tucked a strand of hair behind Lainie's ear. "Well, think about it. Someone doesn't feel good, so you take care of them. You offer them kindness. And then hopefully, they feel better."

Lainie searched her grandmother's face. "You make it sound so simple. What if they make that difficult?"

Nana shrugged. "Then you try harder." She paused. "I have an idea.

I've been thinking about your Bucket List and how I can help. Turns out, one of Papa's friends has a son who works on a parasailing boat."

Lainie's face lit up. "For real? Penny's going to flip out."

"I'll arrange everything," Nana said, then gave Lainie a long, direct look. "But you're not going to do it with Penny."

"What do you mean—" Then Lainie realized where Nana was headed with this. "Nope. No freaking way."

"Alaina . . . *yes.*"

Lainie shook her head. It was supposed to be her and Penny flying high above the water, shouting into the breeze. Not her and Sasha. There was no *her and Sasha.*

"So you're, like, blackmailing me?"

Nana shrugged.

"You don't get it. The point of the Bucket List is that it's only the Summer Sisters."

"But Daniella is in New York, and her mother said she's been doing some things there with friends from her program."

"Don't remind me," Lainie grumbled. She glanced at Nana and could tell there was no way she was going to budge on this. "Fine," she said with a sigh. "I don't like you when you're controlling."

Nana gave her a sideways smile. "Oh, mija. I'm *always* controlling. I'm just so good at it, you don't notice."

Then Lainie's grandmother winked at her and left.

✳

As the boat sped up, out of the river and into the open ocean, Lainie closed her eyes to the spray on her face. The smell of salt and seaweed.

The white noise of the engine mixed with a trio of pelicans flying above them. It was a painfully beautiful, cloudless sky. Almost too perfect, like it was making fun of Lainie for dreading this whole thing.

I should be here with Penny, she kept thinking. *And Daniella. Carly, too, of course. Always Carly, too.*

Instead, she was sitting across from Sasha, Nana, and Mr. Mason. Sasha was either excited beyond words or terrified for her life. Lainie couldn't tell which. The girl simply stared out at the water, twirling a strand of her hair around one finger, over and over and over.

Finally, the boat slowed, then sputtered to a stop. Sam, the son-of-Papa's-friend, turned around and clapped his hands together.

"Okay!" he said. "Are you girls going to do two solo rides, or one tandem?"

"Tandem," Sasha blurted out before Lainie could even decide which was worse. "If I die, I don't want to die alone," she added. But then she broke into a grin, and Lainie realized Sasha wasn't scared at all. She was totally psyched.

The next few minutes were a blur. Lainie and Sasha got strapped into their harnesses on the parachute that was now hovering above the stern of the boat. Nana snapped about a million pictures with Lainie's phone. And then, before Lainie could say something snarky to Sasha, or anything at all, they were suddenly rising into the air, fast, fast, fast. The first thing Lainie noticed was that ocean water was a different color up here. Then she glanced toward shore, where the entire boardwalk of Ocean Park Heights looked like it had shrunk to the size of a toy village.

All the Summer Sisters should see this, she thought. *I'd give anything to have Daniella next to me right now. Penny and Carly down there on the boat, waiting their turn.*

Lainie spotted Nana and Mr. Mason far below them, taking photos.

She heard Sasha draw in a breath and turned to see the girl's face animated and alive. Her cheeks flushed. She looked like a completely different person.

Now the boat was moving, and they were moving, too. Soaring, really.

Sasha let out a *"Woo-hoo!"*

Lainie laughed. Without thinking, she let that laugh become a *"Yee-haw!"*

"This is amazing!" Sasha shouted to the sky as she leaned her head back. "Isn't it amazing?"

"Yeah!" Lainie called back. She glanced down at the boat. Then, off to the right, she spotted some shadows flickering under the water's surface. There were two, one bigger than the other.

"Look!" Lainie said, tapping Sasha on the leg and pointing. "Dolphins!"

Sasha gasped when she saw them. "Oh my God," she muttered, her voice full of wonder.

"Aren't they the coolest?" Lainie asked. "They're my all-time favorite animal."

Sasha watched the dolphins intensely for a few moments. "Mine too," she said. "It's actually one of the reasons we decided to live near an ocean."

Lainie nodded, and they were silent for a few moments. Simply existing together in the same space.

Finally, Sasha asked, "Do you think this is what a kite feels like?"

Lainie let out a laugh. "Probably."

Sasha closed her eyes again, and Lainie took in a deep, deep breath. Deeper than she had in a long time, like she was filling herself up with as much of Ocean Park Heights as she could.

They didn't speak again for the rest of the ride, but it felt okay. It felt like they didn't need to.

⋛ 14 ⋚

LEATHER JACKET, JEANS, AND BLACK DOC MARTENS. Red fingerless gloves holding a book written in French.

Daniella couldn't stop staring at the guy sitting next to her on the subway. Up in the real world above them, it was the hottest day of the year. Almost ninety-five degrees. Why was he dressed like it was February and also 1987?

Glorious Oddball.

Ugh, she really wanted to sneak a photo of him and post it with the hashtag. Too bad Jules wasn't there. Or Carly, of course. They would have the guts to ask and not care if he gave them a dirty look or said something rude. Daniella went through those scenarios in her head, and even that gave her a flutter of panic in her chest. Why did she have to be so pathetic?

But she *was* riding the train alone all the way down to Eighth Street, to meet her friends at Washington Square Park. So maybe she was . . . growing?

"If you can get there without any panic, that's a win," Dr. Richards had said during their last video session, when Daniella had mentioned she was nervous about her weekend plans.

"That's a really small win," she'd said.

He'd shrugged, his shoulders appearing for a moment in his video window, then disappearing. "Small wins are worth celebrating. Then you build on them for the bigger wins."

A bigger win. Like instead of wishing Jules or Carly were with you to do a scary thing, actually doing that scary thing yourself.

Daniella drew in a deep, deep breath, then let it out. She mentally counted to three and turned to the leather-jacket guy. "Excuse me . . ." she said softly, half hoping he wouldn't even hear.

But he looked up at her. "Yes?" His eyes were kind, curious.

Daniella felt encouraged by that. "This is going to sound weird, but I'm doing a kind-of experiment for FotoSlam. I came up with a hashtag—GloriousOddballs—and I've been posting photos of people celebrating their uniqueness, or whatever. Would you mind if I took your picture and posted it?"

The guy stared at her for several long seconds, and it felt like torture. Then one side of his mouth turned up into a crooked smile.

"Sure," he said. "Cool idea."

"Thanks so much," Daniella said, relief whooshing through her.

She held up her phone and the guy looked into the camera, keeping his tilted smile and raising one eyebrow, as if he were trying to appear both suave *and* silly. Cli-*click*.

"Can you tag me so I can repost it?" the guy asked as Daniella opened up FotoSlam. "I'm @KrishnaCade." He spelled it for her.

"Of course!" Daniella said, as the train slowed for the next stop and the guy got up.

"Good luck," he called to her when he stepped off the train.

Daniella waved, then turned back to her phone. She added the photo, the guy's username, and what felt like the perfect caption.

If you ride the subway looking too awesome for this
time period, you are definitely a #GloriousOddball.

After she shared the post on FotoSlam, she clicked on the Glorious Oddballs hashtag. It was something she checked a few times a day, to see if anyone else had picked it up. Jules, Margot, and Adrian had each posted a few photos, but so far, their viral try had been a dud. It was one of the hardest things Carly had ever put on a bucket list. Maybe if they'd all agreed on the final list together, as they always had in the past, they would have cut this task.

Thanks a lot, Carly.

Daniella also didn't understand why Lainie and Penny hadn't posted anything yet. She'd texted them a few days earlier, asking them to. They both said they would when they could, when they saw something that fit the hashtag. Which was feeling more and more like an excuse, making Daniella feel more and more annoyed.

But wait. There was a new photo under the hashtag, right before the one Daniella had just posted. A shot of a dog with crossed eyes and his tongue hanging out.

My pup doesn't even know the word "freak" and
that's amazing. #GloriousOddballs

Daniella's heart sped up as she clicked through to the profile of the person who'd posted it: a boy who was friends with Margot. Okay, one person from Queens. Viral had to start somewhere.

While she was in FotoSlam, she looked at Lainie's parasailing photos and video again.

Now I know what a kite feels like!
#SummerSisters

A pang of jealousy, wishing Lainie had waited for her to come back from New York. Then again, she'd been parasailing before. It fit better with the Bucket List vibe if it was something new. And at least Lainie had gone with that girl Sasha, not Penny. Daniella didn't feel so excluded, knowing the two of them weren't hanging out every second of every day.

Eighth Street was the next subway stop, and Daniella braced herself for what she'd have to do: squeeze past and around strangers, maybe rush against the stream of people trying to get onto the train while she was trying to get off. When she was carrying her oboe case, she felt more protected, with a portable barrier against a crowd. Plus she could use it as a weapon if she had to. She'd carried that thing for years and knew how to swing it in dangerous ways.

As the train began to slow, Daniella stood and gripped the nearest pole, then launched toward the sliding doors the second they opened.

✶

Jules and Adrian were waiting for her on a bench just past the Washington Square Arch.

"She has arrived!" Jules announced with fanfare, standing and bowing to Daniella.

She giggled and felt her face flush. "Sorry I'm late."

"No such thing as *late*," Adrian said. "Let's take a break from schedules and timing and all that crap. This will be like . . . a jazz improv day."

"Yes, please," Jules said, taking Adrian's hand, then Daniella's, and leading them farther into the park. Daniella instantly felt a different energy here than in Central Park, where she and Zoe had finally had their picnic on a ledge above Zoe's favorite playground. They'd taken turns going down the rock slide backward or on their stomachs, like Zoe had done with Carly since they were little.

It had been a really great time, Daniella had to admit. She'd gotten a taste of what it was like for Carly, growing up in her and Zoe's neighborhood with a built-in playmate. But today, Daniella was glad Zoe was at a birthday party all afternoon. No guilt. Nobody texting to ask when she was coming home so they could try another bubble tea flavor.

As they walked, Adrian let out a yawn.

"Late night?" Jules asked.

"*All* night," Adrian replied. "My friend's uncle and his husband have a house in Rockaway, and every year they host this weekend-long party. We took an Uber out there with a bunch of people. Got home, like, minutes before my mom woke up."

Daniella was impressed and a little shocked. "So she never knew you were away all night?"

"Oh, she knew," Adrian said. "But we have a deal. As long as I'm home before the day starts, and I don't do anything stupid, everybody's cool."

"You're lucky," Jules told Adrian. "My parents make me call every four hours if I'm spending the night somewhere else."

Up ahead, the walkway met up with another, larger walkway. At the intersection, a college-aged girl had set up a table covered with handmade jewelry. The pieces glinted with sunlight and color. Daniella slowed down and craned her neck to get a good look at them.

Jules and Adrian kept walking, tugging her forward.

Oooh, let's check these out. Carly's voice. A flicker, a flash, of many moments past. Carly could never walk by someone selling fashion-oriented trinkets without stopping.

Daniella let go of Jules's hand and turned to the jewelry table.

"Hang on a sec," she called to her friends, who reversed course.

"Hi," the girl said to Daniella.

"Hi," Daniella replied "Did you . . . um . . . make these?"

"Yep."

"They're beautiful. I like those earrings."

Daniella pointed to a pair of simple silver hoops that caught her eye. They were strung with tiny opalescent crystals.

"Those look like the ones you wore a few days ago," Adrian said over her shoulder.

"True," Daniella said softly. "But these are bigger, and a different color."

"These chokers are the best things ever," Jules said over her other shoulder, reaching around Daniella to pick up a choker made completely out of metal wire wrapped in different patterns, encircling a red mineral gem. "Daniella, put this one on."

"I don't really wear chokers," Daniella said. "I tried once. It looked wrong on me."

"This choker is not *that* choker," the jewelry maker said.

"I agree," Jules added. "You're putting this one on so we can decide for ourselves." They fastened the choker around Daniella's neck. The girl held up a mirror and Daniella readied herself to awkwardly tell everyone *no thanks*.

She didn't expect to see what she did, or feel what she did, in her reflection. *ME*, she thought, and also: *I love it. I want to wear it every day forever.*

Five minutes later, they were continuing toward the center of the park, Daniella wearing the choker.

"I don't really wear chokers . . ." Adrian mimicked to Daniella, rolling his eyes good-naturedly. "You don't know what you're talking about."

Daniella laughed. "I guess I've always felt like, some things only belong on other people and not me. You know, with more flair and style and . . . specialness. Like you two."

"Well, speaking on behalf of stylish, special people everywhere," Jules said, "style is not something you have or don't have. It's more like . . . a recipe. That you experiment with and change a little bit every time you make it. When you taste it, you know immediately if it works or not."

"Whoa," Adrian said. "Deep."

"Does that make sense?" Jules asked Daniella.

Daniella nodded. A recipe. She wasn't sure what ingredients went into hers, but she did know that being with Adrian and Jules, on a perfect summer day in Greenwich Village, made her hungry to sample whatever she could.

Up ahead, in front of the giant fountain, some guys were performing breakdance tricks for a small crowd. Daniella, Jules, and Adrian stopped to watch for a bit, then pooled dollar bills to drop in their donation box.

"The busking circle of life," Adrian said. "We got some, then we give some. It all comes around."

Jules spotted a young couple heading their way: a woman with a guitar strapped to her back, and a man holding a stack of CDs.

"Crap," Jules said, tugging on Daniella's arm. "Let's get out of here before Harry and his wife try to sell us the terrible album they recorded on an iPhone in their bathroom."

"I'm concerned that you know all that about them," Adrian said as they started moving toward one of the park exits.

Jules laughed. "They used to play a music club I go to, but they got banned for selling weed to the audience. Honestly, I think that was the only way they got people to come to their shows."

Adrian began talking about his favorite club on Long Island, and as they all walked, Daniella just listened. How had she managed to connect so easily with Jules and Adrian, when their worlds were so much bigger than hers?

At a vintage clothing store, Daniella found a jean jacket with embroidered flowers down the arms. *YES*, that little voice said when she put it on. When Adrian was trying on sneakers, she slipped on a pair of chunky sandals to see if she could actually walk in them. By the time they took a break for lunch at a sandwich shop, Daniella was lugging around two shopping bags' worth of thrift store finds.

"Hey, check this out," Jules said, holding up their phone so the others could see. It was the FotoSlam page for the Glorious Oddballs hashtag, filled with more than a dozen new posts from strangers in a couple of hours.

"Wait, what?" Daniella asked, stunned.

"Oh, no way!" Jules said, taking a closer look. "Krishna Cade posted on the hashtag! That's why it's blowing up."

"That's the guy from the subway . . . in that post, there," Daniella pointed out.

Jules slapped Daniella playfully on the shoulder. "You took a picture of Krishna Cade? You *talked to* Krishna Cade?"

"Uh, yeah," Daniella said. "Who is Krishna Cade?"

Jules put their face in their hands. "Like, a very hot fashion designer. A bunch of actresses have been wearing his clothing lately."

"Oh, right!" Adrian exclaimed. "Clea Hollander wore him to the Met Gala last year."

"Yes!" Jules said, relieved.

"Whoa," Daniella said. "So he's sort-of famous." *Glad I didn't know that when I was getting up the nerve to talk to him*, she thought.

"With a huge following on FotoSlam," Jules added. "I can't believe I'm friends with someone who talked to Krishna Cade. I can die happy now."

Daniella beamed.

"That is so freaking cool," Adrian murmured. "So, when can we say the hashtag has officially gone viral?"

"Not sure," Daniella replied. "Is there a rule book for this stuff?"

"Ask your cousin," Adrian suggested. "She's the one who made the list, right?"

Daniella took a sip of iced tea and nodded. Time to change the subject.

"Did you say there was a weekly flea market around here?" she asked Jules. "Let's go there next."

⋆

Lorelei Burdick was one of the most exciting up-and-coming young composers to emerge in the last few years, and the Future Forward

Music Academy was thrilled she'd signed on to be a guest teacher this summer.

Or at least, that's what it said on the academy website. Daniella was supposed to feel lucky that she'd landed a place in this person's music composition workshop. Adrian would be in there, too.

Right now, though, as Lorelei stood in front of the class and asked, "Who hasn't started their piece yet?" Daniella wished she could sink into her chair until it had totally absorbed her.

She scanned the other students, all sitting in a circle. Nobody moved . . . and then, slowly, Adrian raised his hand.

"Who else?" Lorelei asked. "I know there's more. Just so you know, it's okay if you haven't. I understand that creativity doesn't operate on a schedule."

Daniella took a deep breath and raised her hand before she could think twice about it. Then two more student hands went up.

Lorelei nodded, then shifted in her chair to fold her legs under her. "Okay. What's holding you back?"

"I keep starting things and then hating them," one boy mumbled.

"Yeah, that's to be expected. How about this: Don't stop. Even if you hate it. Sometimes you have to hate something for a little while before you can love it."

"Uh . . . okay," the boy said.

"What about you?" Lorelei turned to Daniella and raised one eyebrow.

"I haven't started anything yet because I . . ." Daniella hadn't really thought about why. She simply knew her idea bank was empty. She wasn't sure she even had an idea bank to begin with. "I can't think of anything to write about," she finally admitted.

Lorelei nodded again, unfazed. "That happens. Can I ask you something?"

"Sure."

"When was the last time you felt deeply, deeply sad?"

Daniella stared at her. Was this a therapy session or a music composition class?

"You don't actually have to tell me," Lorelei added, waving her hand. "Just think about the answer."

Ask your cousin, Jules had said so casually, because Jules lived in a world where Carly hadn't died. Daniella had hoped she could live in that world, too, as long as she was with her new friends. But being with them also meant she was *without* everything she normally had in the summer. Carly. Penny and Lainie. Ocean Park Heights.

"Do you remember?" Lorelei prodded.

Daniella felt a pinprick behind each of her eyes. *No crying, no panic attacks, do you hear me?*

"Yes," she said.

"Then tell yourself about it. But not with words. With melodies."

Daniella nodded, closed her eyes, and tried to think in the language of music.

≥ 15 ≤

BOOM.

Boom, boom.

Penny glared at the rattling bathroom door. It was an old house, and who knew how long that door would hold.

"You've been in there for an hour!" Penny's brother Jack yelled as he pounded away. "I have to pee!"

"Go in the outside shower," Penny barked back at him. "You always do that anyway!"

"Mom said I can't anymore, or she'll take off the hot water handle."

Penny sighed. "I'll be done in a few minutes."

She scrutinized her reflection in the mirror. Actually, *officially*, she'd been done a while ago. Hair blow-dried. Mascara and lipstick on. One truly evil pimple covered (sort of) with concealer. For the last fifteen minutes, she'd been staring at herself, full of questions. What did Dex see in her? Did this top make her look trashy? Did it make her curves look even bigger than they were? *Enter Kitten Girl again.*

Penny knew she wasn't *supposed* to hate her newish breasts—that it wasn't very feminist of her to criticize herself for, well, being a woman. But still. It was hard to see this whole new person in the mirror every day. Would she ever get used to it?

Jamie wasn't here—she'd gone out with some kids she'd met at Zohar's party—so Penny couldn't ask her opinion on the shirt. She didn't have time to change now. She just had to believe she looked okay.

Kiss a boy.

The words stood out in Penny's head like a blinking neon sign.

She wished they weren't on the Bucket List. She wished she could simply enjoy hanging out with Dex and let whatever happened happen. Or whatever had *not* happened, depending on how things went down. Penny knew Carly had put that on the list as part of their Boyfriend Goals. Now she had to achieve this thing for them both. Lainie wasn't in the dating zone yet, and even if she were, she was dealing with other things this summer.

Theoretically, Daniella could meet someone in New York. Maybe she already had. Would she even tell them? Penny realized she wasn't sure. Everything about Daniella was getting fuzzy and unfocused, something she couldn't make sense of anymore.

Now came Carly's voice in her head, whispering *It's gonna have to be you.*

Pressure, much? Penny thought back. Did "Kiss a boy" mean *she* had to do the kissing? Like, start it? Ugh, she hoped not. A bead of sweat started creeping down her back.

"Pennnnnnnnnyyyyyy," Jack whined. "How can it take you that long to get ready to go out?"

"Because being a girl is hard," Penny heard her mom say from somewhere else in the house. "Really, really hard."

"You know what's harder?" Jack called back to their mom. "Having only one freaking bathroom in the whole freaking house!"

"Penny," her mom said, her voice louder and closer now. She must be standing outside the bathroom door, too. "If you're meeting this boy at seven, you really should get going."

"I know, I know."

Deep breath. Here goes. Penny opened the door and smiled at her mom for a second before Jack barreled past her into the bathroom.

"It's *so* hard being a girl," Penny said to her mom. "Please tell me it's worth it."

Her mom reached out and smoothed a stray hair from Penny's cheek. "Always," she said, and sighed.

∗

Dex was waiting for Penny at the entrance to the arcade, wearing cargo shorts and a T-shirt with a cartoon of a bear riding a skateboard, holding a surfboard. She could tell he'd tried to get his bangs off his face—there was a lot of hair product in there—but had given up. She was glad he'd given up.

Penny saw him looking expectantly down the boardwalk, then watched his eyes land on her. He was still for a moment . . . and then he broke out what Penny now knew as The Smile.

"Hey, Penny," Dex said when she got closer. The way he said her name . . . that might destroy her. That might make her do something super dumb like reach out and sweep his stray bangs away from his face.

"Hey back," she said, and hoped he couldn't hear her heart thumping.

"What's your favorite game in here?" Dex asked as he led her into the arcade. Suddenly the sounds of the boardwalk—music and seagulls and people screaming on the FunLand rides—were drowned out by electronic machine noises. Chirps and beeps, rings and dings. Occasionally interrupted with a human "Yesss!" or "Arrrghhh!"

"I like the bowling," Penny said. "And Skee-Ball. My dad always insists we play Skee-Ball because he says it's timeless. What about you?"

"I'm a sucker for the claw machines," Dex said. "I know they're pre-programmed to only win a few times a day. But they're so frustrating that when you do finally get something, it feels incredible."

"How often do you win?"

"Well, I play a lot. So let's just say that I have about a hundred stuffies in my room right now. I mostly donate them to a charity thrift store."

"Cool," Penny said with a nod, while also thinking, *OMG, I love you for that.*

They stopped in front of the row of Skee-Ball games.

"I love Skee-Ball, too," Dex said. "But I miss when we were little and the machines spit out all those tickets. I don't like the whole card system."

"Me neither!" Penny agreed. "It was so satisfying to have something you could hold. And then walk around with your haul so everyone could see how much you were winning."

Dex laughed. "Yeah, there's no way to be all 'In your face' about it now."

"We sound like my dad. He's always like . . ." Penny dropped her voice to do her dad imitation, which was famous in her family. "It was better in the old days! When I was a kid, you had to be rude and obnoxious to people's faces! Now you can do it online, and that's for cowards!"

Penny glanced at Dex, who was regarding her with one eyebrow raised. Had she gone too far?

"He's not wrong," Dex said, then added, "That's why I don't do social media." He bent down and used his card to activate two Skee-Ball games, one next to the other. Both games lit up, made a bunch of noises, and the wooden balls rolled down their little alleys.

"Not at all?" Penny asked.

"No. I used to. I was on all the time, actually. But last year, I got in really big trouble for something, and my mom and stepdad took my phone away for a month. I thought my brain might explode. But after a few days, I got used to it, and then eventually I realized I was happier. Like, so much less stressed. I know I sound like someone from a school assembly or something, but it's true. Now I have a phone but no Tik-Tok, no Snapchat, no FotoSlam. Everyone teases me about it, but who cares? You have no idea how many great books I've read lately."

"Wow," Penny muttered, then wondered what Dex would think of the Summer Sisters sharing the Bucket List online.

Dex took a ball from his game and rolled it. It jumped up and missed the fifty-point hole by an inch. "Damn it, so close!" he grumbled.

"So, to get your phone taken away, you must have done something really, really bad."

Dex laughed. "I just made this whole speech about my personal growth journey, and *that's* what you got out of it?"

Penny shrugged. "What can I say? I like juicy details."

She didn't want to say what she'd really gotten out of Dex's story: more proof that he was different, and he was comfortable with it. Sure of himself, but not in an asshole kind of way. Penny realized she didn't simply *like* this guy. She *admired* him.

"Tell you what," Dex said. "If you beat me at Skee-Ball, I'll tell you."

"Deal."

Penny picked up the first wooden ball from her game. She examined it, turning the thing over in her hand. Then she aimed and rolled. It sprung up and landed in the 100-point hole.

Dex's jaw dropped and he looked at her, impressed . . . then suspicious.

"That *never* happens," Penny told him, holding up both hands. "I usually suck at this."

"You lie!" Dex said, then started laughing. "You're a ringer!"

Penny shrugged. "Okay, yeah. It's my secret superpower."

Eight balls later, the final score was Penny's 630 to Dex's 420. As they left the Skee-Ball games and wandered through the arcade toward the wall of claw machines, Dex spilled the tea about how he got into trouble. It involved a bonfire in the woods at a football game, running away from police, and falling into a creek.

"My friends were being dumb," Dex admitted, "but I was dumber because I knew that, and still went along with them."

Great, Penny thought. *You admit mistakes and that's just one more amazing thing about you.*

They reached the claw machines, and Penny stopped dead when she saw one offering a rainbow of colorful plush food items with faces on them.

"I can't believe they have Smushies!" she exclaimed. "I love these!"

"Yeah, they're kind of blowing up right now," Dex said.

Penny eyed one Smushie in the middle of the machine, made to look like a very happy can of soda.

"No way! They have Fizzy. He's totally rare," Penny explained.

Penny swiped her card. She slid the claw so that it hovered above Fizzy the Soda, then pulled down on the joystick to let it drop and hopefully grab Fizzy the right way. When the claw started to come up, the Smushie rose with it for a couple of inches before it slipped out.

"Denied!" Dex said. "Although I have to say, I'm glad you're not a ringer at *everything* here."

"Let's try one more time?" Penny suggested. "I'd love to get one to donate to the shelter."

Dex flashed The Smile and nodded. "Okay, cool."

Penny swiped her card again. She moved the claw right, then up a bit, then left a bit, then down. It dropped and closed snugly around Fizzy the Soda, lifting him up, up . . . then over, over. Penny held her breath.

"Yes!" she said when Fizzy dropped right into the chute.

"All right!" Dex exclaimed, laughing. He reached out and hugged her.

Oh, he feels warm and smells really good.

When Dex drew away, they locked eyes for a moment. His face had never been so close to hers. It took every ounce of self-control for Penny not to turn away out of shyness or being overwhelmed.

Maybe this was it. He was going to kiss her.

Or was he?

Yes.

No.

Crap.

Then, just like that, the moment was over. Dex glanced down at the machine.

"Go get your soda guy," he said.

Penny pulled out the Smushie, and they ambled over to a giant Space Invaders game where they could sit side by side, taking turns zapping the aliens.

"So," Dex began, staring at the screen, expertly maneuvering his space cannon. "What do you like to do in your free time? Besides slaying at Skee-Ball and claw machines."

Penny smiled and tried to hold her own with her cannon, but Dex was definitely better. "Hang out with friends, I guess. I volunteer at a retirement home, talking to the residents, helping out with craft time, doing puzzles, that kind of thing." She paused. *Can I sound any more boring?* "I'm into animation. I have a few other favorite shows besides *Tomcat*. I'd like to make my own characters, but I can't really draw, so I'm learning some digital graphics and editing tools."

Dex nodded. "You can do a lot with that stuff. I made a comic a few months ago. I'll show it to you sometime."

Once Dex had thoroughly beaten Penny at Space Invaders, they climbed out of the game chairs and he turned to her. "Um . . . So you wanna go get something to eat?"

"Sure," Penny said, and they started winding their way out of the arcade.

The sun had set, and the lights of the boardwalk danced all around them. Penny loved the combination of the dark sky over the ocean with the bright glow of shop fronts.

She hoped they could go farther down the boardwalk. There was a taco place all the way at the end, where it was quiet, and the benches on the sand dunes were usually empty. She wanted to suggest that, but felt weird about it. Would it seem too forward?

"Okay," Dex said, "this is what I'm thinking—"

He paused, and Penny waited for him to continue. But he was staring at something. Penny followed his eyeline and saw that the something was a group of kids on the beach side of the boardwalk. A guy and two girls.

And one of the girls was Jamie.

"Dude!" the guy called out to Dex.

"Helmstadt!" Dex called back, and made a beeline for the group. Penny followed, eyeing Jamie. *Go away*, she thought. *Go away go away go away.*

Dex fist-bumped the guy and said, "This is my friend Penny. Penny, this is Finn and his sister, Layla."

"Hi, I'm Jamie," Jamie said to Dex.

Penny watched Dex register Jamie's existence. Her hair, her smile, her *Jamie-ness*. Dex's expression changed. Suddenly he wasn't Dex anymore. He was any one of a million guys who clearly thought Jamie was mega-hot.

"Hey," Dex said, grinning. "I'm Dex."

Penny waited for him to introduce her to Jamie, at which point Penny would stop him and explain that they knew each other. But seconds went by, then more, and he didn't do that. Finally, Jamie said, "I'm actually an old friend of Penny's. I'm staying at her place."

Dex glanced at Penny, and she nodded back at him. Forced a smile. As if she weren't quietly wishing for a time machine so she could have these two un-meet.

"Nakashima, we're so glad we ran into you," Finn said. "Did Brady reach you? He said he's been trying."

"Uh, no." Dex replied, frowning. "Penny and I are hanging out, so I had my phone on Do Not Disturb."

Something inside Penny softened and even started to melt a little. He did like her. Enough to change a setting on his phone for a few hours.

"Well, he's freaking out and ended up calling me," Finn said. "You know his girlfriend back home?"

"Sophia, yeah," Dex said.

"She just dumped him. I guess she heard about him hooking up with someone else on the Fourth of July."

"Oh crap," Dex muttered. He checked his phone, then looked over at Penny. "Brady's my best friend here," he explained.

"We're on our way to check on him," Finn told Dex. "Do you want to come with us?"

"Oh man," Dex said, running his hand through his hair. He then turned to Penny. "Brady's been through a lot lately. I should go make sure he's okay."

"Totally, you should," Penny said, nodding.

"I know it's not the most exciting invitation, but do you want to come with us?"

"No, that's okay," she told Dex. "I wouldn't want to make things awkward. He's *your* friend. And if he's upset . . . You should go."

Penny looked over at Jamie, expecting her to say something along the same lines. But Jamie took a step closer to Layla and Finn.

"I'd like to come, if it's okay," Jamie said.

"Of course," Dex replied.

Wait, what?

"Penny, will you be okay getting home by yourself?" Dex asked, looking concerned.

"Um, yeah. I just—" What was happening? Was Jamie really walking away with Dex? She should go with them. But she couldn't change her mind now. She'd look like an idiot. "I'm fine," she added, waving her hand dismissively.

But she had to swallow hard, because she suddenly felt like she was about to throw up. Or scream. Or both. How had everything just gotten completely turned upside down?

"I'm so, so sorry about this," Dex told her. "But I'll see you at work tomorrow, yeah?"

Penny nodded, and he reached out to give her the quickest, lightest hug. Then he was gone, along with Jamie and Layla and Finn, all absorbed by the boardwalk crowd within seconds.

Suddenly Penny felt like she could cry. Carly was gone and Dex had ditched her for Jamie. To make things even worse, here came Grumpy Gus, scowling his way in and out of the foot traffic, headed straight in her direction.

She could break down into tears the size of seashells. It would be totally justified.

No, Penny told herself, swallowing again. *No crying. Especially not in public. Not over this. Not over anything.*

She squeezed Fizzy the Soda, sidestepped Grumpy Gus, and headed for the taco place alone.

⤳ 16 ⤶

THE SUNDAE MENU AT CAPTAIN CONES WAS
organized by size. At the top was the Captain's Classic Sundae, with
just whipped cream, hot fudge, and a cherry on top. Things got more
complicated from there, starting with the Treasure Chest (which added
nuts and candy pieces) and ending with the Titanic, which floated in a
pool of 7UP dyed blue and came with four spoons.

Lainie took one look at the picture on the menu and felt queasy.

She imagined what Carly had in mind when she put this on the
Bucket List. The Summer Sisters huddled together at a table, taking
turns dipping into the sundae. Or would they have divided up the sundae by section? After they'd finished it, they would have been given
buttons that said I SANK THE TITANIC AT CAPTAIN CONES. It would
have made an awesome FotoSlam post.

Then they'd have pinned the buttons onto their school backpacks.
In the middle of winter, when they were missing the shore and the
Summer Sisters, they could touch them . . . and remember.

"Earth to Lainie. I repeat, Earth to Lainie."

Penny started poking Lainie in the shoulder.

"Sorry," Lainie said. "I was just . . . Let's ask for two spoons instead of four, okay?"

Minutes later, they were sitting at an outdoor table, staring at the biggest sundae either of them had ever seen.

"Can we still check it off the Bucket List if we eat it, then puke it up later?" Penny asked.

Lainie laughed. "Let's say, yes." She gazed at the sundae and felt a pang of sudden guilt. "I still think we should have waited for Daniella on this one."

Penny shrugged. "I don't know how busy I'm going to be at the end of the summer."

Lainie frowned. "Too busy to meet your friends for a ginormous ice cream sundae?"

Penny took a bite, then put down her spoon. "Okay, so maybe I just really, really need a distraction right now. If I focus on the Bucket List, I don't have to think about my disaster date. Or the fact that I want Jamie to grow a third eye."

"You're not mad that we didn't do the parasailing together, are you? Nana really didn't give me a choice."

Penny took another spoonful and shrugged. *Yup, she's mad,* Lainie thought. At least they were doing this one together. It would be better if Daniella were here, too, but Daniella probably didn't care. She was obviously having the best time ever in New York with her cool music friends.

"Hey, you," Penny said. "Start eating! You have most of the banana on your side."

They'd snapped some photos of the Titanic right after it had been delivered to their table, with her and Lainie pretending to be terrified. Once they got about halfway through, Lainie positioned her camera for another selfie. She and Penny both smiled and held out their spoons, ready to take another bite.

"I need a digestion break," Lainie said. She put down her spoon and leaned back in her chair. *Daniella should be here.* With another person helping them eat the sundae, Lainie wouldn't feel like she'd have to roll home.

She glanced over at the family sitting next to them. It looked like there were two moms and a little boy. One of the moms had a copy of the *Ocean Park Heights Herald* open in front of her.

A headline jumped out at Lainie.

TOWN BOARD TO LAUNCH MEMORIAL BENCH PROGRAM ON RENOVATED STRETCH OF OPH BOARDWALK

Lainie sat up straight and leaned over so she could read the article. A section of the boardwalk near her grandparents' house had been totally redone over the winter. There weren't any shops or restaurants on that stretch; it ran past homes and condos, then ended at the jetty and the inlet. Lainie remembered how Carly loved taking her camera down there, snapping photos of the boats coming and going from the river.

Now you could "buy" one of the new benches there as a memorial.

"Oh my God!" she exclaimed, slamming her hand down on the table and startling Penny. "Sorry. But I just had the best idea ever."

Penny leaned back in her chair and sucked on her spoon. "I'm listening."

"It sucked that we couldn't go to Carly's funeral, right? I mean, I know her parents wanted to keep it small. But they had a memorial service in the city, at her school, didn't they?"

Penny nodded.

"We should have a memorial *here*, too," Lainie said. "In Ocean Park Heights."

Penny popped the spoon out of her mouth and made a face like she'd just tasted something bad. "Don't you think that would make everyone sad all over again?"

"Probably. But what's wrong with being sad?"

"Are you seriously asking that?"

"What?" Lainie said.

"Being sad is . . . being *sad*." Penny glanced away. "It . . . blows."

"True," Lainie said. "But sometimes, the Bucket List doesn't feel good, either. It feels like we're kind of, I don't know, *betraying* Carly. Because she never planned for us to do it without her."

"Of course she didn't plan that!" Penny said, with a bitter-sounding laugh. "But she'd want us to. She's glad we are. I can feel it. Don't you?"

Lainie sat back. Did she? Whenever she thought of Carly, tried to imagine her there, she only felt this huge black hole of hurt and loss. And that hole was growing wider, swallowing the bakery and Nana and Papa's house, too.

"I guess I'd like to find some other way to honor Carly," Lainie finally said. "Something that won't end when the Bucket List is done and summer's over." She glanced over at the newspaper again. "Those new benches where they redid the boardwalk? You can buy one to be a memorial for someone. So I was thinking . . . what if we bought one for Carly?"

Penny thought for a moment, then nodded. "Interesting. How much are they?"

"I don't know," Lainie replied. "But probably a lot."

"And that's where you want to have a ceremony?"

"I'm just thinking all this through right now, but . . ." An image popped into Lainie's head. Her and Penny and Daniella gathered around a bench at the edge of the sand. Their families, too. And Carly's family, hopefully. "Yeah. It would be perfect."

This mental picture started to expand. On one side, a table of food—everything Dulcie's was famous for. Lainie would make lots of the guava-stuffed bread, which had been Carly's favorite.

"What would we have to do?" Penny asked.

Lainie thought for a moment. "We make two phone calls. The first is to the OPH town hall to find out how much the benches cost. And then we talk to Daniella."

"Sounds like a plan," Penny said, and they high-fived.

Lainie glanced down at the remains of the Titanic, which was now a blob drowning in blue soda. "I'd say we're each about ten bites away. Do you think you can make it?"

Penny picked up her spoon and held it in her fist like it was a spear and not a flimsy plastic utensil.

"I'm going down with the ship!" she shouted.

⋛ **17** ⋚

DANIELLA STARED AT THE PICTURE IN FOTOSLAM.

Lainie and Penny sat on either side of an empty sundae bowl. Two spoons lay on the table. Lainie was sticking out her tongue in an I-might-vomit pose. Penny was flashing two thumbs-up, but she'd scrunched up her mouth in that goofy way only Penny could. They were both wearing the buttons. I SANK THE TITANIC AT CAPTAIN CONES.

Penny's caption:

> We finished a TITANIC sundae at Captain Cones! And with only two spoons, not four. Hope you can tell what a huge accomplishment this was. Gonna go buy some Tums now. #SummerSisters

The "before" and "during" pictures were also part of the post. It had already gotten a ton of likes. Daniella hearted it as well, adding a YAY YOU GUYS! in the comments.

Then she put down her phone, her chest tight.

She should have been there. They should have waited. Lainie and Penny had already done the Candy Universe trip without her, and she assumed they'd save the other food-related thing for when she got back to the shore.

She scrolled back through Penny's posts to see the ones from the candy store. Just to torture herself. Just to feel her chest tighten even more.

"Daniella, how are things going with your piece?"

She looked up to see Lorelei, her music composition teacher, standing above her. Daniella was sitting on the wall of the courtyard, waiting for Jules, Margot, and Adrian to come out so they could go to the park for lunch.

"It's . . . um . . ."

Lorelei laughed. "Say no more."

"I have a few melodies," Daniella explained. "And I'm doing what you said, about remembering feeling sad." She paused. Lorelei had soft eyes and a permanent semi-smile. She tilted her head when she listened to students. She was tilting it now.

"Actually I don't need to remember because I feel kind of a little sad all the time these days," Daniella blurted out. She blinked back the tears she knew were on their way. *Nope nope nope.*

Lorelei didn't seem shocked or surprised. She just nodded. Like, *Of course you feel a little sad all the time.* It was kind of creepy but also comforting. "Is it that kind of summer?" Lorelei asked.

"Yeah," Daniella said, her voice wobbling. "This program has been great, and I've met so many people. But it's also a summer without a lot of things that are important to me."

Nodding again, Lorelei tilted her head to the opposite side. "I'm sorry you're sad, but I'm glad you have an outlet for it. And guess what? It sounds like you have a title for your composition."

"I do?"

Lorelei held up her hands like she was framing a name in lights. "*Summer Without,* an original piece by Daniella Franco." She dropped her hands and locked eyes with Daniella. "I can't wait to hear it."

Then she turned and headed down the street.

★

Life had settled into a routine at the apartment. Daniella usually got back from the academy after Aunt Tina had come home with Zoe. Daniella would walk in to find Zoe melting into the couch in front of the TV and Aunt Tina in her bedroom with the door closed.

All Daniella wanted to do was collapse onto her bottom bunk and close her eyes, listen to the white noise hum of the air-conditioning unit. But Zoe always looked at her with such longing, bursting to tell her about theater camp that day. To sing one of the songs or show her a few steps of choreography. Daniella would force herself to sit down on the couch to listen and watch. Carly would have done that. Actually, Carly would have joined in the singing and dancing, but Daniella's sister-replacement skills didn't go that far.

As soon as Uncle Chris walked in the door from work, everything shifted. Zoe turned her attention to him. Aunt Tina emerged from her bedroom to start planning dinner. Daniella could tell they were trying so hard to act like a normal family, like there wasn't a gaping hole in front of them every single second. Daniella jumped into the act, too, helping chop vegetables and chatting about her classes.

After they had eaten and dishes were put away, Daniella could finally steal some time alone in her bottom-bunk burrow to zone out on her phone or have a video session with Dr. Richards.

That day, her head was still swimming with Lorelei's suggested title for her original piece. *Summer Without.* Behind those two words, there were more melodies. They felt to her a little like . . . moments. No, wait. Not exactly moments but . . . snapshots. FotoSlam posts with captions, scrolling by on her phone screen. Some made her smile and some gave her that tightness in the center of her chest.

She took out her oboe, assembled it, then dug around in her backpack for her sheet music notebook and a pencil. The individual notes started drifting from her head right onto the blank staffs on the page.

can you vc?

The message alert on Daniella's phone startled her.

Yeah, give me a minute, she typed back to Lainie, suddenly nervous. Wait, why the hell would she be nervous? She hadn't talked or video-chatted with Lainie since they all started doing the Bucket List, but so what? This was Lainie. She propped the phone on the nightstand and fluffed out her hair.

When Daniella picked up the video call, she saw that Penny was also there, in her own little box. *Good, they're not hanging out together right now,* Daniella thought.

"Hey, you," Penny said. "How's NYC?"

"Amazing," Daniella replied. It was a little bit true. "How's OPH?"

Penny shrugged. "It's OPH. Same as always."

Ouch. So me being gone makes no difference?

"But not exactly the same, obviously," Lainie interjected, looking directly at Daniella. At least Lainie had a clue. "We miss you."

"I miss you guys, too," Daniella told them. Then they were all silent. A few seconds ticked by, and Daniella wondered if the Wi-Fi connection was cutting out. But she could see Lainie and Penny moving. Nope, just a plain old awkward moment. Daniella couldn't take it.

"That post from Captain Cones was the best," she lied. "Great job."

"Thanks," Lainie said.

"It'll be at least a year before I can eat ice cream again," Penny joked.

"Dee, your hashtag, though," Lainie added. "I can't believe it's taking off!"

Daniella smiled, thinking, *Then why haven't you posted on it yet?*

Another awkward moment. Daniella fought the urge to leave the chat and text them later that she'd gotten disconnected. She'd rather not talk to her friends at all if it was going to be like this.

Finally, Lainie broke the silence. "Soooo, we have an idea we want to run past you."

She went on to tell Daniella about the new benches, and her vision for a memorial service for Carly at the beach. As Lainie described it, Daniella felt transported to the spot on the boardwalk where the bench might be. The laughing gulls screaming *Hahhh hahhh* above her, the wind raising the hair on her arms. The occasional foghorn bellow of a boat gliding through the inlet.

Talking about Carly made it feel like there were four of them on the chat. "It sounds amazing," Daniella said, wiping the sting of a tear off one eye.

"Do you think Carly's parents would be okay with all that?" Penny asked.

"Yeah, they would love it." Daniella knew this instantly. She thought of Carly's family going through the motions of a daily routine, trying to reshape themselves around the empty spaces and extra silences in the apartment.

She'd gone to the funeral, but she barely remembered it as a hazy time of shock and disbelief. So yeah, she needed this memorial, too.

"The benches cost seven hundred dollars," Lainie said.

Daniella winced. "Ouch."

"Yeah. But we're going to put a donation box in Dulcie's, with a flyer explaining why we want a bench for Carly. That will help. My grandparents said they would give us some money."

Daniella nodded, getting the plan now. "I'm sure my parents will put out a box at the Sea Spray."

Penny added, "And I'll talk to my boss at Anderson's to see if they can collect donations at their welcome center."

"Thanks for organizing this, Lainie," Daniella said, then bit her lip. "I wish I were there to help you."

"Me too," Lainie said. There was something in the way she said it. *Maybe Lainie's summer so far isn't as awesome as the FotoSlam posts make it look.* "But I'll still need help when you get back. I'll put you to work then."

"Yes, ma'am," Daniella said, saluting Lainie.

"Your wish is our command, Girl Boss," Penny added.

Lainie laughed. Maybe they were going to be okay.

"So," Penny said. "Where are we with the Bucket List?"

Daniella let out a long exhale. Maybe she could truly breathe now that they were talking about the Bucket List, together, sort of in person. She reached under the nightstand and pulled out Carly's shell purse, then gingerly removed the paper. It now felt so priceless, it might as well have been the original Declaration of Independence.

They went down the list, recapping which items were checked off and which weren't.

"We should decide what we're all going to do together next month," Lainie suggested. Daniella caught her giving Penny a meaningful look. *Ah, so they HAVE been talking about this stuff.*

"Definitely the eighties movie marathon," Penny said. "That way Daniella and I can fight over which character has the ugliest outfit."

Daniella laughed. She wanted that, too. She wished they could do it right away and not when she finally got back to the shore.

"Hang on," Daniella said, an idea gripping her. "We don't have to do the marathon in person. We can do one of those online watch parties."

"OMG I love it," said Penny.

"How does that work, exactly?" Lainie asked.

"We set it up on our computers," Penny explained. "Then we're all watching the movie at the exact same time. And we video-chat like this while we're doing it. Daniella, you're a genius."

"When are you guys free?" Daniella asked.

✶

Daniella set up the watch party for Saturday night, the only time they were all free. Penny and Lainie both had to work the next day, but they could power through their exhaustion for the sake of the Bucket List. It felt strange, having to schedule everything. In the past, they could make plans at a moment's notice. They'd be lounging on the beach and then, an eyeblink later, riding their bikes to FunLand or the movie theater.

Tina, Chris, and Zoe were out at a barbecue, and Daniella was thrilled to have the apartment to herself. For old time's sake, she made a fort on the floor out of couch pillows and set her laptop on the coffee table. Popcorn, check. Orange soda, check. A bag of Skittles from the newsstand on the corner, check.

Up first was *Sixteen Candles*. It had taken about three hundred text messages back and forth to decide on movies for the marathon. Without Carly there to give them the perfect list, nobody wanted to step on anyone else's ideas. Finally, Penny's mom suggested the three best (in her opinion) John Hughes movies, and that was that.

"Are you guys ready?" Daniella asked once they were all on the call and had their computers open.

"Let's go!" Penny said, crunching a potato chip. Daniella could see her nestled into bed in her little attic room.

Lainie was on the screened porch, and Daniella spotted the familiar fuzzy blanket covered with dolphins that Lainie had been toting to sleepovers since the beginning of time. "I'm so ready," she said.

Daniella hit play.

They watched together (but also, not) as Samantha Baker sighed over Jake Ryan. Penny sighed along with her.

"I mean, how many guys can pull off sweater vests *and* front-pocket khakis?" Penny asked.

"I still think she should have given the Geek a chance," Lainie said. "He's cute."

"I wouldn't say he's cute," Daniella chimed in. "But he's not . . . *not* cute."

"Both of you!" Penny said. "Just, *ew.*"

They laughed at the best parts and joked about everything that was cringe-worthy or outdated. But as the movie wore on, Daniella noticed they were all talking less and less.

"You guys aren't getting sleepy, are you?" she asked.

"Nuh-uh," Lainie replied.

When it was almost over, and Samantha was leaning over her surprise birthday cake to kiss Jake, Daniella heard a loud "GAH!" from Penny.

"It's a good movie," Lainie said, "but I like *Pretty in Pink* better. We should have watched that one first."

"At a marathon, you have to watch movies in the order they were made," Daniella told her. "At least, that's what Carly always says."

Dead silence.

"I mean . . ."

"We know what you mean," Lainie said softly.

More silence. Daniella wanted to slap herself for killing the mood.

"Pee break, and then we start *The Breakfast Club*?" Penny suggested.

"Yeah, good idea," Daniella replied.

Ten minutes later, she was hitting play on the next movie. Trying to decide if she should tell Lainie and Penny about how Krishna Cade reminded her of Bender, Judd Nelson's character from the movie. Maybe they'd heard of him and would be jazzed that she'd met a medium-famous person. A fashion designer, no less. Maybe all that was Carly's doing somehow.

But would that sound creepy or bragging? Were her Glorious Oddballs posts a sore subject for them? It was easier not to go there.

They were all quieter this time. Less talking and even less munching.

"You guys," Daniella said at one point, willing to mention the hashtag posts if it would liven things up. "I have to tell you something funny . . ."

"Oooh, do tell," Penny said.

From Lainie's video window, there was only silence. Daniella enlarged it and saw Lainie's face, smushed into her pillow and half-covered by the dolphin blanket.

"Penny, look. Lainie's asleep," she whispered.

Penny yawned. "Not gonna lie, I'm pretty tired, too. Should we finish the marathon tomorrow?"

"Uh, it's not a marathon if you don't do it all in one sitting."

"I know. I'm sorry. My job is freaking exhausting. Maybe we should just agree that we finished this item on the list."

"Finished?" Daniella exclaimed. "We didn't even watch two whole movies!"

Penny sighed. "Okay, let's change it to 'movie *night*' instead of 'movie marathon.'"

"The rules say we all have to agree on changing an item."

Penny paused, then shot Daniella a glare. "Well, we're changing the rules this year, too, aren't we? Like doing the Bucket List with total strangers instead of the Summer Sisters?"

Anger shot through Daniella. "Excuse me?"

"You know what I'm talking about."

"Yes, I do. And speaking of rules, maybe you guys should have talked to me first before deciding to do Candy Universe and Captain Cones together."

Penny fell silent, which threw Daniella. It was rare for Penny not to have a snappy comeback or funny remark.

"I'm too tired to get into this right now," she said finally. "I'll text you tomorrow."

Penny's video window vanished. Lainie was still passed out cold in her own window. And in *The Breakfast Club*, Bender was saying rude things to Claire while she was trying to eat sushi.

It's not supposed to be this way, Daniella thought. *The Bucket List is supposed to make everything better, not worse.*

She closed out the watch-party link and put away her computer, then reached for the shell purse again. She opened the list and stared at *Late Night 80s Movie Marathon* written in Carly's handwriting.

Carly wouldn't have let her check this one off yet.

But Daniella grabbed the purple pen and did it anyway.

⋛ 18 ⋚

PENNY'S MAYBE-DATE WITH DEX WAS CUT SHORT
(because he was a good friend) and ended with him leaving with
Jamie (because he was a human boy). That was bad enough. Then it
got worse.

The next time Penny saw Dex at work, he acted like nothing had
happened. As if they'd never met up at the arcade and played Skee-Ball
and hugged over winning a Smushie.

He was as friendly as he'd always been, not holding back on The
Smile. He didn't mention Jamie, which was driving Penny a little crazy.
She didn't want to know if something had happened between them, so
she hadn't asked Jamie. But she really *needed* to know.

It was all so complicated.

Penny figured, the only way she could deal with it was her favorite
way of dealing with anything: pretending she was fine.

"Hey, Penny," Dex said when she arrived at the beach one morning.

"Hi, Dex." *I love the way you say my name and I'm saying yours in case you love the way I do it, too.*

Dex looked up at the sky, which was pale gray. "Should be pretty chill here today, with the weather. Zohar's on this shift, too. I guess we'll have time to do a lot of cleanup work."

Penny nodded. "I don't know why people stay away when it's like this. This is my favorite kind of beach day."

"Same," Dex said. "The waves are usually awesome." Then he turned to Penny. "So, you know . . . I owe you food."

Penny caught her breath. "What?"

"From when we were hanging out that night. We were on our way to get something to eat when I had to leave."

"Oh, right," she said casually, as if she'd forgotten instead of thinking about it on a loop for days.

"Are you free after work?"

Penny felt her feet become something besides feet. Blobs of Jell-O, maybe, or swirls of seafoam. It was the question she'd been hoping to hear. She drew in a breath to say *yes* . . . and then remembered something. *Oh crap.*

"My dad's coming in tonight," Penny told Dex. "We're all going to his favorite restaurant for dinner."

Dex's face dropped. "Oh. Okay. Cool."

No, no, no. He might not try again.

"But actually," Penny said, the bubble of an idea forming. "That's not until seven. We could go get a snack or whatever as soon as the beach closes."

"A snack?" Dex raised one eyebrow.

"Yeah, you know. Something fried that sounds gross but turns out to be amazing."

"Ah. Or maybe a bunch of weird stuff thrown into a blender and called a smoothie?"

"Exactly," Penny said.

"It sounds perfect."

Here came The Smile. And then his eyes found hers and stayed there.

Penny swallowed. Hard. She'd never craved a smoothie more in her life.

A couple of hours went by, and Penny was grateful to stay busy with sweeping sand from the restrooms, hosing off beach chairs, and helping the few guests they did have. She didn't have a chance to wonder if things had gone wrong between Dex and Jamie. Between Penny's work and Jamie always being out with new friends, Penny hadn't had a chance to ask her. But why else would Dex want to hang out again?

When she came back to the rental hut, Dex and Zohar were playing hangman on the back of a rental agreement, so she joined in.

"What about a *W*?" she suggested when they started a new round with a ten-letter word.

Suddenly a voice bellowed from the other side of the rental hut counter. "Excuse me? Hello?"

Penny turned to see a bearded guy in a black tank top and matching shorts. Yellow mirrored sunglasses. A yellow-and-black hat like the ones cyclists wear.

"Hi," Dex said. "Can I help you?"

"Didn't you see me waving from the beach? Yes, I need help. Can *you* help me? I don't know! I guess we'll find out!"

Dex's customer-service mode flicked on, and Penny noticed him standing up straighter.

"I'm sorry, sir," Dex told him. "We didn't notice you trying to signal us."

The guy shook his head and rolled his eyes. Then he looked back and forth between Dex, Zohar, and Penny. With his big yellow glasses, he reminded Penny of a huge bug.

"When you kids pick up items on the beach to throw away, where do you put them?" the guy asked.

"You mean, trash?" Dex asked.

"No, I mean *items*. Some people call them trash. I don't."

Dex shook his head and frowned. "I apologize, sir, but I'm having trouble understanding what you need help with."

The guy—already Bug Dude in Penny's mind—sighed.

"I was drinking some hard cider I brought with me. I ferment it myself, and I reuse the bottles because they're specially designed and really expensive. I had two empty bottles by my towel when I went for a walk down the beach. When I got back, the bottles were gone. The people sitting near me said they saw an employee pick up the bottles and take them away. But I need them back."

Dex nodded. "Yes, we routinely sweep the beach for garbage and recyclables that guests may have overlooked."

Bug Dude frowned. "I didn't *overlook* my bottles. I left them with my bag and beach chair. Just tell me where you put them and we'll dig them out, and this will be no big deal."

"We throw them in one of the receptacles at the beach entrance," Dex said.

"Which one?"

Dex turned to Zohar. "Zo, you've been doing the beach sweeps today. Do you remember?"

Zohar shrugged. "I'm sorry, I don't. I use whichever one is less full."

Bug Dude took a deep breath, slowly turning a shade of red that clashed with the yellow.

"Well, you're going to have to look through all of them to get my bottles back."

Zohar looked horrified.

"Look, man," Dex said. "He was only doing his job."

Penny knew the real story, but Zohar wasn't speaking up. Also, this was a really strange thing for a guest to be upset about. She wanted to say what she was thinking but didn't want him to yell at her like that floppy-hat mom did on Penny's first day, or the few other people who she had somehow pissed off in the weeks since. Her mouth was always getting her in trouble.

She took a long look at Bug Dude, and a notion sparked in her head. *He's just like one of my brothers*, she thought. Always thinking they're entitled to something they're not. The next thing she thought was, *And I know how to handle my brothers.*

"Actually, he wasn't," Penny said.

Zohar, Dex, and Bug Dude all turned to look at her with different puzzled expressions.

"Doing his job, I mean. The thing is, you're not supposed to have glass bottles on the beach. The rules are posted over there." She pointed to one sign, then a few others. "Also there, there, and on the back of your Anderson's beach pass."

"Well, yeah, that's for people who want to drink and drink. I wasn't doing that. I was enjoying the fruits of my labor in a beautiful setting."

Yup, exactly like my brother Nick. Always finding loopholes in the rules, never admitting that something he did was wrong.

"That wouldn't have mattered to the beach patrol if they'd come by and seen your empty bottles," Penny said. "They would have been waiting for you to show up and then given you a ticket. Zohar saw your bottles, and the beach patrol was only a few hundred feet away. He did you a favor by getting rid of them."

Bug Dude stared at Penny for a few very long moments.

"That's fine," he said. "I still wish he'd left them alone."

"Okay, well, the next time you're a guest at Anderson's, we'll be aware of your situation."

The guy's stance softened a bit, his shoulders un-hunching.

"I'd still like to find those bottles," he said.

"You're welcome to look through the bins yourself," Penny said. Then she turned to Dex. "Dex, is there any way we can make up the cost of the bottles, so he doesn't have to do that?"

The corner of Dex's mouth turned up into the beginning of a smile. He looked . . . impressed.

"Yes, of course," Dex said to the guy. "We can give you your rental for free, or we can give you a couple of beach passes that are valid any day this summer. Actually, we can do both."

Bug Dude glanced up at the sky, thinking. Penny caught a glimpse of his eyes behind the sunglasses. They looked like normal eyes on a normal person.

"Okay," the guy said. "That sounds fair."

After he'd left the hut, Dex turned to Penny and laughed.

"Now, *that* was awesome," he said. "No joke, I'm going to recommend you for Employee of the Month."

Penny smiled, feeling her cheeks flush and her feet start to dissolve again.

"Seriously," Zohar added. "Way to think fast."

"I guess I did what I always do with my brothers when they're being obnoxious like that," she said. "If you don't freak out, it's no fun for them anymore. And then you really destroy them by being nice."

Here came The Smile. "Can I write that down and put it up on the wall of the hut?" he asked Penny. "Because it might be the smartest thing I've ever heard."

*

The beach closed at 5:00 p.m., and by 5:15, Penny and Dex had clocked out of their shifts and were walking south on the boardwalk.

By 5:17, Penny was already filled with questions. *Is this a date? Why did he wait so long to invite me somewhere again? Why does he have to be so freaking cool? How can he possibly in a million years have feelings for me when we just passed five girls in four seconds who are prettier and look way more fun to be with?*

"Where should we go?" Dex asked.

Penny, surprised by a question that wasn't in her own head, shrugged. "You decide. I'm good with whatever."

It didn't matter what they ate or didn't eat. She simply wanted as much time as possible with Dex.

"How about a pretzel?" he suggested, pointing to the Pretzel Haus.

"Yah, yah," Penny said in a kind-of-German accent. "I know it sounds TWISTED, but I love pretzels!"

Dex stared at her. Possibly bemused, definitely baffled. Or maybe just horrified. What the hell was her problem? A weird voice *and* a bad pun? Penny waited for Dex to turn and flee in the opposite direction.

He didn't run away, but he didn't laugh or smile, either.

"After you," Penny said, gesturing for Dex to step up to the counter first.

She hoped he'd order a Jumbo and suggest they share it. But he ordered a small pretzel for himself, then turned to Penny.

"Same for you?" he asked. She flashed him a thumbs-up.

Separate pretzels. Did that mean something?

Pretzels in hand, they started walking again. The rides at FunLand had opened up an hour earlier, and Penny could see the Ferris wheel spinning slowly over the roofs of the boardwalk buildings.

"I love this time of day at the beach," Dex said. He was gazing up at the Ferris wheel, too.

"Yeah," Penny said. "It's like one version of it is turning into another."

Dex laughed softly. "That's the perfect way to put it." He glanced at Penny sideways. "You're kind of a dork, aren't you?"

She looked away. *Ouch. So there it is.*

Then Dex added, "Like me." When Penny turned back to him, he grinned. "But cooler. I get this feeling that you don't believe in your own awesomeness."

Penny stopped walking and swallowed her bite of pretzel. "Um . . . does anybody?"

"Yes." Dex stated this matter-of-factly, without having to think about it. "Awesomeness isn't some universal standard. It's just . . . liking yourself. Being your own biggest fan."

"Eh," Penny said with a shrug. "I tried, but I couldn't think of a catchy cheer."

She gave him a playful, casual grin, expecting him to laugh. Instead, Dex reached out his non-pretzel-holding hand and brushed her fingers with his.

"Well, *I'm* your fan," he said. "Right now, maybe even president of your fan *club.*"

Is this the way it feels to have your heart zapped by one of those hospital crash cart machines?

On instinct, Penny swept her fingers back over his.

Then Dex wrapped his hand around her hand.

To any one of the dozens of people moving past them, they were simply two teenagers walking along the beach.

But really, Penny was flying.

"IS IT SUPPOSED TO BE THIS GOOEY?"

Lainie stopped mixing the batter to massage her arm. Baking shouldn't be so painful.

Nana came over and peered into the bowl. "Yes, that's perfect."

"My arm is killing me. It feels like I'm mixing concrete."

"The more you work for it, the better it tastes," Nana said, winking at her.

Lainie rolled her eyes, shook out her arm, and went back to mixing. Nana was finally teaching her how to make Dulcie's famous cheddar jalapeño biscuits—for Carly's memorial.

"Can we use the electric mixer next time?" Lainie asked.

"Of course. But you need to make any recipe by hand at least once. That way you really feel every step of it."

"Oh, I feel it, all right," Lainie said, shaking out her arm again, and Nana laughed.

"What are you guys doing?"

Lainie glanced at the door to the kitchen. It was Sasha, who'd been cleaning up out front.

"I'm teaching Alaina how to bake the cheddar jalapeño biscuits," Nana told her. "Would you like to learn as well?"

Lainie shot Nana a pleading look. *Are you freaking kidding me? I've been begging to learn this for years and you're just inviting her in like it's no big deal?*

"Um . . . sure," Sasha said. "Let me hit the bathroom first."

After Sasha went into the bathroom, Lainie leaned in close to Nana.

"I really don't want her here right now," she whispered. "Can't it just be you and me?"

Nana searched Lainie's face. "I'm sorry, Alaina. But how do you think she feels, hearing us in here together while she's out there alone? And maybe if you learn together, she can help you with food for the memorial."

How do you think I feel? Lainie wanted to ask. *Why do you care more about some other girl's problems than mine?*

Instead, she muttered, "I have Penny to help me with the memorial. Sasha didn't even know Carly."

"I thought you were beginning to like her," Nana said, frowning.

"I wouldn't go that far." Okay, so she didn't intensely hate Sasha anymore. She saw her through a different filter now, knowing what she'd gone through. Yeah, they'd shared a great moment of soaring through the air above a dolphin, and okay, there'd been some laughing. The next day, Lainie had brought in a book on dolphin behavior, the best she'd ever found, to show Sasha.

Sasha had taken one glance at it, grunted "Nice," and gone back to drawing a sailboat on the memo board. In the days since, she'd started spending more time than before in her earbuds-and-sketchbook-don't-bother-me zone.

Can't I just have this one perfect morning, all the teaching and learning and baking, without HER?

Lainie was gathering up these kinds of experiences in the bakery and at the house. Covering them in mental Bubble Wrap, tucking them away somewhere safe.

The bathroom door opened and Sasha came out, shaking her hands dry.

"Okay, show me stuff," she said, not at all excited.

Lainie beckoned Sasha over. "Can you finish mixing this? It's super easy."

Nana gave Lainie a disapproving look, but Lainie turned away from it.

✶

Sometimes in the afternoons, once the bakery had closed, Lainie liked to ride her skateboard to the inlet. If she timed it right, she could watch Papa bringing his boat in. He'd spot her waving from the shore and blow his air horn at her. Two short, one long. Her personalized nautical greeting.

Lately, she'd started scouting the renovated stretch of boardwalk and new benches. Lainie knew which one she wanted. It was opposite a house Carly had always liked, turquoise shingles and white shutters, a balcony where Carly said she'd put a bench swing, if she lived there.

As Lainie skated toward the water, she went over the numbers in her head. The donation box at the bakery had now taken in $76.

Daniella's mom had texted her an update on the Sea Spray donations: $112. With the $100 that Nana and Papa had pledged, they were almost halfway to paying for the bench, and it had only been a week. This would happen, for sure.

A real thing that would tell Ocean Park Heights, *Carly was here.*

Maybe also, *Lainie and Daniella and Penny were here, too.*

Lainie paused to check her phone. She'd texted Penny the night before, asking if she'd had a chance to talk to someone at Anderson's about collecting donations for the bench fund. This was the third time she asked. The other two times, Penny had forgotten, but promised to do it the next day.

No answer yet. Lainie typed out a new message: Hey, checking to see if you asked about the donations. She paused, then added: Like you said you would.

Lainie added the winky-face emoji, but she was officially annoyed now.

She went north on the boardwalk, toward the bench she wanted. This was one of the best stretches of beach in Ocean Park Heights. A lot less crowded, the breeze usually stronger, the waves a little bigger. It was a popular surfing spot, too.

A handful of kids were out there at the moment. Lainie spotted three boys and two girls in a cluster. Then, a little farther out, one dark-haired guy surfing alone on a bright yellow board. When the next big wave came along, he was positioned perfectly to catch it. Lainie watched as he stood up and rode gracefully toward shore for several long seconds before tumbling into the water.

Someone started whooping and clapping at him from the beach.

Lainie narrowed her eyes so she could see better, because the someone looked familiar. *Oh.* The someone was Penny. And that surfer must be The Guy. Dex.

She looked down at her phone and saw that Penny had read her last texts but hadn't replied. Lainie sent one more message: Sorry to be a pain but I really need to know ASAP.

Then she peered out at Penny on the beach, watched her pick up her phone, glance at it, then put it back down on her lap.

"Ughhh!" The sound surprised Lainie. Did she actually make that noise out loud? It felt like it had escaped from some place inside her that she didn't even know existed.

Now she did . . . and now that noise was free.

"Screw you!" she shouted at Penny because Penny was too far away to hear.

As Lainie hopped off her deck and started marching across the beach to where Penny was sitting, she thought about how her private baking session with Nana had been invaded by Sasha. About the bookshelves in Nana and Papa's living room, slowly being emptied into storage boxes and garbage bags. About Daniella being in New York and not in Ocean Park Heights. And about Carly being . . . nowhere. Ever again.

Don't scream. You might not be able to stop.

"Hey!" Penny called when she looked up and saw Lainie coming toward her.

"Hey," Lainie said, keeping her voice cold and flat. "Thanks for ignoring my texts."

Penny frowned, confused for a moment, then got it. "Were you just . . . *watching* me?"

Lainie shrugged and shifted her deck from one hand to the other.

"Not on purpose, I'm not *stalking* you or anything. I was scoping out the memorial benches."

Penny stood up, brushing sand off her legs. "Okay. Sorry I keep forgetting about the donation box."

"*Forgetting?* How can you forget? That's like saying . . . you're forgetting about *Carly*."

Penny glared at her. "Uh, no," she said. "It's totally not. How could you think I would ever?"

Someone let out a "Woo-hoo!" and Penny glanced out at the water. Lainie followed her gaze to Dex, who'd caught another wave.

Lainie sighed. "Well, obviously you have other things on your mind."

"So I'm not allowed to have a boyfriend?"

Lainie raised her eyebrows, surprised. "You guys are, like, official now?"

Penny let out a soft laugh. "Yup. Can you believe it?"

Lainie could see how excited Penny was. Maybe on another day, or in a different summer or a parallel universe, Lainie would ask Penny what it was like, how she knew she was ready for an actual boyfriend. But here and now, Lainie couldn't get there.

"That's great, Pen," she sneered. "Congrats. I don't want to cut into any of your making-out time or whatever, so I'll find someone else to help me with Carly's memorial."

Penny rolled her eyes. "Lainie, come on. You know I want to help. You know I *will* help."

"Do I?" Lainie snapped back. "Because if making me ask you again and again to do one simple thing is your idea of helping, I don't need it."

A shadow of hurt flickered across Penny's face, and she shook her head. "And I don't need you getting all bitchy with me about this. I said I was sorry." Then she looked out toward Dex again. "Thanks for being so mean about Dex, too. It's only, like, the coolest thing that's ever happened to me."

Lainie's jaw dropped. "I'm being *bitchy* and *mean*?"

Penny threw her hands up and let them slap down at her sides. "Yes!"

Lainie saw something in the corner of her vision and turned to see Dex coming toward them, yellow surfboard under one arm and a huge grin on his face. She glanced back at Penny.

"It's okay if you've moved on to cooler things," Lainie said to her. "And I know you don't want your summer bummed out by some depressing ceremony. If I'm the only one who still cares about Carly, I can handle that."

"Come on, Lainie," Penny said, sighing. "You know that's not true."

"Oh, yeah? Then prove it!"

Lainie spun around and stormed away, the stretch of empty beach between her and Penny getting wider every second.

✳

Although the OPH skate park was only a dozen blocks inland, Lainie rarely went. It was always full of local kids who already knew one another, and thanks to an epic argument she'd had with one of them a few years ago, she never felt welcome. At home, things were different: She was friendly with some of the park regulars and loved having a safe place to work on tricks, especially when she was feeling stressed out or pissed off. Ocean Park Heights was perfect for street skating, but sometimes in the summer, Lainie really missed being able to burn off energy in a half-pipe.

Screw it, Lainie thought as she skated away from the beach and toward the park, practically vibrating from the fight with Penny. *I'm going.*

When she got there, she breathed a sigh of relief to see only a few skaters, and pulled out her phone to switch it to a front pocket—she was less likely to fall on that side. There were two missed phone calls from Nana. A voicemail, too. Lainie hit play.

"Alaina." Her grandmother's voice sounded all wrong. Heavy and flat. "Please come home as soon as you can. It's Papa . . . there's been an accident with the boat."

⋛ 20 ⋚

YOU CAN DO THIS, YOU CAN DO THIS.

Youcandothis.

Daniella followed the flow of students into Lorelei's classroom, running her thumb over the familiar seams in the handle of her oboe case. Today, they were expected to play at least thirty-two bars of their works-in-progress, then get feedback from everyone. And hopefully not puke from the stress.

Daniella thought her piece was okay, maybe even *good*, up until the final bars. She'd tried to take the melody in many different directions, but none of it sounded original. There was already too much other music in her head, too many pieces memorized over too many years of playing. She'd been awake until four in the morning, trying to remember all the sounds of Ocean Park Heights, then build a rhythm out of them.

But she couldn't, and now she was exhausted on top of dreading the idea of playing this thing for other people.

"What's the worst thing that could happen when you perform your piece?" Dr. Richards had asked her at their last video session.

"Everyone hating it," Daniella replied.

"And why would that be so terrible?"

Daniella hadn't been able to come up with an answer. She just knew that it would be, period.

"I'm sure some of you are apprehensive about today," Lorelei said now, when everyone in the class had settled into their seats. "That's normal, and I'll say, that's healthy. We *should* have doubts when we're composing. It's part of the process. Sometimes you can't do your best work until after you push through those doubts."

Daniella glanced up and noticed several of her classmates, including Adrian, nodding. She had to admit, Lorelei did have a way of making you feel less like a freak. Maybe this would be fine. Or at least, maybe she'd be able to show her face at the academy again.

"I'm going to call on students randomly," Lorelei continued. "So be ready to go at any time."

Daniella held her breath as Lorelei closed her eyes and stabbed her finger at a class list in her lap.

"Micah!" she called out once her eyes were open. "You're our opening act today."

Micah, a trombonist, nodded somberly. He walked to the podium at the front of the class, put his sheet music on the stand, and started playing. He didn't even hesitate. Daniella wondered where he got the ability to do that. *If only you could order it online with two-day shipping.*

The piece was beautiful and dramatic and sounded like something that could be performed by a chamber group tomorrow. Lorelei reminded everyone what it meant to give "constructive criticism," but she didn't really need to. Everyone in the class took turns gushing about Micah's piece.

Which of course, made Daniella even more convinced that hers was terrible.

A boy named Grey went next. He squeaked out a few disjointed melodies on his clarinet. The students tried to sound positive in their reactions. *I can hear in the notes how much you care about this work. I like the end but I'm confused about the beginning.*

Daniella watched Grey's face as he took the hits. He nodded, expressionless, but she could see in his eyes that he was quietly devastated.

That was when her heart picked up its pounding. Faster, heavier. Daniella tried to take a deep, calming breath but it caught in her throat, making her cough. She covered her mouth with a shaking hand . . . and then she could feel that thudding in her ears. The back of her neck. Her whole body, really.

You can do this, she whispered to herself.

"Daniella?" Lorelei called, looking at her class list. "Do you want to show us what you've got so far?"

"Sure," she managed to say, her voice quivering.

Maybe if she acted like a person who actually *did* want to show them what she had, she'd magically become one. Maybe if she stood up and put one foot in front of the other, over and over, carrying her oboe and sheet music notebook, it would happen by the time she got to the chair on the podium. She could at least try.

Daniella made it halfway there before she froze. Her heart was beating so fast now, she'd started feeling dizzy. The room was rocking back and forth. She put a hand on her chest to steady herself.

"Are you okay?" Adrian mouthed to her.

Lorelei came over to Daniella and touched her shoulder. "Sweetie, do you need to step out and get some air?"

Daniella nodded, loving Lorelei so much in that moment, she could have hugged her. "Um, yeah," she choked out. "I think I didn't eat enough breakfast or something."

"Then please, go have a snack and boost that blood sugar," Lorelei told her. "Come back whenever you're feeling better."

Daniella nodded as normally as she could, then walked out of the classroom as normally as she could. As soon as she reached the hallway and closed the door, she didn't have to be normal anymore. She took in big, gulping breaths, then rushed to the front entrance. She wasn't sure if the fresh air would actually help, but at least she could be away from everyone.

The afternoon sun was hitting the courtyard square-on. Daniella felt like someone was shining a spotlight on her panic attack, so without thinking about the consequences, she started walking toward the park. If she was lucky, the play structure would be empty. She could huddle up there and simply . . . be.

Alone. Invisible.

Not caring what people thought of her. Not always wondering, *What would Carly think of this?*

On the way, Daniella passed a homeless woman sitting in the entryway of a shuttered store. She looked up and peered at her through cloudy eyes. Daniella felt sure the woman was judging her, could tell she was a misfit. She didn't want to make it worse by crossing the street or walking faster. She looked away and continued on, feeling this stranger's gaze.

Finally, she arrived at the playground and as a gift from the universe, it was mostly empty. Daniella crawled onto the platform and found a half-shady spot. She hugged her knees to her chest and put her face down in between, then just breathed. *In for four, hold for seven, out for eight.* Again. And again.

As her heartbeat slowed, the pounding in her ears started to fade, and the noises of the neighborhood around her grew louder. The *squeak-creak* of a swing chain as a man pushed a baby back and forth. An echoing *thump-thump-thump* from two teenagers bouncing basketballs. Some car engines sputtered and some purred, and off in the distance, coming from all directions, Daniella could hear people shouting and calling and laughing. There was no rhythm to the voices, and that felt like a rhythm of its own.

Without realizing she was doing it, Daniella started to hum, picking up the beats of the swing and the basketballs. The other sounds started to give her the melody, guiding her from one note to another as they rose and fell.

This could work, she thought after she realized she was humming the same riff over and over. *This could be the section I need in my piece.*

Twenty minutes later, she walked back into class.

Everyone's head turned, and suddenly she was on display again. Lorelei raised her eyebrows hopefully as she asked, "Daniella. Are you feeling better?"

"Yes," Daniella replied. "And I'm ready to play."

*

"I'm telling you," Adrian said to Margot and Jules as they stood in the courtyard after dismissal. He put his arm around Daniella. "It was the most exciting thing that's happened in the program so far."

Daniella shook her head. "It really wasn't."

"It *totally* was," Adrian insisted. "You looked so messed up, I thought we were going to have to call 911. You run from the room, and then you come back and absolutely *slay* with your piece. Look, I still have goose bumps!"

Adrian held out his arm, and they could all see he wasn't lying. Daniella still had Lorelei's expression burned behind her eyelids. She saw it every time she blinked. Impressed and proud and . . . actually moved. She'd said that. *Daniella, that was so very moving. I can hear how much of yourself you've put into it.*

"You're going to play it for us, right?" Jules asked.

"Even better, maybe you can play it outside the subway entrance and make a ton of cash!" Margot added.

Daniella laughed, but then shook her head. "It's not that kind of piece."

"Dani! Hey!"

It was a familiar voice, ringing out above the chatter of other students as they poured out of the academy building. Daniella scanned the crowd.

"Over here, dummy!"

Daniella spotted Zoe standing by a wall. And Aunt Tina. Both of them waving.

She waved back, thinking, *Crap, oh crap, oh crap. I don't want you guys anywhere near this place.*

She pasted on a smile and made her way over to them.

"Hi, sweetie," Aunt Tina said. "We had to run an errand in this neighborhood, and Zoe really wanted to surprise you."

"And take you for some fro-yo," Zoe added.

Jules came up behind Daniella and rested their chin on her shoulder. "Hi, I'm Jules," they said. "One of Daniella's groupies."

"We're fans, too," Adrian said, pulling Margot over to them.

Daniella felt herself flush. With embarrassment. Nerves. A dash of disbelief that anyone would call themselves her fan or groupie, even as a joke.

Tina smiled and introduced herself and Zoe.

Before Daniella could grab her aunt and cousin to steer them away from her friends, Adrian exclaimed, "Oh, you must be Carly's mom!"

Daniella stole a glance at Aunt Tina's face, just in time to see her expression change from light to dark, a lamp switching off. After what seemed like forever but was probably two seconds, Tina said softly, "That's right."

"We've been helping Daniella with Carly's Bucket List," Margot chimed in, and Daniella winced.

Tina frowned, swallowing hard. "I . . . beg your pardon?"

"Can we go?" Daniella said heatedly, reaching for Zoe's hand. "I'm starving and need fro-yo *stat*." She tugged Zoe toward the courtyard exit and onto the sidewalk, not daring to look back at her friends.

"Daniella!" Aunt Tina called as she caught up to them. "What did that girl mean?"

"Margot?" Daniella made a dismissive gesture with her hand. "She gets everyone confused when I talk about Ocean Park Heights. She must have meant Lainie."

Zoe stopped short. "Lainie made a bucket list for this summer?" she asked.

"Yeah," Daniella replied. *They'll never know it was Carly's.* This lie wasn't as big as the whopper she was telling her friends. This lie was to spare Tina and Zoe from a whole awkward, probably painful thing. It was okay. *Right?*

"Why didn't you tell me?" Zoe's eyes grew wide and somehow, darker. "I've always wanted to help with the Bucket List. Carly would never let me."

"Honey," Tina said to Zoe, putting one hand on her shoulder. "This is something Daniella's doing with her friends."

Zoe was still staring at Daniella. "I thought *I* was one of your friends."

They were standing in the middle of a sidewalk, but Daniella felt cornered.

"Of course you are! I, uh, didn't think you'd be into it. Lainie and Penny and my friends here are all older, and some of the Bucket List stuff is pretty weird."

Zoe scoffed. "Wow. That's amazing."

Lainie frowned. "What do you mean?"

"Carly used to say the *exact* same things when I asked her about the Bucket List. And now you're blowing me off, just like she always did."

Zoe spun around and started walking in a huff, several feet ahead.

As Daniella watched her, she couldn't help thinking, *Well, you wanted a substitute sister. Sounds like you got one.*

"Don't worry about her," Tina said softly to Daniella. "She'll be fine once we get to the yogurt place."

Daniella nodded at Tina, but her thoughts started spinning faster as she walked.

I never thought for a second about including Zoe in the Bucket List.

Also, now I'm a big fat liar to my music friends AND Carly's family. I am a horrible person.

A car horn blared and someone screamed Daniella's name. She shook herself back into the here and now, realizing that she'd stepped off a curb toward oncoming traffic.

Back on the sidewalk, Aunt Tina was holding both hands to her chest. Heaving deep, ragged breaths. Her eyes wide and locked on Daniella.

Daniella rushed to her. "Sorry!" she blurted out. "Sorry, sorry, sorry!"

For all of it.

⋛ 21 ⋚

PENNY'S LITTLE BROTHER, JACK, WAS WHINING.

"I don't get why we do this at the *beach* in *summer*. If it's a Christmas card, it should have snow in it."

"*Holiday* card, not just Christmas," Nick said, slapping Jack on the butt. "And it's not snowy where, like, half the US celebrates anyway. You're following the white establishment narrative of a totally commercialized day on the calendar. Get woke."

They were trudging across the sand toward the water, and Penny was already sweating in her jeans and long-sleeved white top. That was the holiday card photo look her mom had picked for this year. *At least the shirt's baggy,* Penny thought, feeling the fabric whip against her skin in the breeze.

Her mom led the way up ahead, walking with the photographer friend she'd hired. Her dad trailed behind everyone else. She glanced over her shoulder at him, and he winked at her.

"Right here!" Mom called, once she'd reached the spot she wanted.

"Jack and Penny, you stand in front, I'll be in back with Dad and Nick."

Penny and her brothers started to arrange themselves, their backs to the ocean, the sun right above them like an overhead spotlight. As their dad finally caught up, he took a long glance at his family.

"Lisa," he said to Penny's mom, "your daughter is now as tall as you and Nick are. She can't be in front anymore."

Mom gave him a dirty look. "It'll look fine. Better than if we have Jack by himself or make Penny kneel."

Penny stepped out of formation and glanced at the photographer. *A little help here?*

"I, uh, have to disagree," the photographer said to her mom. "Penny could stand with Nick on one side, you and Adam on the other. Then Jack in front, in the middle."

Mom sighed. "I just want to make sure it doesn't ruin the photo composition I have in mind. And also you can see all our bare feet. That's part of the vibe I'm going for."

Penny's dad laughed. "It's a family photo! Why does it have to have a vibe?"

"It's an *artistic* thing."

He laughed again, but harsher this time. "I am so tired of hearing that excuse for wanting everything a certain way. And come on, admit it. This photo is to pretend to everyone that you have a perfect, happy family that spends summers at the shore. *And look how down-to-earth we are! We're not wearing shoes!*"

Penny exchanged glances with both of her brothers. What was happening?

"You didn't hear them snapping at each other all morning?" Nick whispered to her. "She wants to go away to an artists' colony in

October, but he says it's too long to be gone."

"Mom broke a dish in the kitchen," Jack murmured.

Nick put his arm around his younger brother and said, "Come on, let's go look for sea glass."

As Nick and Jack moved farther away, Penny's mom was marching up to her dad, getting in his face.

"You're an ass," she said. "I'm not the one pretending here."

"Let's call it even and say we both are," her father replied.

Mom shook her head. "I simply wanted to get a good picture of all of us together, in this place we love. But apparently, that's too much for you."

She pushed past him and started walking up toward the dunes, back in the direction of home. Then she stopped and turned to face him again.

"And, Adam? In case it's not obvious, this kind of crap isn't hurting only me. It's hurting our kids . . . and the way they feel about you. Think about that the next time you want to be a jerk about something."

Then Penny's mom was gone. Dad turned to look at Penny, with an expression like he'd just been slapped in the face. Then a question in his eyes: *Is that true?*

Duh, Penny wanted to call to him. Instead, she walked over to her brothers.

"Come on," she told them. "Let's get out of here."

✶

After she'd gone home and changed into her own clothes, Penny got on her bike and pedaled toward Dulcie's. She didn't want to be anywhere near her family, but she also didn't want to be alone. When she saw the big CLOSED sign on the window, she remembered that it was Monday, and the bakery wasn't open. She doubled back toward Lainie's grandparents' house.

Penny could see Lainie and her grandparents on the screened porch. They were going through drawers that had been pulled out and placed on a table between them.

"Knock, knock," Penny said, leaning her forehead against the screen.

"Lucky Penny!" Lainie's grandpa exclaimed with a beaming smile.

"Hi, Papa Arturo," Penny replied. "Nana Dulcie," she added, waving at them. Then she waved at Lainie, but Lainie didn't wave back. "Hey, Lainie," Penny said gamely. "Looks like we're both off work. Want to go do something?"

Penny saw Lainie glance at her grandpa, then her grandmother. She whispered back and forth with them a couple of times. Finally, Lainie rolled her eyes, got up, and came outside.

"Why, is Dex busy?" Lainie asked, her voice twisted with sarcasm.

Penny sighed. "I have no idea what Dex is doing today. You and I haven't hung out in a while and I thought maybe we could go to the boardwalk."

Lainie glanced back at her grandparents. "As if this summer wasn't crappy enough already, Papa's hurt. He crashed into another boat and fell. He hit his head pretty hard."

"Oh God . . . is he okay?" *And why didn't you call me?* Penny wanted to add.

"We think so," Lainie replied. "He checked out fine at the ER, but Nana's trying to talk him into getting some more tests, just to be sure.

He's supposed to take it easy, so I should stay here in case he needs me."

Lainie paused, biting her lip so hard Penny expected it to start bleeding.

"I also have some stuff to do for the memorial," Lainie added.

"What kind of stuff?" Penny asked. "I can help."

Lainie gave her a loaded look. "Like you helped with the donation box at Anderson's?"

Penny felt a flush of heat at the back of her neck. "Are you seriously still obsessing about that? I took care of it. They were totally happy to put out a box."

"How much have they collected so far?" Lainie asked.

"I, um, haven't checked yet. I was going to do it yesterday . . . but kind of forgot."

"I knew you would," Lainie said, nodding sadly, "so I called them myself. Fifty-four dollars, by the way."

Confused, Penny tried to process that. "Then why did you ask me how much—never mind. I see what you did there."

"Am I the only one who cares about this memorial?" Lainie asked. "You can tell me the truth. It's okay if I am." She glanced out toward the boardwalk and the ocean, a faraway look on her face that Penny couldn't read. After a few moments, Lainie added, "You're obviously too busy to deal. And Daniella . . . I don't know. Every time I text her with updates, she's like *Okay, great* or sends a thumbs-up."

"Lainie, she's in *New York*. What else do you want her to do right now? When she gets back, I'm sure she'll follow your orders or whatever."

Lainie stepped back. "My orders? Are you saying I'm being a dictator about this stuff?"

Is she? Penny asked herself. *No, that's maybe too mean. But she is really pissing me off right now.* "Okay, not a dictator," she replied. "Just a total control freak."

Lainie froze. Possibly trying to decide whether to scream or flip Penny off or something worse. But then she grew suddenly calm, which was even scarier.

"It's fine," Lainie said, her voice cool as ice. "I get it. You don't want to get all sad planning something for Carly when you could be out having fun with your boyfriend. Because what could possibly matter more than sitting on the beach, watching some guy surf, and then yelling *Yay*? Well, don't worry about it. I can ask Sasha to help me."

"*Sasha?*" Penny echoed, confused. "Don't you still sort-of hate her?"

"No," Lainie said. "She's okay. And it would probably help her to get involved with something like this."

Penny shook her head, trying to make all the pieces of what Lainie was talking about come together into something that made sense. "Help her with *what*?"

Lainie smirked, and Penny realized she'd taken some kind of bait.

"Forget I said that," Lainie said, waving her hand. "I'm not supposed to tell anyone her story."

This hit Penny hard. Was she just "anyone" now?

"Oh, I get it," she began, hearing the bitterness in her own voice. "Carly's not here anymore. We don't *have* to be friends."

Those words hung between them in the silence that followed. Not fading as quickly as others.

"I—" Lainie started to say, her eyes wide. Her expression then turned hard and cold. "I guess you're right."

Penny nodded. "Since I'm so *unreliable*, I'm sure Sasha will be a much better partner." She turned to leave, but something inside her wanted more, and she turned back. "I think we should drop the whole Bucket List thing, okay? I'll see you at the memorial . . . assuming I'm still invited."

She turned around quickly, before she could say anything else. Before Lainie could say anything else.

At least I'm the one walking away this time, Penny thought as she headed for home.

⇝ 22 ⇜

"FIFTY NEW POSTS WITH THE GLORIOUS ODDBALLS hashtag!" Jules exclaimed, scrolling through FotoSlam. "Look at this pic of a girl with her pet pig. They're both wearing the same glasses and it's the best thing I've ever seen."

Jules passed the phone to Daniella and Margot, who broke out laughing. They'd taken over a rickety little climbing bridge on the playground, hanging their legs over the side.

"How many does that make so far?" Daniella asked.

"Way over two hundred," Adrian replied. "But the really cool thing is, the posts are from everywhere. California. Canada. England. There was one from Australia, right?"

"Yup," Jules said. "Daniella, we've got *reach* with this thing."

"I think you're officially in viral territory," Adrian said to Daniella.

"Really? I mean, I guess if it's on three different continents. And at this rate we should get to at least three hundred, right?"

"Definitely," Adrian said.

"That sounds viral enough to me," Jules said.

Daniella took the shell purse out of her backpack. "Thank you, Krishna Cade! I'm going to check it off the Bucket List."

"Ooh, can we watch this sacred ceremony?" Jules asked.

Daniella smiled. "Sure. Welcome to the incredible, spectacular sight of me making a purple check mark on a straight black line."

She pulled the list and pen out of the shell purse, unfolded the paper, then uncapped the pen. She held it up, above the list, then slowly lowered it and made the check mark.

Jules, Adrian, and Margot applauded.

A lightning bolt of memory hit Daniella. It had been almost exactly a year ago. Lainie, Penny, and Carly in Daniella's backyard, sitting around the fire pit as Daniella made a big, silly deal out of checking off a Bucket List item. It was *Have a boy win something for you at a board-walk game.* She remembered that moment better than she remembered the boy (Andrew Greer, *cringe*), the midway game (ring toss), or the prize itself (a pink stuffed whale, *also cringe*).

Daniella would have given her left pinkie to relive all that. Just once. A few ordinary seconds at the time, and now they were legendary in her mind. *If only there were a way to know these things are special when they're happening,* she thought. Then: *Wait, one's happening now, isn't it?*

She looked for the details of this new moment—ones that might sharp-focus the memory. Jules's nose ring, which was an iridescent blue star, and the red stamp on their hand from a club they'd gone to last night. Margot's ponytail swishing every time the bridge moved, the way she wiggled her feet like she was shaking energy out of them. Adrian's sneakers with all the doodles on the soles, the scar on his left arm that he never talked about. The cloudless sky above, and the ocean of humidity that swirled around them all.

Daniella closed her eyes to seal it in. She'd only known these people a few weeks, but they were keepers, no question. Margot, Adrian, and Jules would be part of her life for a long, long time. She never had that kind of *aha* experience with the Summer Sisters; she'd been so young when they all started playing together. *Little kids just assume that friends are forever.*

"So what's left?" Margot asked, leaning in to peer at the list.

Daniella shook herself out of her thoughts and scanned Carly's handwriting. "Not sure. Maybe the music video one?"

"That seems like a lot of work," Jules said, stifling a yawn. "And someone you know was out dancing way too late."

Daniella nodded. "Yeah, you're right. I'm not up for that kind of planning right now." She glanced at the list again. "Nobody's kissed a boy yet . . . but we'll leave that one for Penny. She says it could happen any day."

"Go, Penny!" Adrian said, raising a fist.

"There's *Chalk art a whole driveway.* That would be easier for Penny or Lainie since there aren't a lot of available driveways in Manhattan. Although they've both been pretty busy and haven't gotten to it yet."

"Wait," Margot said, gazing at the blacktop in front of them. "Does it have to officially be a driveway?"

Daniella stared at the list. "I don't know." *I would give BOTH pinkies to be able to ask Carly about this.*

"What if the thing being chalk-art-ed is, like, bigger than a driveway? Then that would count, right?"

Daniella glanced at Margot, then at the blacktop, and instantly caught Margot's drift. "How big are you thinking?" she asked.

"I don't know. Maybe the whole thing?"

"Are you serious?" Daniella asked, laughing.

"Of course I am," Margot said. "There are four of us, and we could get more help if we needed."

Daniella scanned the blacktop, picturing it covered in drawings and doodles and writing. In her heart, without even having to think about it, she knew Carly would have loved it.

She smiled at her new friends. "When can we start?"

*

The next morning on the way to the academy, Daniella bought four boxes of jumbo-size chalk. Margot brought a portable speaker, and Adrian and Jules brought drinks and snacks. They were ready to go as soon as they were dismissed for the day.

As they walked to the park together, Adrian asked Daniella how she felt about her piece for composition class. Daniella had recorded it in Zoe's closet the night before, then quickly emailed the file to Lorelei before she could change her mind. Clicking send had pushed her to the edge of a panic attack, but she talked herself down.

"I have no idea if it's any good or not," Daniella told Adrian. "But it was the first thing I've ever composed from start to finish. That's something, right?"

"Are you serious?" Adrian said. "That's *everything*. Dude, I didn't get that far. But I handed it in anyway."

Daniella nodded, wondering if Dr. Richards was going to call *Summer Without* a "big win" when she told him about it at her next video session.

When they got to the park, Margot scoped out the blacktop. "Let's each take a corner and slowly work toward the middle," she suggested. "Daniella, you pick first."

Daniella stared at Margot, grateful for the way she took charge of things. That part of her was so much like Carly. She took a pack of chalk and headed to the far corner, just left of the basketball net. Without thinking about it, she grabbed the purple chalk and started drawing a giant heart.

A few minutes later, Daniella saw a pair of sneakers come into her field of vision and glanced up. It was a little boy, maybe seven years old, watching her.

"Can I help?" he asked.

Daniella tried to imagine herself, Penny, and Lainie covering one of their driveways in Ocean Park Heights with this chalk. Maybe they would have come up with a theme. Or it might have been random, all emojis and rainbows and fish and cats and stick people and whatever else seemed funny in the moment. If one of the other kids on the street asked to help, would they let him or her? Probably not. But here, on this corner in New York City, there was no answer but yes.

"What's your name?" Daniella asked.

"Cory," the boy said.

"I'm Daniella. Pick a color, Cory, and get to work."

The next hour was a blur of pavement, chalk dust, dirty hands and knees, and Margot's emo-heavy playlist blasting through the portable speaker. Other little kids had joined them, and slowly, slowly, all four corners were getting close to meeting in the middle.

At one point, Daniella felt her phone vibrate in her pocket. She heaved herself up off the blacktop and checked the screen. The caller ID said FUTURE FORWARD MUSIC ACADEMY. Daniella's first thought was *I'm in trouble.* Then: *But I didn't do anything!* Followed by: *Or did I?*

After rushing to a shady spot far from the music, she took a deep breath and answered it.

"Hello?"

"Daniella? It's Lorelei. Is this a good time?"

Daniella glanced over at the crazy scene she'd created in the park and said, "Yeah, sure."

"I wanted to let you know that I loved your finished composition. It is simply beautiful and very . . . powerful."

Daniella froze for a second, wanting to make sure she'd heard right. "For real?"

Lorelei laughed. "Indeed for real. With your permission, I'd like to recommend it to the academy director for the recital at the end of the program. Every year, they choose a student piece to be performed. This year, I think it should be yours."

"Performed?" Daniella asked, having a hard time even saying the word. "By who?"

"One of the chamber groups. Hopefully your group, if that's not too strange. We'd work with you on the arrangement, of course. What do you think?"

Daniella closed her eyes, and the music from Margot's speaker faded into the background of street noises. Instead, she heard *Summer Without*, but not simply as an oboe piece. She heard it larger, wider, stronger, one sound coming from four instruments. The hair on her arms stood on end.

"I think that would be great," she said. Then in her mind, she added, *I also think it would give me the biggest panic attack I've ever had, but I'll deal with that later.*

After Daniella thanked Lorelei and said goodbye, she put her phone away and walked, a little wobbly, to the center of the blacktop. She couldn't wait to share her news with the others, but there was a Bucket List item to finish first.

✷

Two hours later, Daniella stood with Adrian, Margot, and Jules at the top of the play structure, surveying their creation. It looked like a field full of stars, hearts, and flowers that danced, floated, and even crashed into one another. Adrian had connected the four sections of the blacktop with what looked like waves of turquoise water.

Cory had helped for a while. So had an older woman Daniella often saw at the park, feeding crackers to pigeons while chatting to them in another language. A group of guys came by and made a big deal out of not being able to play basketball, but Adrian had told them off and then one of them had come back to help.

"It's so freaking cool," Jules said.

"Yeah, but what actually is it?" Margot asked. "It's not anything in particular."

"I think it's whatever you want it to be," Daniella suggested, and the others agreed.

"I took some pics and videos while you guys were drawing," Adrian added, holding up his phone. "Sending them to you."

Daniella started to snap photos of the entire blacktop from their high-up view. She chose the two best ones, then posted them, along with a few of the shots from Adrian, to FotoSlam.

> Chalk art a whole driveway? Blah. We chalked a
> whole NYC playground blacktop. Hope it doesn't
> rain for a few days! @LuckyPennyA77
> @Alaina_RC #SummerSisters

After the post showed up, Daniella glanced over at Adrian, Margot, and Jules. It didn't feel right not to give them a shout-out. She went in and edited the caption, thanking and tagging the three of them, too.

Adrian's phone let out a happy little *Ping!* and he glanced at it.

"Ooh," he said. "We're in the caption along with the Summer Sisters! This is a huge moment for me!"

Daniella laughed and swatted him playfully on the arm.

"Don't let it go to your head," she teased.

"Oops," Adrian added. "I think you forgot to tag Carly."

"Did I?" Daniella made her best surprised face, then checked the post. "You're right. Good catch."

She swallowed hard and tried to keep her hands from shaking as she edited the post with another tag. Carly's old FotoSlam account, @CarlyRose212, had been taken down. So Daniella typed @*CarlyRose213* instead. She'd made that typo before. She could always say she'd done it again.

✶

The next morning, Daniella felt like she might actually be gliding as she walked from the subway station to the academy. Her parents had squealed with delight when she told them her news about the recital.

213

Lainie and Penny had both responded to the chalk art post with heart emojis. And she hadn't felt a moment of panic during the entire train ride downtown.

She turned in to the academy courtyard and noticed that most of the kids had already gone inside. But Adrian, Margot, and Jules were standing on the front steps. Staring laser beams at Daniella.

"Hey, guys," she said, stopping short. "Were you waiting for me?"

"Yeah," Adrian replied, his voice flat.

"Why didn't you tell us that Carly died?" Margot asked bluntly.

Daniella froze. "What?"

"Carly," Jules repeated slowly. They didn't look as angry; just hurt and confused. "We were browsing your friends' FotoSlam feeds and saw some posts from last winter. From when she . . . passed away."

Daniella's heart thudded, then kicked into high gear. As she stood there, not sure what to say or do next, she could feel the pounding spread into her limbs and up into her head.

"You were looking at Lainie and Penny's old posts?" she echoed, wanting to make sure she'd heard the right thing. When Jules and Margot nodded, Daniella added, "That's a little creepy."

"Not as creepy as pretending your cousin is still alive." Adrian narrowed his eyes, tilted his head. Probably trying to figure out who, exactly, he was looking at.

Daniella took a few steps backward. Her hands started shaking. *He's right. You were pretending, and it was creepy. And wrong.*

Jules took one step toward her. "Who wrote this Bucket List we've been doing?"

Daniella was about to answer, *Carly did!* But she thought about the explanation that would have to follow. Was that creepy, too? Would they understand?

"It's a little—" she began, but didn't know which words should come next. "I'm sorry—"

Now her throat had closed up and she couldn't find enough air to breathe, let alone keep talking.

The only other thing she could do was turn around and run.

⋛ 23 ⋚

PENNY'S DAD WAS A FAST BIKER, BUT PENNY HAD gotten faster since the last time they did a sunset-root-beer ride. Now she was the one cruising in the lead, turning to look over her shoulder every minute to make sure she hadn't lost him.

"Dad, come on! We only have twenty minutes and there might be a line!"

It was their thing: pedaling to the river side of Ocean Park Heights to get a bottled root beer at the old-fashioned drugstore and watch the sun go down. When Penny was little, they did it every Friday, as soon as her dad got to the shore for the weekend. This was their first one so far this summer.

By the time they reached their favorite spot on the river, sodas tucked into their bike baskets, the sun was just starting to sink. They found a bench and sat down.

"You okay?" Penny asked, noticing her dad trying to catch his breath.

"Fine," he replied, coughing into his hand. "A little out of shape."

"That's what you get for staying in the city every weekend."

Penny's dad shot her a look. "You make it sound like I'm doing that on purpose."

She shrugged. "Aren't you? You're not, like, a prisoner somewhere."

"What I mean is, I think *you* think I don't want to be here with everyone."

"That's what Mom thinks," Penny said.

"Well, she's wrong." He stared out at the sky, which was now four different shades of orange. "Can we drop the subject? It's nothing you have to worry about."

Penny glanced at her father, at how tired he looked. Beaten-up and worn down. *You don't have to protect me,* she wanted to tell him. *I'm not a little kid anymore and I can deal with the truth.*

But she said nothing. They watched the rest of the sunset in silence, drinking their root beers and listening to the water lapping at the hull of a dinner cruise boat docked nearby.

"Are you having a good summer, Peanut?" Penny's dad asked.

"Yes," she replied.

"Your mom tells me there's a *boy*. Do I need to have THE TALK with him? Ask him about his intentions?"

Penny looked at her father with horror. "Uh . . . sure, if you want me to run away and change my name."

He laughed. "I would never. I promise. Although I do hope to meet . . . who would I be meeting?"

"Dex Nakashima," Penny said, as casually as she could. Inside, she was cringing. She wasn't ready to talk about Dex to her father.

"You guys work together?" Dad asked.

"Yup. He's really cool." *Can we drop this subject, too, now?*

Dad nodded, and mercifully, stayed quiet as they finished their sodas. Penny tried to remember what she and her father usually talked about on these Friday outings. She'd complain about Nick and Jack. Tell him about whatever fun/weird/hilarious thing happened at the house/beach/boardwalk. But in those dusky minutes as another summer day slid into evening, she couldn't think of one thing she could share that her dad would appreciate or help with.

Maybe it was enough to simply sit there, being in this very specific space they'd always occupied together.

When it was time to pedal home, Penny went slowly, letting her father be in front. She heard his cell phone ring and watched as he stopped to answer it. She stopped, too, and lingered nearby to wait for him, but he walked some distance as he spoke to whoever had called.

Eventually he was done and they continued on to the house, where Mom and Kathy had just finished cooking dinner. Jamie and the boys were in the backyard, setting the table.

"Good," Mom said as Penny and her dad walked into the kitchen. "I was wondering if you guys would be back on time."

"Dad had to take a phone call," Penny said, hoping her mom would ask him who it was.

"Work emergency," he added casually. "Looks like I'm going to have to go back on Monday."

Penny's mother froze. She fixed Dad with a death glare. "You were planning to stay all week," she said.

"I know," he replied. "And I'm sorry."

Penny glanced back and forth between her parents. Why wasn't Mom fighting this? *If she won't, I will.* "Dad," Penny began, "just say you're officially on vacation and you can't come in, period."

He smiled sadly at her. "I wish it were that simple, Peanut, but it's not. Your mother knows."

"Actually, I don't," Penny's mom said. Not angry. Perfectly calm. Penny knew from experience that a perfectly calm Mom could be a quietly furious, low-key terrifying Mom.

"Then I'll explain it to you after dinner," Dad said, turning toward the back door. "Can we eat?"

After he went into the yard, Penny's mom and Kathy exchanged a loaded glance. Then Kathy said, "Yes, let's eat," and ushered her mother outside.

When the meal was over, Penny felt thoroughly weirded out by how normal it had been. Like her mom and dad were putting on a show called *Remember How It Was When You Guys Were Little*? Dad cracked jokes, Mom talked about the painting she was working on, and Nick and Jack had their 347th hand-fart contest.

Penny was the only one who didn't play along.

After dinner, Mom and Dad went for a walk, the way they'd often done in the past at the shore. Also strange. Jamie and Penny cleared the table while Kathy went inside to watch baseball on TV with the boys.

"That was nice, wasn't it?" Jamie said. "Your family's always fun to be with."

"Not lately," Penny muttered.

Jamie nodded but didn't look Penny in the eye. "Yeah, I hear things have been rough."

"They fight a lot."

Now Jamie did look at her. "I'm sorry I can't give you advice in that department. Growing up with a single mom can suck, but at least I don't remember my parents fighting."

Penny nodded, thinking about how Jamie was so damn *kind*. She'd spent years trying to be sweet and caring like Jamie. She got started volunteering at the nursing home because that was something Jamie did. *Actually*, Penny realized, *I've been looking up to her for as long as I can remember.*

She bagged the garbage and walked it toward the bin on the side of the house. Up ahead, she heard voices from the front yard and stopped to listen.

"Just admit it!" Penny heard her mom say, her voice quivering.

"I'm not going to do this with you right now," her dad replied.

"Okay. But for the record, the screwing around would be painful for me, but it wouldn't destroy me. The *lying* would destroy me."

"For God's sake, Lisa, you sound like someone on a soap opera."

"I wish I were. You're not denying anything, so I assume I'm right."

STOP IT, Penny yelled at them, but inside her own head. *Wait. I can make you stop.*

She lifted the lid of the garbage bin, tossed in the bag, and slammed it shut. The sound echoed, and Penny was sure everyone on the block could hear. *Good.*

Her parents' voices went silent. Penny moved forward, toward the yard, far enough for Mom to see her face. *Yes, it's me. And I know.* Then she ran back up the side of the house and inside, not stopping until she flopped facedown on the bed in her tiny attic room. She decided to give herself five minutes to cry, checking the time on her phone.

Penny let out a series of long, muffled sobs into her pillow until the five minutes was up. Then wiped her eyes and opened *Tomcat*

Vigilante on her laptop, watching one episode blend into another until she fell asleep.

The next morning, everyone woke up to find Penny's dad gone. He'd left a note on the kitchen table that said, simply, *I'll call soon.*

✶

"Hey, you," Dex said. "You seem a little distracted today. Everything cool?"

"What?" Penny glanced up. They were cleaning a pair of lounge chairs that were covered in bird dung. "Oh yeah. Absolutely." She pointed to her chair. "Do you think the gulls had some kind of target-pooping contest here last night?"

Dex laughed, which made Penny smile, which let her forget about the drama back at her house. "Are you still up for the water park after work?" he asked.

"Duh!" Penny replied.

On one hand, she couldn't wait to hang out with Dex. On the other hand, she felt slightly nauseous at the thought of being in a swimsuit in front of him. Penny knew, in theory, that she shouldn't be worried about this. He was officially her boyfriend now (*HOLY CRAP, HE IS MY BOYFRIEND*). If his feelings for her changed because of how she looked in a two-piece, he wasn't the guy she thought he was.

But reality beat theory, every single time.

"Okay," Dex said, stepping back from the lounge chairs. "We showed those gulls who's boss. Until tomorrow, at least. Come on, I think the gate's opened."

He held out his hand, and Penny took it. They walked into the hut so they could be ready for the first guests of the day, and she wondered how long she could keep her fingers laced with Dex's before they had to untangle themselves for something silly like a beach umbrella or rental form.

The answer: about thirty-seven seconds.

"Any discounts for friends and family?"

It was Jamie, leaning on the counter, grinning wide. Wearing a very white, extremely tiny string bikini.

"Hey," Penny said, then glanced over at Dex, who was already grinning back at Jamie. "What time are you guys leaving today? I want to make sure I get a chance to say goodbye."

"We're not," Jamie replied. "Leaving, I mean."

"What?"

Jamie shrugged. "My mom says your mom *needs* her here. For moral support and all that."

Penny knew she was supposed to say something along the lines of *Awesome* or *Yes, my mom's needs are definitely what I care about most right now.*

"So you're sticking around for a while?" Dex asked in a way that made Penny's stomach drop, the way it did on the Tower of Power free-fall ride at FunLand. "How have you been since that night we went to Brady's?"

Jamie laughed like the question was some kind of private joke between them. "I've been good. Better now that I don't have to leave."

Penny saw something she hoped was a hallucination or something in Jamie's eye.

Did she just WINK at him?

"Excellent, excellent," Dex said. "Can we set you up with a chaise longue or beach chair on the house?"

Jamie giggled and said, "Sure!" before Penny could process anything else. Now Dex was grabbing an umbrella from the stack and leaving the hut, gesturing for Jamie to follow him. Penny watched as he led her to the chaise longue closest to the water and put the umbrella in the pre-planted stand next to it. Then, instead of coming right back to the hut, Dex *stayed*. Talking and laughing. Laughing and talking.

They were too far away for Penny to hear, but she had no problem seeing their body language. Jamie twirling her finger through her ponytail. Dex standing with one hand on his hip, as if he were posing for a photo. Then Dex came jogging back to the hut and Penny thought, *Finally!* But he didn't come inside. Instead, he grabbed Kiani and jogged back to Jamie's chaise to show her his surfboard.

"Great," Penny said out loud to nobody. It was so obvious, what was happening.

She stared at Dex. She thought about her dad's note.

He's going to dump you, Penny said to herself. *Better start preparing now. Maybe he'll say he was never your boyfriend to begin with. He'll tell you whatever he has to, in order to feel okay about asking Jamie out.*

Right then, a mom with three little kids came up to the hut, and even though Penny wished she could tell them to go away, she had to do her job. By the time they were gone, Dex was busy helping some other guests on the beach.

She needed to talk to someone besides her pathetic, paranoid self. She needed to talk to Carly.

Penny took out her phone and found Carly's listing in the contacts. Of course she hadn't deleted it, or the hundreds of texts between the two of them, or even that two-minute-long voicemail that was only a butt-dial. She squeezed her phone tight, then closed her eyes and tuned out the voices and the seagulls and the roaring waves. Maybe, if she concentrated really hard, she could *feel* what Carly would say if Penny could call her.

But she felt nothing.

The next thing Penny knew, she was dialing Daniella.

"Penny?" Daniella's voice sounded soft and far away.

"Hey," Penny said.

"Are you okay?"

"Yeah, I just needed . . . You're not in the middle of a class or something, are you?"

"Sort of," Daniella said. "I'm supposed to be in African drumming right now, but I'm actually in the bathroom."

"Are *you* okay?" Penny asked.

Daniella paused. Penny could hear a sniffle. She'd been crying. "Not really."

"Tell me," Penny said. "What's going on?"

There were suddenly loud noises on Daniella's end of the line. "I'm sorry," Daniella whispered. "Some people came in. I'll try to call later."

She hung up, and Penny stared at her phone. She clicked back to her Favorites screen.

I can't call Lainie, she decided. *I can't vent to her about Dex. Not after that fight.*

Penny turned her phone completely off and stuffed it in her backpack. She wasn't going to need it today. There was nobody on the other end of the line who could help her.

⋛ 24 ⋚

LAINIE AND SASHA STOOD IN THE ALLEY BEHIND
Dulcie's, waiting for a big pink truck.

"Exactly how pink is it?" Sasha asked, rummaging in the pouch
where she kept her colored sketching pencils. "Are we talking a strawberry ice cream pink, or a super-ripe watermelon pink?"

"Umm . . . definitely more watermelon."

Sasha pulled out a fuchsia-colored pencil and held it up. "Not a
color that makes me think of fancy Colombian coffee."

"It will," Lainie said. "Trust me."

Nana bought only one type of coffee for the bakery, from one specific vendor—Ramón, a friend-of-a-cousin-of-a-friend, who sourced his
beans from a small grower in the Norte de Santander region. He'd bought
his van used from a professional dog walker and never repainted it.

Lainie watched as Sasha opened her sketchbook and started doo-
dling with the pencil. She got it now: Art was how Sasha dealt with . . .
being Sasha.

Although hopefully that's getting easier, Lainie thought. *While being Lainie is getting more difficult.*

She was planning to use this time in the alley to ask Sasha for help with the memorial. Lainie hadn't heard from Penny in days. But she couldn't bring herself to talk to Sasha just yet. Sasha was still running hot and cold with her, sometimes chatty and sometimes quiet, like today. Lainie couldn't shake the feeling that needing this girl in any way was some kind of defeat.

Before Lainie even tried to get up her nerve, she heard a rumbling and turned to see the pink truck heading down the alley. When it pulled up, the driver leaned down and held out his hand for Lainie to high-five.

"Ramón!" she said, reaching up to slap his palm. "This is Sasha. Her dad's buying the bakery."

Ramón and Sasha said hello to each other, then Ramón turned back to Lainie. "Are you telling me this could be my last delivery to you and your grandmother?"

Lainie felt something in her throat close up. That word. *Last.* It had been floating around her brain all summer, but kept its distance, blurry and gray. Now it was coming into focus. Full color. Getting more and more real.

Ramón suddenly looked concerned. "Oh, honey, I didn't mean to upset you."

That was when Lainie realized she had tears in her eyes. She quickly wiped them away and pulled her mouth into a smile.

"It's okay," she told Ramón. "I'm fine. Can Sasha watch you bring in the order so she knows where everything goes?"

Ramón nodded, and Lainie turned quickly away from him.

"I'll be back in a few," she told Sasha.

She rushed inside the bakery and leaned with both hands against one of the kitchen's metal counters.

You are pathetic, she told herself. *If you fall apart during a coffee delivery, what are you going to do at the end of the summer?* She tried to picture herself walking out her grandparents' front door for the last time and getting into the car to drive home, knowing she'd never be back. It didn't feel like something she could physically do.

But she'd have to, somehow.

Lainie lifted one hand and slammed it on the counter. A loud clang, then the noise echoed and lingered. Filling the kitchen with sound that matched how she felt. Lainie did it again, this time with her other hand.

"Alaina Calderon!"

Lainie spun around to see her grandmother standing by the door to the front room. Glaring at her.

"You stop that," Nana said, her voice cool but sharp. "You're acting like a child."

Lainie stared at Nana for a moment. "How am I supposed to act, when my life is completely falling apart?"

Now there were tears stinging the corners of her eyes. Lainie slowly wiped each one away with a finger, waiting for Nana to come to her. Wrap her in a hug. Kiss her forehead and whisper that she wished she could make it all better.

But Nana didn't move. Instead, she pointed a long, strong finger at Lainie.

"Your life . . . is *not* falling apart. Yes, you are going through some hard things. Take a look around: so are other people, too! Sasha is fighting for her mental health. Carly's parents lost a child. And your grandfather . . ."

227

Nana's voice crumbled into silence.

"What?" Lainie asked, taking a few tentative steps toward her grandmother. "What's wrong with Papa?"

"He called me five minutes ago to tell me his head was hurting him," Nana replied, taking a deep breath. "Hurting him a *lot*. And then he started talking nonsense. I hung up and called 911. They're taking him to the hospital right now and I'm going to meet them there. Wes is on his way to pick me up."

Stunned, Lainie watched Nana hurry into her office, grab her purse, and come back out.

"Is he going to be okay?" she asked, approaching her grandmother and touching her hand. "I mean, the doctors already said he was, right?"

Nana shrugged. "I don't know, mija. When I walk into that hospital, they might tell me that the man I've shared my life with for forty-three years, my Arturo, might be gone. Or that he's still here in body, but not in spirit. Or that he'll come home but never be the same again."

Lainie could see how hard her grandmother was trying to keep herself from breaking down.

"I could say that *my* life is falling apart," Nana said, looking Lainie square in the eye. "But I don't. Because life is never falling apart. It's never perfect, either. Not for anyone. Life is just . . . *life*."

A car honked out front. Nana dashed toward the door.

"That's Wes," she said over her shoulder to Lainie. "I'll call you as soon as I know something."

Then she was gone.

Papa, Lainie thought, thinking of how she'd said goodbye to him that morning. She'd been in a rush and hadn't had time to give him the usual hug-kiss combo. Instead, she'd waved on her way out. He'd waved back, grinning like it gave him endless pleasure and pride to simply look at her.

Now she could be losing *him*, too?

Lainie started crying, and then she was suddenly running. Through the front of the bakery, out the door, and toward the boardwalk. She wanted to feel the ocean breeze brush her face, her hair waving behind her. That way, if she kept crying, the tears would dry quickly. She didn't even know where she was going or where she *wanted* to go. Nothing in Ocean Park Heights felt like a safe place anymore.

When she came to the corner of Daniella's street, she almost turned there. To go see Carly, because Carly would listen and tell Lainie everything would be okay, then wait with her for the phone to ring. But Lainie stopped herself in time. *Stupid. Even if Carly were here, she wouldn't be able to protect you from what might happen to Papa.*

Up ahead, she could see the Ferris wheel rotating and people at the top of the Tower of Power. FunLand must have just opened for the day. Lainie found herself at the entrance gate.

The shortest line was for the pirate ship ride, where you rocked back and forth, higher and higher, until you half levitated out of your seat, convinced this was going to be the one time the seat belts malfunctioned. It was perfect.

Five minutes later, she was sliding into the back row of the ship, next to a dad and his two sons. She'd been on this ride dozens of times, a hundred maybe, with Penny or Daniella or Carly, or two of them or all three of them. Never by herself.

The ship started moving. Swinging gracefully, like it was trying to rock everyone to sleep. Then the swinging got faster, and someone screamed. Lainie took that as permission. On the next swing, she screamed, too. As loud as she could into the salty air.

She was sad and scared for her grandfather. Mad at her grandmother for being mad at *her*. At Sasha for getting the life Lainie wanted and not even appreciating it. At Daniella for not being here for this summer and Penny for not understanding her.

I'm pissed at you, too, Carly. But am I allowed to be?

By the time the pirate ship started slowing down, Lainie was all screamed out.

Also, a little dizzy and very close to puking.

She walked for a bit, until she felt right again, getting a frozen lemonade in a souvenir cup. Nana hadn't called yet and Lainie needed to stay distracted. So she ambled toward the game booths, where the employees called out to her as she passed.

"Prize every time! Show us what you've got!" one shouted.

Another yelled: "Hey, you look like you can pitch a softball pretty well. Look at all these milk cans that need to be knocked over!"

Lainie ignored them. Until she reached the balloon dart game and stopped, looking up at the prizes hanging from the ceiling. The giant rainbow llama was still there.

She knew there was more than one. This wasn't the exact same giant rainbow llama they'd all seen on that first night of summer. It probably wasn't the same one that had been there a week ago, or even the day before. But *this* giant rainbow llama was clearly staring at her, its shiny plastic eyes daring her to go for it.

Really, Lainie simply wanted to throw something hard, and maybe have it break something. She stepped up to the booth and dug out a five-dollar bill from her pocket, put it on the counter. The teenage boy running the booth took the money and placed five darts in front of her.

"Pop one balloon—" he started to say.

"Win a small prize. Pop three, win the biggest one. I know the rules."

The boy laughed awkwardly. "Okay, then. Whenever you're ready."

Lainie squeezed the dart, letting all her anger and frustration and sadness transfer into it from her hand. Then she threw it, hard. It hit a balloon, then bounced off. The second dart did the same.

She knew the tricks: the balloons were only half inflated to make them harder to pop, and the points on the darts had been filed down. But it felt so good to make a hard, fast motion like that. To experience the release of letting something out, throw by throw. *I could do this all day*, she thought.

Lainie hurled the third dart even faster than the other two, and it went straight into the sweet spot of a blue balloon. *Pop.*

"Nice!" the boy said.

"Thanks," Lainie replied, catching her breath. She threw the last two darts and missed, enjoying it so much, she temporarily forgot there were prizes involved.

"You can pick something from the 'small' row," the boy told her. "Or do you wanna play again and try to trade up?"

Lainie checked her pocket. "I don't have enough cash," she said, then glanced wistfully at the llama.

"Are you going for something specific?" the boy asked, catching the glance.

"I was, yeah," Lainie said, trying not to sound as disappointed as she felt.

The boy narrowed his eyes and peered at her, curious. "You work at Dulcie's, don't you?"

Lainie nodded.

"Those chocolate chip cookies are insane," he said, then tilted his head to examine her for a few more seconds.

"What's wrong?" Lainie asked, suddenly self-conscious.

"Here," the boy said softly, looking left and right to make sure nobody was watching. He reached under the counter and pulled out five more darts. "The owner there gave me an extra cookie once, when it was my birthday."

Lainie nodded. "Yeah, that sounds like my grandmother." She looked at the extra darts. *Why not?* She definitely wanted to throw something, to feel that relief, a few more times.

When she let the next dart fly, it popped a red balloon. No problem. Like she was a darts champion.

The second and third darts missed, but the fourth hit. *Pop.*

"Whoa!" the boy said. "Congrats! You get your pick of prizes."

"The llama," she said, realizing that her voice was a little scratchy from the pirate-ship screaming. She cleared her throat. "I want the llama."

"You got it," he said, and used a pole with a hook on the end to pull the llama down from its spot. He handed it to Lainie, and she hugged it to her chest. The thing was almost as tall as she was.

"Thank you," she said to the boy, gazing deeply at him for a second to let him know how much this meant. She didn't care if he thought she was weird.

She brought the llama over to a railing at the edge of the boardwalk, overlooking the beach. Placed her (it was totally a *her*) in front of the railing and backed up, trying to frame the picture.

"Okay, Eloise," Lainie said to the llama (it was totally an Eloise), "this is an important picture and it has to be just right."

She laughed at herself. *Talking to a stuffed llama.* But she felt lighter now. More able to believe that Papa was going to be okay. Maybe everything else would be okay, too, eventually.

After taking a few photos, Lainie was about to put her phone away when it started ringing. It was Nana.

She took a deep breath and answered the call.

⋛ 25 ⋚

THE LAST NOTES OF THE CHAMBER PIECE FADED. All movement stopped—the hands, the arms, the fingers playing instruments. In the new silence, Daniella looked up at the ceiling of the rehearsal room and found the vents. She imagined that the music she and the other kids had just performed had floated up through those vents and out of the building. Now it was drifting through the city, finding people who needed to hear it.

Mr. Novikoff slowly scanned the room, scrutinizing each of the four students for a few seconds. Daniella, *Minecraft* Boy, and the viola player all looked away. Margot was the only one who met his eye.

"*That*," he said, "was very close to perfect. Thank you. You may go."

Everyone broke into relieved whispers and smiles, then started packing up their things. Daniella didn't bother putting away her oboe. That would mean extra time in the same room as Margot. She tucked it close to her body, grabbed her backpack and case, and rushed out of the room.

Whenever one of her (former) friends glanced at her, Daniella would turn away. She'd become an expert at avoiding the disappointment in their faces. The secret: pretending she'd never met them to begin with.

*

That afternoon, Daniella went straight uptown to the apartment. It was actually a relief to sit on the subway, surrounded by strangers. She didn't have to worry about lying or not lying to them. She could be anyone to them. Maybe a girl who lives in the city all the time. Maybe someone who's visiting from, like, England. If Carly were there with Daniella, they'd make up a whole story about themselves. They'd even talk in English accents.

She took out her phone and checked FotoSlam for any new posts from Penny or Lainie, not sure she even wanted to see them. She already felt more alone, more left out, and more unable to have normal friendships than she ever had in her life.

Phew, no fresh photos or videos. For now.

Then, out of habit, she checked the GloriousOddballs hashtag. Dozens of new posts had appeared in the last day from people all over the world. Daniella knew she should have felt excited and satisfied. Even Carly would have been impressed—Carly never had any luck making anything go viral, and she sure had tried. Now so many different faces stared up at Daniella from the screen, inviting her in to whatever made them feel like a freak. Shouting about it as one voice in a chorus.

Daniella kept scrolling, past the new photos and all the way down to the earliest ones on the hashtag. There she was with Jules, Adrian, and Margot on that first day at the playground. Just like that, she felt it again: the rush of finding people who *got* her. Of trying on a version of herself that finally fit.

Now the recital was going to be an ordeal. She was having her original piece performed . . . but who would be there to cheer her on?

Two faces popped into her head. *But . . .*

Were things truly different between her and Penny and Lainie, or was she imagining it? Did they talk about her when they hung out together? Were they realizing that Ocean Park Heights was more fun with only the two of them?

Her thumbs twitching, Daniella started typing a message to Lainie and Penny. Then she deleted it, letter by letter. Then wrote it again exactly the same.

hey guys how's it going

Almost immediately, Lainie replied with a hi.

Daniella waited for Penny to answer, but after a minute or so, she still hadn't. Maybe she was busy at work and would see the thread later. Daniella took a deep breath before she started another text:

so guess what? there's going to be a recital during the last week of my program and they picked this piece i composed for my chamber group to perform. it would mean a lot to me if you guys came to NYC to see it. like, really a lot

Nothing happened for a long moment. Then under Lainie's name, three dots popped up to show she was typing. Daniella watched them for a few seconds. Then a few more. If Lainie was still typing, it meant she was trying to explain why she couldn't come. Writing *Totally! I'll be there!* wouldn't take this long.

Then the dots vanished.

And there was still no reply from Penny.

Daniella stared at her phone for a little longer, then swallowed hard and put it away to keep herself from sending another message. She was too tempted to write something like:

Okay, I can take a hint.

I know you're annoyed with me but I'm annoyed with you guys, too.

I know you're busy doing stuff together that's a lot more fun. So it's fine. But also SCREW YOU.

She shouldn't have come to New York this summer. If she'd stayed at the shore, she wouldn't have drifted apart from her friends. This was a giant bonehead mistake and why did she ever think it would be anything else?

When she felt her heart start fluttering, she checked the light-up map of the subway line on the wall of the train car. Two more stops. She had to hold on for two more stops if she didn't want to have a full-on panic attack right here, possibly becoming the next big meme. Daniella closed her eyes and took her four-seven-eight breaths, thinking about her forest, not caring how strange it looked.

Many breaths later, she'd made it. All she had to do next was get off the train, climb up into the daylight, and sit somewhere until she was okay to go back to the apartment.

"Daniella?"

She'd just emerged from the subway steps, and there was Aunt Tina, coming out of a drugstore. Daniella stopped short, which caused a man to bump into her from behind.

"It's a sidewalk!" he snarled. "Keep moving."

Tina took Daniella's hand and pulled Daniella toward her. "Are you okay?"

Daniella nodded but found she couldn't draw in a deep enough breath.

"Honey, your hand is shaking!" Tina put her other palm on Daniella's forehead, frowning with concern.

Daniella wanted to (a) throw herself into Tina's arms or (b) run away, down the street, and hide in the nearest alley. *I was getting better. Now look at Aunt Tina's face. That's my fault.*

"I'm really fine," Daniella said, trying to make her voice sound airy. "Or I will be. It's really . . . hot, and I'm super tired."

Tina tilted her head, and Daniella noticed her aunt's lip tremble. "You're still having panic attacks, aren't you?" When Daniella shrugged, Tina asked, "Does Dr. Richards know?"

"Yes," Daniella said, but it was another lie. *Wow, they're really flying out of you these days.* The truth: She'd totally forgotten about her last appointment. Now she felt her throat close up, and leaned against the building for support.

Aunt Tina took out her phone and made a call. *Oh no. She's calling my dad, damn it, damn it.*

"Hi, it's me," Tina said. "I need you. We're outside Yorkville Pharmacy."

Daniella was confused for a moment, then realized Tina must have called Uncle Chris. Not her dad. That was something, at least.

By the time Chris and Zoe got there five minutes later, the attack had passed. Daniella had taken back control of her breathing and was sipping from her water bottle.

"Are you both okay?" Chris asked.

"I'm fine," Daniella said.

"She's not." Tina sounded impatient. "She was having a panic attack. Can you take her home? I have to go . . . I don't know, for a walk or something. I need to be . . ."

Uncle Chris nodded. "It's all good, sweetheart. Just come home when you're ready."

Tina turned and headed away from them.

"I'm really, really sorry," Daniella said to Chris. "I was much better when the summer started. But things have been . . . hard here."

Daniella glanced over at Zoe, who looked worried. *Yes, you've been one of those hard things,* she thought. *But not on purpose.*

Uncle Chris searched Daniella's face. "Are you telling me, you've been having panic attacks the whole time you've been staying with us?"

Daniella stared down at the sidewalk and nodded.

"Why didn't you tell us?"

Now Daniella shrugged, still not able to meet her uncle's eye. Or Zoe's—whom she'd made an accomplice. "You guys have already been through a lot. I didn't want to make things worse."

Chris put his arm around Daniella's shoulders.

"Daniella, I hate that you had to deal with all that on your own." He paused, a faraway look in his eye. "And having you here, helping you with whatever you need . . . trust me, all of that makes things *better.*"

"It would be worse without you," Zoe added.

Now Daniella took a long glance at them both. "Seriously?"

"A hundred percent," Chris said. "Do you want to talk about what happened today to trigger the panic?"

Daniella swallowed hard. Took a deep breath, mostly to make sure she wasn't about to lose it again.

"I think my friendships with Lainie and Penny are going away," she finally said. *Drifting out with low tide. I can't reach them in time.* "And I totally messed things up with my friends from the music program."

Chris nodded. "That would do it."

Zoe stepped forward and squeezed Daniella into a hug. She didn't let go right away.

"Thanks, Zo," Daniella said into Zoe's hair.

Zoe finally released Daniella, and Daniella could see her eyes were glassy with tears.

"I'll always be your friend, even if you mess things up with me," Zoe said. "We're stuck with each other anyway because we're cousins."

This made Daniella laugh. "You're not wrong."

"You're fr-ousins," Chris said.

"Sisters from different misters," Zoe added.

Sisters. Somehow, Daniella had forgotten that being like-a-sibling worked both ways. If she managed to *be* one, that meant she also *had* one. In Zoe. And it was becoming natural instead of a thing that took effort.

Daniella laughed again. A woman with a tiny dog wearing tiny booties jostled by them.

"We should get out of people's way," Chris suggested. "Let's head home."

"Bubble tea first?" Zoe asked as they started walking. "I'm up to number thirty-two on the menu."

"Sure," Daniella replied, then an idea popped into her head. "You know, something like that would be a fun Bucket List item. Maybe next summer, there will be a chance for us to do it together."

Zoe's face lit up. "Totally! That would be amazing. I'm not going to let you forget you said that."

Daniella flicked Zoe on the shoulder. "Oh, I know," she said.

They all continued down the block. As Daniella let herself feel the warmth and the buzz of what had just happened, she had a weirdly comforting thought:

I'm okay, but in some ways I'm also NOT okay, and all of that feels . . . okay.

⸘ 26 ⸘

WHEN IS HE GOING TO KISS ME?

Do we have to be on our own, where nobody else can see us?

Am I supposed to give him some kind of a signal that I WANT him to kiss me?

What if I just kissed HIM?

What if there's a really good reason why we haven't kissed yet, like he's realizing he doesn't like me that way or I'm too weird or I'm too young or I'm not skinny enough or I gross him out in general? What if he likes Jamie?

And seriously, what if I just kissed him?

Penny was officially driving herself to distraction, but for the next few hours, she had to pretend she wasn't. Dex had suggested they go to Teen Night at one of the restaurants in town. She couldn't wait. Also, she was terrified.

"Have fun," her brother Nick had said. "That's the best hookup scene I've ever been to."

"Ooh, Penny's going to hook up!" Jack had added, then turned to his big brother. "What exactly counts as hooking up?"

Nick started explaining, and Penny immediately pressed her hands over her ears and ran out of the room, singing as loud as she could.

Dex had offered to pick her up at the house, but Penny chose a more neutral location. Penny's mom and Kathy were out shopping, but Jamie was still home. She was meeting up with some new friends, but hadn't left yet. Plus, the chances of Nick and/or Jack doing something fatally embarrassing were 99.999 percent.

As Penny walked to the meeting spot a few blocks away, she thought about what would have happened if her dad had been home. Would he have insisted on meeting Dex? Given her some horrifying speech on *being safe* or told her she couldn't wear that black crop top?

Penny was super pissed at her dad. For missing most of what was happening this summer. For making her mom so sad. For making Penny hate him a little. And, if it were true, for being a cheating cheater. Were her parents going to get divorced? Was that going to be her story now?

She tugged the neckline of her top up, and the bottom seam of it down. When Penny had first seen the top at a store on the boardwalk, it looked to her like something Jamie would wear. She'd thought, *Why can't this be something I would wear, too?*

Penny was really regretting asking that question.

"Hey, you," Dex said, grinning wide, when they found each other. "You look great."

"Thanks," Penny replied. "You too."

Dex was wearing an open button-down shirt over a white tee, and jeans with the bottoms rolled up. He'd put some fabulous-smelling product in his hair, so now it looked *on-purpose* messy instead of *this is what the ocean did* messy. All Penny wanted to do was run her hands through it.

Dex gestured for them to cross the street, and Penny followed. They'd worked together all day, but the beach had been busy and they hadn't had much time to talk.

"Who was your favorite guest today?" Penny asked.

Dex shrugged. "I guess those four women on their annual girls' trip, with the matching muumuus."

Penny laughed and waited for him to ask her the same question. She already had an answer waiting (that family from France). But instead, Dex added, "Let's not talk about work, okay? It was pretty stressful and I'm trying to shake it."

"Sure," Penny said, an odd squeezing sensation in her stomach. Then, without thinking about it, she reached out and took his hand in hers. Penny caught Dex glancing down at their joined hands, then up at her face, then down at the ground.

"So, make sure you have some music requests in mind," he said. "The DJ at this thing will play whatever you want."

"Cool," Penny said. "I'll start making a mental list. Do you have one?"

"Yeah," he replied.

Penny waited for him to continue, to start naming his favorite songs which would hopefully be her favorite songs, too. But he didn't. Usually, it felt like she and Dex could keep a conversation going forever, like hitting an air-hockey puck back and forth, back and forth. Their banter sliding easily from one to the other. So . . . *why is he so quiet right now?*

Maybe he's just tired.

Maybe he's not feeling well and has that summer cold Mom's always talking about.

"Oh good," Dex suddenly said. "Looks like the line to get in is pretty short."

He pointed toward the Blue Reef Inn, half a block away. Penny could see a cluster of kids outside.

As they moved closer, Dex let out a laugh. "Even better, Luke's at the door. He's one of my surf buddies."

Dex let go of Penny's hand and approached his friend for a fist bump. Luke waved Dex and Penny inside, skipping the line to pay the cover charge.

"That was the closest thing to a VIP experience I've ever had," Penny whispered to Dex as they climbed the stairs to the restaurant's second floor.

Dex laughed. "Well, that's because you're a Very Interesting Penny."

Then he gave her The Smile. That squeezing feeling in Penny's stomach began to let up.

But Dex didn't reach out for her hand again.

✶

Teen Night was hot, crowded, and loud. Penny and Dex danced along with everyone else to the summer's biggest songs, and a few from summers past. Dex was a good dancer—funny, but with lots of rhythm and a few sweet moves. Penny was relieved to find that she could match him in that department. She caught other girls looking at Dex, then looking at her with envy, which felt unfamiliar and thrilling.

I'm having fun! Real, actual, fun! She wasn't even worried about

As each song wound down, Penny glanced at Dex and imagined him taking her hand and pulling her off the dance floor, out onto the deck overlooking the river. That was the hookup spot, according to Jack. The way Penny envisioned it, Dex would lead her to the railing, and they would only look at the stars above them and not the other couples eating each other's faces a few feet away. Then he would kiss her. (Or she would kiss him. She was ready to do it, if she had to.)

And it would be movie-worthy perfect.

"Watermelon Sugar" was about to end when Dex looked up at the door and flashed a smile at someone. Three of his friends had walked in and were waving at him to come over. *Please, please don't*, Penny thought. Dex glanced at Penny, then looked back at them, shaking his head no.

But all through "Bad Guy," Dex's eyes kept darting over to his friends, checking out what they were doing.

He's looking for something to do that's more fun than dancing with me.

When the song ended, Dex once again spotted someone he knew. His face lit up and he leaned in to shout at Penny over the music.

"Jamie's here!" he said excitedly, then pushed past Penny to the door.

Jamie was standing with that girl Layla and a couple of others, scanning the room. When she saw Dex coming toward her, she laughed. Penny could see them leaning in close, talking. Then Dex put his arm on Jamie's back to lead her into the thick of the dance floor. Jamie gestured for her friends to follow, and before Penny could even process what was happening, she, Dex, Jamie, and their friends were all dancing together in a cluster.

Penny on one side. Dex and Jamie on the other.

Penny continued to dance and smile, but inside, she was one massive freak-out. She hadn't told Jamie about her plans with Dex, so was this only a coincidence? The worst luck ever? Or were Dex and Jamie texting each other, and that's how Jamie knew they'd be there?

The room started spinning, and Penny tried to blink it still again. There was sweat dripping down her back. A wave of nausea hit her, and she immediately stopped dancing and backed up, out of the cluster, off the dance floor. Rushing onto the deck, Penny took in big gulps of air until her foot hit something, and she looked down to see a boy and girl huddled on the floor with their arms around each other.

Fantastic.

She moved away from them and found a spot against the railing where she could half collapse, and breathe, and feel kind of normal again. What the hell had happened in there?

A few seconds later, Penny felt a hand press gently on her back.

"Are you okay?" Dex asked.

She nodded, but when she tried to say *Totally!,* she couldn't get the word past the huge lump in her throat. She took a deep breath, then another.

When she could finally speak, she glanced back up at the stars—the stars she and Dex were supposed to be gazing at right before they kissed—and muttered, "It's cool if you don't want to go out anymore."

Dex frowned. *"Excuse me?"*

"I can tell you really like Jamie. I get it." Penny took another breath, long and slow this time. "I mean, look at her. And look at me."

Dex opened his mouth to say something, then froze. Which told Penny everything she needed to know. If she was wrong about him, he wouldn't have hesitated. Right?

"I agree," Dex said. "Jamie is amazing, and—"

"No!" she interrupted. No way could she hear any more. "I'm not going to get dumped. If I'm not going to feel like puking from humiliation every time I think about you, *I* have to do the dumping!"

Dex took a step back, looking hurt and confused. "You're breaking up with me?"

Penny felt a rush of clarity. Maybe it was because she'd taken control of the situation. Maybe it was the fresh ocean breeze after being in the day-heat for so long.

"I can't be with someone if I never know where I stand with them," she told Dex. "It's too stressful."

Dex shook his head, still puzzled, but then his expression softened. "Wait, is this about what's going on with your parents?"

Blindsided, Penny couldn't answer right away. When she finally found the words, she muttered, "What do you know about that?"

"You've seemed really off and distracted the last couple days. I asked Jamie if you were okay and she told me there's all this intense stuff going on with your family. She . . . uh . . . said your mom and dad might split up."

Penny wasn't sure which sentence was more painful to hear: the one about her mom and dad, or the one about Dex talking to Jamie about her. It was official, then: She had nobody she could trust with secrets anymore.

"So . . . " she began. "You could have just asked *me*, but you went to Jamie instead?"

"I *did* ask you! You said you were fine, it was nothing, blah, blah, blah." He laughed a little, but it was definitely a sad laugh. "You could have told me, you know," he said, growing serious. "Don't you trust me enough to tell me what's going on in your life?"

No, because it's not happy and fun, and I want our time together to be happy and fun.

No, because it would have bummed you out when you can spend time with someone like Jamie, who doesn't have a family that's a mess.

Because talking about it to anyone would make it real.

Dex was staring at her. Waiting for a reply. Waiting to understand.

Finally, Penny said, "No, I don't trust you. And that's why we have to break up."

Quickly, before she could think twice, she started walking past Dex on her way back inside, half expecting him to grab her arm and try to stop her. But he didn't. Which must have meant that everything she'd said was totally fine with him.

Asshole.

She rushed down the stairs and out of the Blue Reef Inn. Her top started to ride up as she ran, and she gripped it, vowing to wear baggy flannel shirts for the rest of her life.

Once she was outside, Penny slowed her pace to a fast walk, eager to put as much distance as she could between herself and Teen Night. She wasn't allowed to be out at night by herself, but she wasn't ready to go home yet. Next door was Village Pizza, which had long tables outside under a pavilion.

Penny simply wanted to sit. Breathe the night air. Maybe feel human again.

But her fingers had other plans. They reached for her phone and found a familiar name on it.

"Hello?" Lainie said when she picked up.

And Penny started sobbing.

⇟ 27 ⇞

PENNY CLIMBED INTO THE BACKSEAT OF WES'S CAR. He'd barely pulled away from Village Pizza when Lainie felt her friend face-plant into her shoulder.

Lainie reached out to hug Penny, and Penny started crying again.

"Thank you for picking me up," Penny muttered, sniffling.

"You're welcome," Lainie said. "And I'm sorry about Dex. I really am."

Penny just nodded, wiping her nose.

"It sounds like you did the right thing," Lainie added. "If he always made you feel like he wasn't sure about you, or that you weren't good enough, then what's the point?"

What is this advice coming out of my mouth? Lainie wondered. It wasn't from her own experience, that was for sure. Maybe she'd read it in a magazine, or overheard Nana saying it to someone. Whatever it was, it seemed to be helping. There was no longer a faucet of snot and tears flooding Lainie's T-shirt.

"Where's your house, Penny?" Wes asked, raising his eyes to the rearview mirror.

Penny leaned forward so Wes could hear her. "It's number twenty-eight—" She stopped. Turned to Lainie. "I'm still not ready to go home. My mom's going to ask me all these questions and my brothers are going to enjoy this way too much."

Lainie nodded. "I get it. We can hit a drive-through or something, but then I have to get back to the hospital. I want to be there when Papa gets out of surgery."

Penny took Lainie's hand. "Can I come?"

"What?" Lainie asked "Why?"

"You just, like, came to my rescue," Penny replied. "Now I can keep you company while you're waiting. Unless that would be annoying, or whatever."

Lainie looked at Penny. When Penny called, Lainie had almost run out of things to keep herself busy. She'd scrolled through her entire FotoSlam feed from the last week, played fourteen rounds of *Candy Crush* on her phone, and rewatched her favorite episode of *The Great British Bake Off*. Nana had gone downstairs to talk to a social worker and do paperwork for the hospital, saying she'd be back in a few minutes. It had been over an hour.

"It would totally not be annoying," Lainie told Penny. "You would be coming to *my* rescue."

$$\ast$$

In the surgery waiting room, there was now a little girl sitting at the miniature table in the kids' corner. She looked up when Lainie and Penny walked in.

"Hi," she said. "You want to color with me?"

Lainie glanced at Penny. Penny gave a *why not?* shrug. They walked over to the table and sank down into the tiny chairs. Penny's knees almost bumped her chin.

"You can color this page with the kittens," the girl said to Lainie, tearing two sheets of paper out of her book and sliding them across the table, along with a few crayons. Then she turned to Penny and said, "You get the bunnies."

"Thanks," Penny said, smiling. "I'm Penny. What's your name?"

"I'm Madeline. I'm stuck here because my brother's having an operation and my mom couldn't find a babysitter."

Lainie started coloring one of the kittens, orange with blue stripes. "Nice to meet you. I'm Lainie."

"You have to say, 'I'm Lainie,' and then tell why you're stuck here."

"Ah, okay," Lainie said.

This kid reminded her of the first time she played with Carly, Daniella, and Penny on the beach. The way Carly made sure that by the time they'd finishing building their sand creation, everyone knew everything about everyone else.

"I'm Lainie, and I'm stuck here because my grandfather was on his fishing boat, and another boat crashed into him. He fell and hit his head. Really hard. They're trying to fix it right now."

Madeline stopped her coloring and stared at Lainie. "If you break your head, do they put a cast on it?"

Lainie had to think about that one. "No, I don't think so."

"Go ask them at that counter," Madeline said, pointing at the nurses' station.

"No, thanks."

"Ask!" Madeline insisted. "Don't be shy!"

"*You* do it," Lainie snapped back.

"I don't want to," the girl said, then put her hand on Lainie's coloring sheet and pulled it back toward her.

Lainie glared at the girl, resisting the urge to say, *You don't have a lot of friends, do you?*

"Hey," Penny said, touching Lainie's elbow. "Before I forget, I have something for you."

She put her purse on the table, opened an inside pocket, and pulled out a fifty-dollar bill.

"My dad gave me this when he came to visit," Penny continued. "I want to donate it to the bench."

"Penny, you don't have to do that."

"But this is his guilt money and I don't want it. Or need it! I love earning my own cash, even if I have to keep working with Dex." Penny made an *ugh* face.

"I'll take the money!" Madeline said.

"Nice try," Lainie told her, then turned back to Penny and held out her hand. "I'm sorry for what I said about you not caring about the memorial or Carly—"

"It's all good," Penny said, slapping the fifty into Lainie's palm. "I understand why it seemed that way."

Lainie put the money in her pocket, and they fell quiet. Penny shivered and tugged at her top again.

"You look good in that," Lainie said.

"Really? All I can think of is the skin that's showing. And how I wish it weren't right now."

"Take my sweater," a voice said. Lainie and Penny turned around. It was Nana, removing her red cardigan and holding it up for Penny. "It's frigid in here with the AC."

Lainie and Penny launched out of their tiny chairs. "Anything yet?" Lainie asked.

"They said the surgeon should be coming out soon. But she wouldn't tell me more than that." Nana gave Penny a hug, then handed her the sweater. "I'm so glad you're here, Penny. You're a good friend."

Nana sat down in a nearby chair. Lainie and Penny sat next to her.

Madeline and her mom were called up by the nurse and ushered through a set of heavy double doors. Before she disappeared, Madeline turned around and called to Lainie and Penny, pointing to a piece of paper on the table. "We're going to see my brother in the recovery room! I decided you can do the kitten page after all."

Lainie and Penny waved goodbye.

"This is weird," Penny said quietly, "but that girl kind of reminded me of Carly."

"Same!" They both laughed a little, then Lainie scanned the room. She could almost *see* the worry and desperation and grief that hung in the air. She asked Penny, "Is this what it was like for her parents, do you think? When they were waiting at the ER in the city?"

"Maybe," Penny replied, taking a deep, shaky breath.

"We never even got a chance to talk about that night," Lainie said.

After a moment, Penny said, "Yeah. I wasn't sure what we were even *allowed* to talk about." She paused, hugging the sweater closer to her. "I remember that Daniella's mom called my mom. She told me while I was studying for an algebra test. The first thing I thought was, *Maybe my teacher will let me skip this test.* Isn't that disgusting?"

"You were in shock," Nana said matter-of-factly. "Our brain is always trying to protect our heart."

Lainie nodded. "I did something just as strange. As soon as my mom got off the phone, she made me a giant cup of hot chocolate with whipped cream, and she never does that. When she told me Carly was gone, the first thing I did was pick up the mug and drink the whole thing, because I didn't want the whipped cream to melt."

Lainie turned to her grandmother. "What if it's bad news, Nana?" she asked. "What are you supposed to do?"

Nana smiled sadly. "I'm old . . . and I've lost many people I loved." She took a deep breath and stared up at the ceiling. "I guess there's nothing you're supposed to do or *not* supposed to do in that moment. You're simply receiving information. Then, good or bad, you focus on what comes next."

She glanced back down at Lainie, a single tear sliding down her cheek. Lainie reached out and wiped it away, then took Nana's hand.

The three of them sat in silence for a few more minutes, until an elderly man walked into the waiting room. He was carrying a big brown shopping bag with handles and wearing a badge that read HOSPITAL VOLUNTEER. The man approached Nana and asked, "Excuse me, are you Dulcie Muñoz?"

"Yes," Nana told him, raising her eyebrows.

"Someone left this for you at the front desk."

He handed Nana the bag, then winked at Lainie and Penny before leaving.

"What is it?" Lainie asked.

Nana took out a folded piece of paper. Lainie recognized it as an order slip from the bakery, with a note written on it.

"Oh, my goodness," Nana said as she read the note. "Sasha put together a care package for us, in case we're stuck here awhile."

Penny flashed Lainie an impressed look. Nana started pulling boxes of treats from the bag. One box had the words *My Attempt at Cheddar Jalapeño Biscuits* written on top.

"I'd be scared to try those," Lainie said.

"Stop, you," Nana muttered. "I'm sure they're delicious."

She opened the box, picked up a biscuit, took a bite, and chewed slowly.

"Well?" Penny prodded.

Nana swallowed and gingerly put the rest of the biscuit back in the box. "It's the thought that counts."

Penny and Lainie cracked up. Maybe Sasha had a long way to go (maybe even forever) until she could bake well, but she'd made them laugh when they really, really needed it. For that, Lainie would always be grateful.

They were digging into a box of cookies when the double doors flung open. An impossibly tall man dressed head-to-toe in surgical scrubs emerged. He glanced at the nurse, who pointed at Nana. Lainie shivered as the doctor walked toward them.

"Mrs. Muñoz?" he asked.

Nana froze with a cookie halfway to her lips.

≳ 28 ≲

IF ONLY I COULD PRACTICE ONE MORE TIME.

If only I could check how I look in Carly's big mirror, because this one doesn't show my feet. Would it be weird to ask?

If only I could be video-chatting with Jules, Margot, and Adrian right now. They would tell me to chill out.

If only they hadn't picked my piece.

If only I were a normal person who could actually handle stuff like this.

Daniella was dressed. Her hair was done. Well, maybe not *done*, but combed out with some product to keep it from being a frizz-fest. She knew all the recital pieces by heart, and the night before, had actually dreamed she was playing them. At the Ocean Park Heights bandshell. By herself. To Grumpy Gus.

There was no time to analyze *that*. She had to leave soon. Aunt Tina, Uncle Chris, and Zoe were all going to ride with her to the academy, and Daniella's parents would meet them there.

"Honey, are you almost ready?" Aunt Tina said through the bathroom door. "Chris and Zoe already went downstairs."

Daniella felt her body flush with energy. Not the good kind. This kind was spiky and scraped her on the inside. Almost on cue, her heart started beating like a bird frantically flapping its wings. Her hands shook and her throat closed up.

"I need a few minutes," Daniella squeaked out.

She sat down on the edge of the bathtub and stared at a single square of floor tile. *In for four, hold for seven, out for eight.* After six of those, Daniella still felt her thumping heartbeat in every part of her body. Plan B: She squeezed her eyes shut and tried to find her mind-forest. But she couldn't picture it, as if the forest refused to show itself to her today. Maybe it was finally sick of her needing it all the time.

Daniella sat still, trying to figure out how she could bring herself to stand up, open the door, ride the elevator downstairs, and walk to the subway. Let alone sit in her oboe chair onstage with people she'd lied to and play the music of her heart.

Then she heard a floorboard creak right outside the bathroom door.

"Aunt Tina?" Daniella asked, her voice coming out light and faint.

"Yes," Aunt Tina said through the door. "But I'll leave you alone. I was just worried."

Daniella heard Aunt Tina start to walk away and instinctively called out "Wait!" The floorboards were quiet again. "Can you . . . can you help me?"

Tina opened the bathroom door and went straight to Daniella. Pulling her to standing, wrapping her in a hug. Tight, tight, tight.

"I'm sorry," Daniella murmured. "I should know how to handle these by now."

"Shush, now. Losing Carly was traumatic. There's no schedule for getting through that."

It was odd, hearing Aunt Tina say Carly's name. Daniella realized she hadn't heard her say it once all summer.

Tina sighed heavily. "I wish you'd told me how much you've been struggling. You seemed to be having so much fun, playing your music and exploring the city with your new friends."

At the mention of *new friends*, Daniella flinched.

Tina noticed. "What happened?"

Daniella started chewing on her bottom lip as she thought about the answer. "I think I applied for the academy because I didn't want to face the summer in OPH without Carly. But from the day I got here, I missed it so much, and I still missed *her*."

Tina let out a little laugh. "You mean, coming to stay with Carly's family, in her apartment and city, didn't make it easier to cope with losing her? Honey, no surprise there."

Daniella managed a smile. "Yeah, you have a point. But it wasn't all bad. When I met Jules, and Margot, and Adrian, it was like . . . I'd found a crew who helped me be *me* again."

"Your people."

"Yeah, my people. But then Penny and Lainie started getting closer and I felt left out . . . I'm basically a total mess."

Tina tucked a loose curl behind Daniella's ear. "You're not a mess. You're fourteen. It's okay to have more than one group of friends. And you're still grieving someone very special to you."

Daniella paused, wondering if she should tell Aunt Tina everything.

"There's something else." She took a deep breath. "I didn't tell my academy friends about Carly."

Tina bit her lip and Daniella watched her swallow hard. "That's understandable."

"I mean . . . I told them about her. As a person. As my cousin and best friend who created the Bucket List. But I made it seem like she . . . hadn't died. Then they found out, and they think I'm a twisted, lying weirdo."

Daniella put her face in her hands but peeked out at Tina. Tina searched Daniella's face, and Daniella wondered what her aunt might be looking for.

Aunt Tina took her phone out of her pocket and started typing a text message. "I'm telling Chris to go ahead with Zoe on the subway," she said. "You and I are taking a cab. This way, we have a little extra time, and the ride will be less stressful." Tina sent her text and put her phone down on the edge of the sink. "Now . . . I'm going to count to three, and on *three*, I want you to jump up and down as fast as you can.

"Huh?"

"Just, go with me on this. Jump up and down, and shake out your hands. Wiggle your fingers. Flip your hair." Daniella hesitated, and Tina added, "I'll redo your hair after. It'll look great, I promise. You ready?"

"Um . . . sure," Daniella said.

"One, two, THREE."

Daniella did as she was told. She went into high-power mode, jumping and wiggling and shaking.

After ten or fifteen seconds, Aunt Tina called out, "Stop!" and put a steadying hand on Daniella's shoulder. They both stood there, Daniella panting, Tina's eyes shining with energy.

"How do you feel now?" Tina asked.

Daniella ran a mental body scan on herself. Her heart rate was slowing. She wasn't shaking. There was this new feeling . . . not calm, really. But the sensation of setting something free.

"Better," Daniella said once she caught her breath.

Tina smiled. "I always had Carly do that when she was super stressed out."

Daniella frowned. "Carly would get stressed out?"

"Oh, all the time. She was great at hiding it when she was with her friends or even you, Daniella. But when she was with *us*, she'd let it out in unhealthy ways. She'd snap at us and lose her temper, throw things around her room."

Daniella was quiet, trying to get that image of Carly into focus.

"Um, I really can't picture that," Daniella said. "I always thought of her—I still think of her—as someone who had it all together, all the time."

Aunt Tina shrugged. "Nobody is that person." Then quiet tears slipped from her eyes. "But Carly did have a way of throwing confidence out there, didn't she?"

"For real."

Tina closed her eyes and put both hands over her heart. "I really, really, miss her. Every second. Sometimes it's . . . it's too much."

Daniella hugged her aunt. Then an idea struck her. "Hey, Aunt Tina? Can I show you something?"

She led Tina into Zoe's room and dug the shell purse out from under the mattress. Daniella sat down on the bed and Tina joined her.

"I found this the first night I was here," Daniella said, sliding the Bucket List out of the purse and putting it in Tina's lap.

Tina opened the paper, her eyes darting quickly across it, trying to make sense of what she was reading.

"When—" Tina asked.

"I don't know. Sometime in the winter, I guess. I knew she liked to plan ahead, but sheesh . . . that's a little intense."

Tina laughed through tears. She'd started crying again. Then she really studied the list. "Why are some of these checked off?"

Daniella grinned at her aunt. "Are you ready for this?"

✶

"Hello, everyone! My name is Josef Novikoff, and I'm pleased to welcome you to the Future Forward Music Academy."

Daniella stood backstage, clutching her oboe to her chest.

Mr. Novikoff started droning on about how special the academy program was and how hard all the students were expected to work. Then he launched into a story about a summer program he attended when he was in high school. *Snore.*

Daniella heard a whisper in her ear.

"Oh, for the love of Ludwig, he's going to put everyone to sleep before we even start playing!"

Daniella turned to see Jules leaning against the wall next to her, wearing a vintage black suit, a crisp white shirt, and a bolo tie. They had re-dyed their hair, so now it was white on one side and black on the other.

"I know," Jules said, spreading out their arms to provide a better view of the ensemble. "I took the dress code to the next level."

"Jules?" Daniella whispered. "I thought you guys weren't talking to me anymore."

262

Jules frowned. "Uh, no. I think it was the opposite? *You* stopped talking to *us*."

"Because you and Adrian and Margot were so pissed at me."

"We weren't *pissed*. Okay, yes, we were at first. Because it seemed pretty messed up. Then we realized you've probably been going through a lot. But every time we tried to approach you, you pretended you didn't see us."

"Oh," Daniella said. "Wow, I really am a dumbass."

"Well, maybe a little. But we miss you. Adrian and Margot would probably say the same if they weren't stuck on the other side of the stage."

Jules leaned out into the wings a bit, gesturing to where Adrian and Margot were standing in the opposite wings. Mr. Novikoff had arranged for everyone to enter from both sides. Jules pointed to Daniella and gave a thumbs-up. Margot and Adrian both smiled and waved back.

Maybe this is going to be okay, Daniella thought.

"I'm so embarrassed . . . and so sorry," she said.

"No worries. We can figure it out later. This is your night."

Daniella looked out at the stage and felt her chest tighten again. How big was the audience? Where were her mom and dad sitting? It would help to know these things.

Mr. Novikoff had finally finished his introduction, and now the academy director was saying a few words.

Daniella couldn't see the recital hall seats from where she was, so she moved to the back wing and inched her way toward the edge. Then she peered out at the audience. Scanned the faces. Didn't see any she recognized, until . . .

There was Mom and Dad. Tina and Chris. And Zoe, who already looked bored out of her mind.

Daniella was about to disappear back into the wings when she spotted two more familiar faces.

Her breath caught. Her heart jumped. Heat rushed through her.

All in the best way possible.

⋛ 29 ⋚

LAINIE HAD NEVER BEEN INTO CLASSICAL MUSIC. Her mom took her to a philharmonic Christmas concert once—she fell asleep and spilled hot cocoa on the red velvet seat. But this was different (thank God). Fifty teenagers on a stage in New York City playing the theme from the *Avengers* movies. She'd never seen Daniella perform like this, in a large group, part of a whole.

Daniella had come onstage with the rest of the orchestra and looked right at her and Penny. She'd smiled at them, her eyes shining with tears. It was the kind of smile that meant so many things at once.

Lainie's phone vibrated and she glanced at it. A text from Penny.

which one is Jules? I'm looking for turquoise hair and I don't see it

Lainie looked up, gave Penny a dirty look, then turned back to her phone and started typing.

are you seriously texting me from the next seat over?

yah, it would be rude to talk

it's rude to text!

you're the one with your phone in your lap

that's in case Nana has any updates for me

It hadn't been easy for Lainie to leave Ocean Park Heights, even if it was only for the day. Papa had survived surgery to stop the bleeding in his brain, and was now in ICU. Nothing was guaranteed, the doctor had said, but her grandfather was expected to make a full recovery. Nana wanted to stay busy and keep the bakery open, and Mr. Mason and Sasha were there to help. But it still felt weird, not being there, too.

Suddenly the *Avengers* theme was wrapping up and everyone was applauding. A teacher stepped up to the podium.

"Thank you all for being the superheroes who support your children in their love of music and commitment to their art. When students arrive at our summer program, we know most of them have ventured out of their comfort zone. We teach them African drumming and how to play the gamelan. We make them dance! We also ask them to stretch even further by composing original pieces while they're here. Every summer, we select one student composition to perform, and I'm very pleased to be introducing you to the composer of this year's piece, Daniella Franco!"

Penny let out a "Woo-hoo!" and Lainie slapped her on the knee.

The teacher beckoned to Daniella, who slowly stood up. She looked out at the audience and locked eyes with Lainie. Lainie nodded at her, trying to send her friend some telepathic encouragement.

You've got this, Dee.

Daniella walked to the podium, adjusted the microphone, and took a deep breath. She dug a folded piece of paper out of her pocket and began to read from it. Lainie could see her hands trembling.

"Hi," Daniella began, her voice froggy. She cleared her throat and started again. "Hi, I'm Daniella. Thanks for coming to our recital."

Another round of applause. Lainie watched Daniella take in a deep, deep breath before continuing.

"I can't speak for everyone else, but when I heard that we'd all be taking a composition class as part of the Future Forward Music Academy, I kind of freaked out. I've never composed anything before. I always figured, I'm not a person who thinks about music that way. But what I realized, thanks to our teacher Lorelei Burdick, is that I never composed anything because I didn't have anything I really needed to say. Well, now I do." Here, she paused for another breath. "At the beginning of this year, I lost someone really special to me."

Lainie glanced over to Carly's family. Carly's mom dabbed at her eyes with a tissue. Carly's sister, Zoe, was holding up her phone, recording a video of Daniella's speech.

"Her name was—is—Carly. I live in Ocean Park Heights in New Jersey, and she and I spent every summer there together. Then we met two other friends, and we were like . . . you know how they say, friends are the family we choose? We all chose one another. After Carly passed away, things started changing really fast. Suddenly I didn't have some of the things in my life I was used to having. And it was hard, but what I realized, coming here and meeting new people, was that losing stuff that's familiar to you is not always a bad thing. Sometimes you need to lose that stuff in order to discover new stuff. Like, who you are, and what you want."

For Lainie, that one line echoed. *Losing stuff that's familiar to you is not always a bad thing.* She knew Daniella was talking about herself, but a light switch flipped in Lainie's head.

She was losing so much. Her grandparents' house, summers in OPH, the bakery. Her friendships with Penny and Daniella were already changed forever. Could all of this actually help her in some way? It would be great to be able to believe that.

"So," Daniella continued from the stage, "this piece is called *Summer Without*, and it turns out, I had a lot to say. I'd like to dedicate this piece to my chosen family, my Summer Sisters: Carly, Lainie, and Penny."

Lainie and Penny exchanged a look as the audience applauded. Zoe yelled, "Go, Daniella!" Then Penny slid her arm through Lainie's, and they settled in to listen.

Daniella walked to her chair, sat down, and picked up her oboe. The first high, heartfelt notes made the hairs on Lainie's arm stand on end. The melody reminded her of the call of laughing gulls, and how sometimes they don't sound like they're laughing at all but rather, crying out in loneliness.

The violin came in. Lainie thought of how you hear different music as you walk down the boardwalk, one store playing something, and then the next store blasting something different, so that the two songs mix together for a few moments. Daniella's piece was a bit like that, and so sad . . . but then slowly, it wasn't. It started to grow and swell as the viola and cello joined in, and the rhythm picked up.

It sounded, to Lainie, like hope itself. She glanced at Penny, who was listening with her eyes closed. On the other side of Penny, Zoe was still recording with her phone.

The piece ended in a surge of sound, the notes somehow high and low at the same time. Lainie could feel the vibrations of it through her whole body. Everyone was silent, letting this floaty, otherworldly feeling sink in. Then the entire recital hall burst into applause. Daniella put down her oboe and looked out into the audience, right at Lainie and Penny. She smiled, then wiped away a tear from each eye. Before Lainie knew it, she was standing up and clapping, and Penny was joining her.

Zoe stood, too, still recording it all on her phone. Then her parents, then Daniella's parents, then the rest of the audience. The applause went on for what felt like a week.

Once everyone sat down again, and Mr. Novikoff came up to the podium to introduce the next piece, Penny leaned in to whisper to Lainie.

"A standing O," Penny said. "That must feel amazing."

"She deserves it," Lainie replied.

"I wish I did something that people would stand up and cheer for. Setting up a beach umbrella doesn't really cut it."

"Penny," Lainie said, "I mean it when I say, I'm pretty sure you have a standing ovation in your future."

"Hopefully not for dropping a tray in the school cafeteria," Zoe wisecracked from her seat.

✶

Three pieces later, Mr. Novikoff came out and declared the recital officially over. All the students on stage burst into cheers.

Lainie turned to Penny. "Is it obnoxious if we beat Dee's parents to the stage?"

"I have no problem with being obnoxious." Penny took Lainie's hand and together, they rushed down the aisle, then up some steps, toward Daniella. They were locked in a three-way hug before most students had even put away their instruments.

"That was amazing!" Lainie told Daniella.

"I can't believe you guys came!" Daniella exclaimed at the same time. "I mean, I'm happy. Just surprised."

"You *did* invite us," Penny said.

"Yeah, but . . . you guys never answered. I figured you didn't want to come, but didn't know how to say it."

Penny and Lainie exchanged a look. "Oh my God, we never answered," Penny said.

"You're right, I didn't know how to respond," Lainie told Daniella. "I wanted to come, but not with Penny. We got into a huge fight and weren't talking to each other."

Daniella's eyes went wide. "A *fight*?"

"And I was lost in boy drama. But then Lainie's grandpa had an accident with the boat and—"

"He *what*?"

"It was scary for a little while, but he'll be okay," Lainie said, then elbowed Penny. "And the two of us are okay, too, now. We should have answered your message."

"Let's make it part of the Summer Sisters code," Penny suggested. "Every message gets a reply, no matter what."

Daniella laughed, and Lainie could see how relieved and happy she was. "I love that rule," Daniella said.

"Same," Lainie added.

A kid with black-and-white dyed hair came up behind Daniella and tapped her on the shoulder. When Daniella turned around, she and the kid started squealing at each other, then hugging. Then, two more kids appeared—Lainie recognized them as Margot and Adrian from Daniella's photos—and there was even more squealing and hugging.

Daniella broke free from Margot and grinned at Lainie and Penny.

"Summer Sisters," she said, "meet the Glorious Oddballs."

Lainie laughed. Out of the corner of her eye, she saw one more person standing near them.

It was Zoe, recording everything on her phone.

⫸ 30 ⫷

PENNY LEANED HER FOREHEAD AGAINST THE CAR window and tried to count the lights on the Lincoln Tunnel ceiling as they whipped past her. It creeped her out to think they were driving underneath the Hudson River. She needed a distraction.

"Mr. and Mrs. Franco, thanks again for bringing us along today," Lainie said, leaning sideways against Penny in the backseat.

Daniella's mom turned around from the front passenger seat, still radiant with pride even behind her sunglasses. "You're so welcome, girls. I know it meant a lot to Daniella."

Penny gave up on counting the lights; they were zooming by way too quickly. Instead, she closed her eyes and thought about the lunch they'd had with Daniella, her family, and Carly's family. It was at a tiny Italian restaurant owned by a friend of Carly's dad, and their table took up the entire place. After stuffing their faces with chicken parmigiana and garlic knots, Daniella, Lainie, and Penny had taken a walk on their

272

own through Bryant Park, behind the New York Public Library, and over to Times Square.

It was the first time they'd ever spent time together away from the shore and Penny had felt weirdly . . . older. In a very good way.

After a minute, the car emerged from the tunnel and into bright, natural light.

Lainie yawned. "Wake me when we get to back to OPH," she said, closing her eyes. Penny smiled, amused. It was weird to see Lainie tired, or resting at all. She was always going, going, going. Focused on what was in front of her, whether it was on a skateboard or planning a memorial or completing a Bucket List item. Maybe New York City really did bring out a different side of people.

Soon they were on the Garden State Parkway heading south. Penny looked over her shoulder at the disappearing Manhattan skyline. What did Carly think whenever she drove in the other direction at the end of each summer? Did she see those tall buildings and think, *home*?

Carly, I was in your 'hood today. I felt closer to you. And to Daniella and Lainie, too.

Penny's phone suddenly rattled with an incoming text from Zoe. It was addressed to both her and Lainie.

figured you guys would want these

Three different videos popped up, one by one, on Penny's screen. She watched the first few seconds of each one: Daniella's introduction, the performance, and after the recital when they were all talking and hugging. Penny knew instantly that she would connect them into a longer video to give the Francos, as a thank-you for bringing her to the city. She loaded the clips into a video editing app on her phone.

An older clip in the app's gallery caught her eye: footage she'd taken of Dex surfing. She pressed play, watching him catch a medium-size wave, then hop off Kiani into waist-high water. He looked at the camera and did a goofy-adorable dance for Penny. She could hear herself laugh in the video.

WTF? Why was she torturing herself like this? Sure, Dex had seemed perfect. And he'd liked her, at least for a while. But now she knew it wasn't that simple. People don't show you their true selves right away. Or they change, or their feelings change. Any couple that stays together for more than a month seems like a miracle.

Carly, I loved having a boyfriend, but I hated the way he made me feel about myself. I hope you understand.

Penny had asked for a week off from work for a "family emergency," and Keri had agreed, no questions asked. It was a half-real request: Lainie and Daniella had both needed her. Hopefully, by the time she came back to her job, she'd be able to handle being around Dex all day without feeling queasy.

She opened the surfing video again and hit the trash can icon, the video vanishing from her screen with a satisfying *ka-chunk* sound. Then she popped in her earbuds and watched Zoe's videos from start to finish. The lighting wasn't great, the audio muffled. She'd make them look and sound better.

Wait. The Bucket List.

Make a music video.

Earlier that day, Penny, Lainie, and Daniella had wandered through Times Square and talked about what was left on the list. They'd agreed to wait until Daniella got back to the shore, and maybe by then, they'd have some ideas for how to tackle the few things they still had to do.

What if there was already an idea sitting on Penny's phone? She'd been playing around with animations and filters on the editing app. She could try to make something. If Daniella and Lainie didn't like it, they could do another together.

Penny popped a fresh stick of gum in her mouth and shifted in her seat to get more comfortable. There was work to do.

✶

As the Francos' car bumped across the river bridge into Ocean Park Heights, Lainie woke up with a start. She looked around, her eyes wide, her hair car-nap-crazy. Penny burst out laughing.

"Lainie!" she cried overdramatically. "Talk to me! Do you know where you are? What day is it? Who's the president of the United States?"

Lainie narrowed her eyes. "Did I actually sleep all the way home?"

"Yup," Penny said. "You even snored a little."

"Sorry," Lainie muttered, shaking her head.

"It's fine. Better than fine. I had a chance to work on a little project." Lainie raised an eyebrow.

"Here, check it out." Penny handed Lainie her phone, then leaned in to watch over Lainie's shoulder as Lainie pressed play.

Penny had added a title screen that read SUMMER WITH in big, funky letters. Then the word OUT slid in from the right side, forming the title of Daniella's piece. During Daniella's introduction, the video was in black-and-white. When it cut to the performance of Daniella's piece, it changed to a light blue tone.

"I threw in some stuff," Penny said.

Summer Without was still the beautiful composition Daniella had created, but in this video, with animated doodles and filters that slowly changed from faded colors to bright, electric ones, it was a total statement. When the performance ended and the video cut to Penny and Lainie hurling themselves at Daniella, everyone hugging and crying, Penny had added some sound effects of waves crashing on a beach. Then everything faded out, into a final screen that simply read *#SummerSisters.*

Lainie was silent for a few moments, staring at the now-blank phone screen.

"Is it stupid?" Penny asked. Lainie shook her head. "You think Daniella will be mad that I messed with the video of her piece?"

Lainie paused, then shook her head again. She turned to Penny.

"This is so . . . freaking . . . cool."

"Is it?"

"Uh . . . *yeah*! How did you do all that in the car?"

"I have a couple of good apps," Penny said, shrugging. "Then I found a couple more. It was really pretty easy."

"Maybe for you," Lainie said. "You're good at this stuff. Like, *really* good. The colors changed to the beat and everything. It was practically professional."

"Thanks," Penny said. "You know, there's a place in Philly that runs film and animation classes for high-school students. Maybe I should check it out."

"You should *definitely* check it out," Lainie said. "Promise me you will."

"Yes, ma'am."

The car slowed, and Penny glanced up to see that they were at her house. *Damn it.* She didn't want to get out and face her annoying brothers, and her sad mom, and perfect, boyfriend-stealing Jamie.

"Dee will be back in two days," Lainie said, putting her hand on Penny's shoulder. "Summer's not over yet."

Penny nodded and slowly got out of the car, waving to everyone as they drove away. Then she headed toward her house, trying to think positive.

There was a Bucket List to finish. A memorial to pull off.

Summer's not over yet.

Maybe it could still be saved.

⋛ 31 ⋚

THE PLAYGROUND LUNCH SPOT SUDDENLY FELT much smaller to Daniella.

Probably because Jules, Adrian, and Margot were all huddled on top of her.

"It's a farewell pile," Adrian explained. "When hugging just doesn't feel affectionate enough."

"I love it," Daniella croaked. "But I also can't breathe."

Everyone crawled off her but stayed close. On the blacktop below, there were still traces of their chalk art that had not yet been erased by rain.

"You guys better come visit me," Adrian said. "If you don't . . . I have a whole gallery of low-key embarrassing photos of us from the summer, and I'm not afraid to post them."

"Maybe we can all meet up at Thanksgiving," Jules suggested.

Daniella perked up. *Thanksgiving.* "Hey, you know, my family usually comes here for the holiday. So yeah, that would work."

"It's a plan," Margot said. "Even if I have to take the train or hitch-hike or something, I'll be there."

The last day of the program had been only a half day, where the students could get feedback on their recital performances and fill out questionnaires about their experiences. Mostly, though, it was a time to say goodbye. Daniella had already packed up most of her things at the apartment so she could hang out with her friends as long as possible.

"Hey. Check it out."

Adrian lifted his chin and they all turned to see Dimitri, the falafel guy, walking toward the play structure, a large brown bag in his arms.

"I hear you finished your music school," he said. "I'm giving you sandwiches for free today."

He handed up the paper bag, and they gave him a round of applause. "Dimitri, you simply rock," Jules said, digging inside.

Dimitri shrugged. "They are just small sandwiches. Not the big ones I sell. I need to make *some* money today."

He turned and started walking back to his cart.

"We'll miss you, Dimitri!" Daniella called. "Thanks for all the awesome lunches this summer!"

Dimitri gave a *forget about it* kind of wave, grunted, and kept walking.

Daniella turned to her friends. "I'm sure he's crying on the inside."

They all laughed and passed around the little foil-wrapped bundles, warm and heavenly-smelling. Daniella watched as the others began to eat, taking in every detail she could. The way Margot would inspect her food before each bite. Jules constantly adjusting the spiked choker they wore every day. Adrian flipping his hair from one side to the other. Pigeons flapping their wings as they landed on the blacktop. A baby in a stroller, crying softly.

Somehow, this had all started to feel like home. Not like a *house* home. But a *me* home. A place where a part of Daniella had always lived, and (hopefully) always would.

"So, what happens when you get back to the beach?" Adrian asked her.

"We're raising money for a memorial bench for Carly. When it's ready, we'll have a ceremony and a little party. Still a few things to plan, so I'll be busy helping Lainie and Penny with that. Oh! I almost forgot!"

Daniella took out her phone and pulled up the video Penny had sent her that morning.

made this music video. hope you like it. OK if we post?

Daniella had watched the video on the subway. It made her sob right there in the middle of morning rush hour and she didn't even care.

"Turns out, my friend Penny is some kind of freaky genius filmmaker," Daniella told her friends as she held out the phone for everyone to see. She pressed play on the video and turned up the volume. Jules, Margot, and Adrian huddled in, smiling as soon as they saw the introduction screen.

When the video was over, they all applauded.

"Is it cool with you guys if we put it on FotoSlam as part of the Bucket List? You're in that last section, so I wanted to make sure."

"Duh," Adrian said.

"Why wouldn't we be cool with it?" Margot asked.

Daniella glanced over at Jules, who was quietly gazing at the phone. "Hello? You okay?" she asked, waving her hand in front of their face.

Jules bit their lip. "It really tells a story, Daniella. Even though I wish you'd shared it from the beginning, I'm happy I know it now . . . and I'm extra happy we got to be, like, part of it."

"Same," Adrian said. "If we all come back to the program next year, can we do the Bucket List with you again?"

It caught Daniella off guard. Next year? Bucket List *again*? She hadn't thought past the summer.

"Yeah, maybe," she said softly, not meeting Adrian's eye.

"I'll take that as a no."

Wait. Stop. I don't want to ruin this.

It was time to be honest for a change.

"I'm sorry," Daniella admitted. "I'd definitely like to come back to the program, but I'm not sure about another Bucket List. We only did this one because Carly had started writing it before she . . . We wanted to do it for her, you know?"

And we barely survived it as friends, Daniella added in her head. Besides, Carly was the only one good at coming up with ideas for the list.

Adrian nodded. "I get it." He paused, then smiled mischievously. "Next year we could come up with our own Glorious Oddballs tradition."

Daniella reached out and hugged him. "I love that idea so much."

"So, what's left on the Bucket List for you to do when you get home?" Jules asked.

Daniella thought for a second. "Well, nobody's kissed a boy yet."

"I thought someone had that covered," Margot said.

"Penny thought she did. But then, she didn't. I don't know the whole story. Carly hated having unfinished items on the list, but she picked a tough one. I guess we'll have to roll it over to next year. I mean, if we *do* do it next year."

"You can move something to the next list?" Jules asked.

"Oh yeah, it's one of our rules," Daniella said. "Carly was obsessed with seeing a humpback whale breach. We try every year but haven't done it yet."

"Will you have time to try again?" Margot asked.

Daniella shrugged. "Hopefully. But some things are just . . . all about luck. So, who knows?"

"Carly will make it happen for you this year," Jules said, taking Daniella's hand. Daniella nodded. She didn't miss that fake world she'd created for her friends, where Carly was still alive. Having their support was a thousand times better.

They sat and ate and talked for as long as they could. Finally, both Jules and Adrian had to leave. They climbed off the play structure one by one, then started hugging one another goodbye.

Don't cry, don't cry, don't cry, Daniella told herself as she was squeezing Jules, then Margot, then Adrian as tight as she could.

"Let's all walk to the subway station together," Margot suggested. They moved as a group, this little cluster of people who were so different on the outside yet forever connected, sharing some mysterious and unique strand of DNA.

Daniella glanced back at the park just once, to soak up a last bit of memory, before putting one foot in front of the other down the sidewalk.

★

"Is this everything?" Uncle Chris asked Daniella as he took her duffel bag and oboe case.

"Yeah," she replied. "And my backpack, but I'll carry that down myself."

"Good," Zoe said. "Let's leave, already! I want to be at FunLand right when it opens."

Tina, Chris, and Zoe were driving Daniella back to Ocean Park Heights, then staying for a week of vacation. They hadn't talked about it, but Daniella knew they were also coming to be part of Carly's memorial.

"Joe called the garage and asked them to bring up the car," Tina told Chris and Zoe as they headed out of the apartment.

Daniella started to follow. When she reached the closed door to Carly's room, she stopped. The sign was still there. COME IN! WE'RE OPEN!

Tina looked over her shoulder at Daniella, then paused, watching her for a moment.

"Do you want to go in and take a look around before we leave?" Tina asked. "When we get back from the shore, I'm planning to pack up some things in there. Not everything. Just enough to make room for my desk."

"Your desk?" Daniella asked, trying to picture where that would even go.

"Yeah, I've decided to start up my graphic design business again. It'll be nice to spend the day working in Carly's room." Aunt Tina paused, swallowed hard. "Like I'm hanging out with her, you know? Maybe some of her creativity will rub off on me."

A shadow flickered across Tina's expression, but then she smiled.

"I'm sure it will," Daniella told her aunt. "And I'm okay. I don't need to see her room before we leave. I already have what I need. Thanks for letting me keep this."

She patted the shell purse slung across her shoulder.

"Of course!" Tina said, her face brightening. "Really, it belongs to you. To all you girls." Her voice cracked a bit at the end.

Daniella took Tina's hand on one side, Zoe's on the other. "Come on," she said. "I can't wait to feel sand on my toes again."

≳ 32 ≲

LAINIE CLOSED THE DOOR OF NANA'S LITTLE OFFICE
at the bakery.

She went to the bookshelf and pulled out the copy of *Be Mine by the
Sea*, one of the trashy paperback romance novels Nana kept there. She
used to have these books at home, but Papa would always borrow them
to read on the boat . . . and then lose them.

Tucked between two pages of *Be Mine by the Sea* was the envelope
Lainie had slowly been filling with cash all summer. She'd just visited
the Sea Spray Café and Anderson's welcome center to collect the past
week's donations. It was time to count and hope, hope, hope this new
batch would put them over the top.

Six hundred seventy, six hundred seventy-one, six hundred
seventy-two . . .

Lainie's heart started racing.

. . . Six hundred ninety-eight, six hundred ninety-nine, seven
hundred.

YES.

She stepped back to admire the money pile and dance out her glee for a few seconds.

Once that was done, she started counting a new pile with the rest of the cash, which ended up being forty-three extra dollars for food and decorations.

Lainie packed the bench fund into a big fresh envelope, then tucked the rest of the money back into Nana's book for later. Next stop: Ocean Park Heights Town Hall.

When she burst into the front of the bakery, Sasha was standing at the espresso machine, pouring foam milk into a cup. She and Lainie were watching the bakery for the last few hours of the day while Nana was at the hospital and Mr. Mason was running errands.

"Hey," Sasha said to Lainie. "I'm practicing how to make different designs with the milk. Does this look like a seashell?"

Sasha put the cup on the counter and Lainie peered in.

"Wow," Lainie said, genuinely surprised. "It totally looks like a seashell. Where did you learn to do that?"

Sasha shrugged. "I watched a couple of online videos on how to make other designs, but this one I just figured out. You think people will like it?"

Lainie blinked. Sasha was actually serious, maybe even *excited*, about decorating lattes and cappuccinos with milk art. Excited looked good on her.

"Super cute, Sasha," Lainie said. "You know, you're a really talented artist."

Sasha raised one eyebrow. "So talented, you keep erasing or

throwing out whatever drawings I do for the bakery?"

Lainie felt her face flush. "That was me being an asshole." She paused. She hadn't meant to say that. But maybe she needed to, because it was like she'd unlatched something inside her. "I hope that once your dad is officially running Dulcie's, you decorate the signs and the memo board and whatever else. It'll keep the bakery . . . special."

Sasha shrugged stiffly, as if she couldn't bear any kind of compliment. Then she zeroed in on the envelope Lainie was holding against her chest.

"Let me guess," Sasha said. "You hit your goal?"

"Yup. I'm on my way to town hall right now to fill out the forms."

"Why are you hugging the money like that? It's disturbing."

Lainie laughed. "I know. I guess I'm really happy and I kind of love this envelope right now."

Sasha smiled and looked her up and down. "I'm glad you're happy, Lainie."

Lainie's heart swelled. "I'm glad that you're glad."

The door opened and a pair of customers walked in.

"Are you going to be okay here on your own for a bit?" she asked Sasha. "I shouldn't be gone long."

Sasha waved Lainie toward the door. "I'll be fine. Go."

She will be fine, Lainie thought as she left the bakery. And then she also thought: *I can't believe I'm thinking that.*

The envelope tucked snugly into her pocket, Lainie rode five long blocks up, three short blocks over, to the peach-colored brick-and-glass Ocean Park Heights Municipal Building. She locked up her skateboard at a rack underneath a flagpole flying the American flag, the New Jersey state flag, and the Ocean Park Heights flag.

Lainie rolled her eyes when she saw the town seal fluttering above her. It was the one thing she never liked about OPH: a blue circle with two very angry-looking jumping fish in the middle. When Lainie was seven, she made her own version of the town seal with colored markers: a yellow smiling sun, an ocean wave, the Ferris wheel, and an ice cream cone, all inside a huge pink heart. Nana had driven her here, to the municipal building, and she'd popped her drawing, along with a letter to the mayor, in the mailbox.

The mayor had written a nice note back, thanking her for her suggestion and promising to consider it. The letter came with a coupon for a free round of golf. Not miniature golf. Regular-size, adult golf. Lainie had been pissed off about that for a year.

She stepped through the double glass doors and approached the front desk.

"Good morning," Lainie said in her best polite, professional voice. "I'm here to purchase a boardwalk memorial bench."

The receptionist, a woman about her mom's age, looked amused. "You'll want to see Mr. Berry. He's down the hall that way, third door on the right."

Lainie thanked her, then headed in the direction the receptionist had pointed. According to the sign, Marcus Berry was the director of recreation facilities. The door was ajar, and Lainie could see someone sitting at the desk, typing on a computer. She took a deep breath and knocked.

"Hi," she said when he looked up.

"Well, hello there," he replied. "How can I help you?"

Lainie stepped into his office. "I'm here to purchase a memorial bench."

Mr. Berry studied Lainie for a moment. Then he shifted position, leaning on his desk and clasping his hands together. "What's your name, young lady?"

Lainie sighed. She hated *young lady*. It was right up there with *sweetheart* and the worst of the worst, *little miss*.

"I'm Alaina."

Mr. Berry nodded as if that would have been his guess. "Well, Alaina, I'm glad to hear you want to purchase a memorial bench. However, I have some unfortunate news. The new benches have all been purchased."

Lainie stared at the red-and-blue stripes on Mr. Berry's tie, trying to make sense of what she'd just heard. "I don't understand."

"We had ten new benches available. Once they were announced, they all got snapped up pretty quickly. We sold the last one about a week ago."

Lainie shook her head. "But I've been raising the money since last month! It took a while, but I came in the second we had enough. Can you double check to see if there are any left?"

"I'm positive there aren't."

Make him understand, Lainie. Go there if you have to.

"The thing is, this was going to be a memorial for my friend. She . . . she died in January."

Mr. Berry looked pained. "I'm sorry for your loss. Really, I am." He paused, then added. "I wish you'd come in earlier to get the form. We'd have reserved a bench for you, and you could have brought us donations as they came in."

Lainie clenched her teeth, locking her mouth shut. If she opened it, she was going to scream. Mr. Marcus Berry didn't look like the kind of guy who could deal with that.

You're so stupid to think you had it all figured out. The regret was like a vise around her heart.

"Okay, I understand," she heard herself say. She also heard the shakiness and polite-pretending in her voice. "Thank you."

Lainie backed out of the room and walked quickly down the hall.

When she got back outside, she wasn't sure what to do next. The plan had been: (1) Go straight to the boardwalk and find the bench they'd given her, then (2) Snap a photo of it, and (3) Send it to Penny and Daniella with the text message, *Come meet me at Carly's bench!*

Now that wasn't going to happen. One more thing the universe decided to take away from her.

"Screw you," Lainie muttered. Then, without thinking but simply *needing* something to do with this red-hot energy that was suddenly everywhere in her body, she kicked the base of the flagpole.

The metal made a whimpery *plonk* noise when the rubber sole of her sneaker hit it.

Lainie kicked again, harder. "That's for the bench," she said.

Another kick. "And for Papa getting hurt."

A car drove by, and Lainie bent down to unlock her skateboard, hoping the driver hadn't seen any of the weird and probably illegal things she was doing.

And wanted to keep doing. She kicked the flagpole again, this time with her other foot. "Here's one for the bakery and the house not being ours anymore."

Lainie paused, breathing hard. She figured she had one more good kick in her, before she broke a toe or got arrested or both. She knew what she wanted to spend it on.

"I freaking hate you for what you did to Carly."

Plonk.

Somewhere in there, Lainie had started crying without realizing. She took a few minutes to catch her breath, wipe tears and snot with the back of her hand. She stuffed the envelope into her pocket, then took out her phone.

She needed to talk to Penny and Daniella. She typed out the message and sent it, then looked up. The woman from the front desk was standing at the glass door of town hall, watching her.

Ugh. How much had she seen?

Lainie waved, hopped onto her skateboard, and got the hell out of there as fast as she could.

≷ 33 ≶

AS DANIELLA WALKED TOWARD THE BEACH TO meet her friends, she tried to figure out how Ocean Park Heights could suddenly be two things at once.

It was home, of course. The place where her house, and her parents, and her school and community were. A pocket of the planet where every street, almost every storefront, held a memory.

Since she'd returned from New York, though, everything about it felt new. As if someone had clicked a refresh button on the entire town, including the air, the sky, and the Atlantic Ocean itself. Was that possible?

Daniella knew she herself had been rebooted and reloaded. Even her walk had changed. When she caught her shadow traveling along with her on the pavement, it was standing straighter. More confident, maybe. More sure of who it was and where it wanted to go.

When the street dead-ended onto the boardwalk, Daniella saw

Penny and Lainie up ahead, waiting for her. She went straight up to Lainie and hugged her.

"I'm sorry, Lainie," Daniella said.

"It's my own stupid fault," Lainie mumbled into Daniella's shoulder.

"Stop," Penny said, swatting Lainie on the back.

"It's true," Lainie said as she pulled out of the hug. "I didn't think all the benches would be taken."

"I get that you're bummed," Penny said. "But there's got to be another way to make a memorial."

"Like what?"

Penny shrugged. "Can we do a search online? I bet there are lots of ideas out there."

"Come on," Daniella said. "Let's take a walk."

Daniella was bummed about the bench, too. She'd been looking forward to visiting it whenever she needed. To sit and imagine Carly was there with her, not simply her name on a plaque but really *with* her in some way.

They started wandering up the boardwalk. When they passed one of the newly installed benches, Lainie glared at it. "I forgot that these would be here," she said. "We should have met up at the Sea Spray or FunLand."

Penny shook her head. "I don't want to go anywhere near Anderson's Beach right now. Dex is probably just getting off work and we might run into him."

"Well, that's fantastic," Daniella said, huffing an exasperated sigh. "So we can't go *anywhere* on the boardwalk? What the heck happened to you guys this summer?"

Lainie shrugged. Penny looked down and scraped her flip-flop across some sand on the concrete.

These next few weeks are totally not going to be what I imagined, Daniella thought. Suddenly the memory of that last morning with all four Summer Sisters unspooled in her head like a high-def movie.

"The jetty," she muttered.

"What?" Penny asked.

"We could go hang out on the jetty," Daniella repeated.

Or was that off-limits, too? They'd never talked about whether they'd go to Rock Island for their Labor Day sunrise this year.

Penny grinned. "Let's do it," she said, and started marching across the beach.

Lainie raised her eyebrows at Daniella and they both followed after Penny.

"I may have been in the city all summer, but I can still run faster than you!" Daniella called to Lainie. She knew Lainie couldn't resist a challenge like that.

"No way," Lainie shouted, speeding up. They both flew past Penny, who laughed and then raced to catch them.

Daniella closed her eyes for a moment as she ran. When was the last time she'd felt the breeze in her hair, the brightness of a wide-open sky above her? Then she heard her friends laughing and knew she was truly home.

When they reached the rocks, all three girls paused, not sure who was going to lead them farther. Had it always been Carly, going first onto the jetty? Was it so automatic that they'd never even thought about it?

"Come on," Daniella said, taking a step onto the first rock. Then another, then another. Lainie and Penny followed. They stayed silent at first, like this was serious business. Then Lainie paused and gazed out at the entrance to the inlet.

"Papa would be bringing his boat in right about now," she said, then bit her lip.

Daniella reached out and squeezed Lainie's shoulder. "Maybe you guys will have a new routine in Florida," she said. "Like, a game or something where you can spend this part of the day together."

Lainie softly laughed. "He said they'll have shuffleboard and bocce ball at their condo."

Penny stepped up beside them. "Sounds . . . fun. Dorky, but fun."

They took one more, big step, the biggest really, and landed on Rock Island. Daniella sat down, felt the spray on her ankles, then drew in a deep breath. Without a word, Lainie lay down on her side, with her head in Daniella's lap. Daniella started stroking her hair, then felt Penny scooch over next to her. Daniella leaned against Penny. They stayed there for a few long minutes, not talking. Not needing to.

Daniella turned away from the water to brush some hair out of her eyes, getting a glimpse of Lainie's grandparents' house and the rides at FunLand in the distance. She could see a few of the newly installed benches at the edge of the beach.

Her eyes tracked over to the boardwalk opposite the jetty. Little sparks of an idea started firing in her head.

"Hey, Lainie?" she asked, poking her finger in Lainie's ear.

"What?" Lainie replied, slapping Daniella's hand away.

"Did you notice that there's no bench right there, across from the jetty?"

Lainie sat up and looked at where Daniella was now pointing. "I didn't notice. But I guess it makes sense. Who wants to sit looking at the jetty? You can't see much of the water from there."

"True," Daniella said, but the sparks were still going off. "But you know . . . I bet that spot has a great view of Rock Island."

"What's your point?" Penny asked.

Daniella paused, trying to form her idea into words. "What if we asked the town about adding another bench? Right there at the jetty. Wouldn't that be the perfect spot for Carly?"

Daniella watched Lainie's face as she processed that suggestion, intrigued at first, but then doubtful.

"They'll probably say no," Lainie said.

"But they might say yes," Penny countered.

"Only one way to find out," Daniella added. "It can't hurt to ask. And if it *is* a no, we'll go from there. Okay?"

Lainie nodded, then stared at Daniella, amused.

"What?" Daniella asked.

"Nothing. It's just, I've never seen you be all 'fight the power' like that."

"For real," Penny added, grinning wide. "We're glad you're back, Dee."

Lainie's phone dinged, and she glanced at it. "It's Nana. She wants you both to come over to the bakery and take home some stuff."

Penny jumped up and quickly made the leap-step to the next rock. "Good. I'm starving."

$\star$

As they made their way up the boardwalk, Daniella felt Lainie tug on the back of her shirt.

"I almost forgot this," Lainie said, then reached into her purse and pulled out a crumpled plastic bag. It had three red licorice shoelaces at the bottom, half drowning in colored sugar and chocolate dust. "Your favorite, right?"

Daniella took the bag. "You saved this from Candy Universe?"

Lainie nodded. "I know that was like a month ago, and the laces are probably gross by now . . ."

"Thank you!" Daniella pulled out a lace and stuffed it in her mouth. "Mmm, not gross at all."

Suddenly Penny froze in her tracks and held up a hand. "Hey . . . guys?"

"What?"

Lainie and Daniella turned. A man in a plaid flannel jacket leaned against the boardwalk fence, reading his paper while sipping on a bright yellow smoothie. His hair was combed back and his small, round sunglasses perched on the end of his nose. Gray pants, black socks, yellow wing-tip shoes.

Grumpy Gus.

"It's a sign," Penny whispered, her breath hot in Daniella's ear.

"Of *what*?" Lainie whispered back to her.

"I don't know." Penny shrugged.

Daniella thought about that line on the Bucket List, Carly's slanted handwriting. She could picture Carly giggling to herself as she wrote it. *Take a photo booth pic with Grumpy Gus.*

Or maybe Carly was daring herself to finally talk to him after all those years of being terrified.

Penny took a deep breath and stood up straighter. "I'll go ask him," she said, "but you both have to come with me."

"Wait, seriously?" Lainie said.

"Deal," Daniella added.

Penny cleared her throat and approached Grumpy Gus. Daniella had to admit, the smoothie definitely made him less intimidating.

"Um . . . hello . . . sir," Penny said softly.

Grumpy Gus looked up from his paper. "What?" he muttered, squinting at Penny, as if she were standing fifty feet away instead of right there.

"Hi, I'm Penny. These are my friends Daniella and Lainie."

Gus's eyes slid from Penny to Daniella to Lainie. "Congratulations," he said.

Words started tumbling out of Penny's mouth. "We've seen you around for years, and we know your name is Gus, and you've lived in OPH your whole life—my friend Daniella here has, too—but we've never learned your last name."

He looked at Penny for a long moment, then said, "Waverly."

Penny smiled. "Really? That's, like, a perfect name for someone who lives at the shore. It's nice to finally meet you, Gus Waverly."

Wow, Daniella thought. *Penny gained some mad people skills this summer.*

"So here's kind of a funny story . . ." Penny continued.

She went on to explain to Gus about Carly and the Bucket List. Daniella could see something in Gus's eyes. He was honestly interested, even amused, as Penny described the Titanic sundae, and how one day Lainie was so mad that she accidentally won the giant rainbow llama, and about how they'd never seen a humpback whale breach.

Then Penny went for it. She told him about the photo booth. He stared stone-faced at her, then at Daniella, then at Lainie. Finally, he stood straight up, walked to a nearby trash can, threw out his paper and smoothie cup, and turned to them.

"Come on, then," he said, and started walking up the boardwalk.

Penny looked at Daniella and Lainie, her eyes wide as frisbees. *OMG,* she mouthed. Then they all followed Gus up the boardwalk to the arcade, and inside to the photo booth.

By unanimous vote, they chose the Galaxy background.

By another unanimous vote, they posed for one serious photo, one smiling photo, one goofy photo.

Gus stood in the back and the girls crouched down below him.

"One more!" he said after the third photo was taken. "How about peace signs?"

Peace signs it was.

They piled out of the booth and waited for the photos to slide into the little compartment.

"You saved the day, Gus," Penny said. "Thank you so, so much. Things were looking bleak before we ran into you."

"Oh yeah?" Gus asked. "Why is that?"

"It's a long story," Daniella told him.

"I like stories," he said.

Lainie, who'd been mostly quiet, suddenly piped up. "We've been planning all summer to buy one of those new memorial benches for Carly. I finally had enough donations and went today to fill out the form, but every bench has already been claimed."

"But we have an idea," Daniella added. "There's a spot across from the jetty that doesn't have a bench, and it would actually be the perfect spot for Carly. Or for, you know, her bench."

Gus peered down the boardwalk, toward the jetty. He nodded slowly.

"Let me make a phone call," he said.

"Huh?" Penny asked.

"To the mayor," Gus added, matter-of-factly. "She and I . . . we go way back. High school. We used to surf together, actually."

Daniella glanced at Penny and Lainie. *Was this really happening?*

"I bet she'd meet with you. And then you can do your thing with that story, which is one of the few things I've heard in a long time that didn't piss me off. If you can talk me into one of those photo booths, I'm sure you can talk the mayor into adding an extra bench where you want it."

Gus bent down and pulled out the photo booth strips. "Hey," he said. "Look at us! I'm going to keep this right here."

Then he tucked one of the strips into the inside pocket of his jacket and patted it, as if it were a newfound treasure.

≥ 34 ≤

OKAY, PENNY. THEY DIDN'T MAKE YOU EMPLOYEE
of the Month for nothing.

Gus—Penny wondered if they could even call him Grumpy Gus
anymore, since he'd been the opposite of grumpy to them—had called
the mayor like he'd promised. The girls had a meeting scheduled for
the next day.

Penny didn't have any clothes at the shore that were meeting-with-
a-mayor appropriate, so she borrowed a dress from her mom. It was
a little tight in the bust, which was horrifying. She turned around in
front of the mirror in her mom's bedroom, trying to figure out what to
do. A sweater? A different dress?

The door opened and Jamie poked her head in.

"What is it?" Penny snapped.

Ever since Teen Night, Penny had been avoiding Jamie as much as
possible. When she couldn't, she made it clear she wanted nothing to
do with her. She didn't want to know what Jamie was doing, or where

she was going, and especially who she was with.

"I hear you have a big meeting," Jamie said. "I have something that would look great on you."

"No, thanks," Penny said.

Jamie stared at her for a second. "Fine," she said, and turned to leave. Then she froze, spun back around, and came all the way into the room. "Can I ask you what I've done, exactly, to make you hate me?"

Penny kept her eyes on the mirror. "I don't hate you," she told Jamie, but it came out 100 percent fake. "I have to go."

Penny marched past Jamie, down the hall, and through the front door, grabbing a sweater from the coatrack. She paused on the porch, then heard the screen door slam behind her.

She didn't look back when she asked, "Jamie, why are you following me?"

"Because you've barely talked to me for days. The least you could do is tell me why."

"You know why."

"I really don't!"

Penny sighed and turned around. Jamie looked truly confused. *God, is she really that clueless?*

"Okay, fine," Penny began. "I know I was the one who broke up with Dex, but that was actually really, really hard for me. I couldn't be around you. But I guess I'm feeling better about it now. You and he can go out, date, whatever. Get married, for all I care."

Jamie was silent, frowning at Penny. Clearly baffled. Then she did something Penny didn't expect: She started laughing hysterically.

Penny backed down the porch steps. She couldn't believe Jamie could be so insensitive. Or was she just cruel?

"No!" Jamie cried out. "Don't leave! I'm sorry, I was just surprised."

"By *what*?" Penny asked.

Jamie sunk down onto one of the porch steps. "You broke up with Dex because of *me*?"

"Mostly, yeah. I didn't want him to dump me first. He clearly has a crush on you, so, I mean, go ahead. Go for it. I'm not stopping you."

"Penny," Jamie said slowly, staring right into Penny's eyes. "I don't like Dex. I mean, I like him, he's a great guy. But I don't *like him* like him."

Penny laughed a sarcastic laugh. "Um, it totally seems like you do. And he definitely likes you back."

Jamie shook her head, then took a deep breath and exhaled. "I can see how you'd think that. But actually . . . I don't like Dex that way because I . . . um . . . only like *girls* that way. And he isn't a girl." After a pause, she raised her eyebrows and added, "Although he does have better hair than most girls I know."

Some machine inside Penny's head started spinning extra fast, trying to make sense of this information. "Wait, what? You're only into girls?"

Now Jamie smiled. Sat up taller.

"Yup. I sort of thought you knew. I've been out for a while. And I've had a crush on Layla since that Fourth of July party. I finally got up the nerve to ask her out and we're going to FunLand later."

Penny sat down on the step next to Jamie. "So wait, why were you and Dex hanging out so much that day on the beach?"

"Oh . . . that? Dex noticed a Pride pin on my bag and asked me if I was out to my family. His sister is dating a girl and doesn't know how to tell their parents. He knew it was an awkward question, but his sister has really been struggling and he's desperate to help her. I thought that was really sweet."

Penny found herself sighing deeply. Yes, it was really sweet. And it sounded totally like Dex.

"I'm such an ass," she said, putting her face in her hands. "I'm sure he hates me."

Now she was on the verge of crying. For Penny, crying always felt like a cliff that you should stay far away from, unless you really needed to throw yourself off it. When she'd heard about Carly, for instance. But free-falling like that wasn't going to help her at this moment.

"I doubt it," Jamie said.

"I should go," Penny murmured. "But thank you. And I'm sorry for being a horrible person to you."

Jamie smiled. "I get it. We're all good."

Penny stood up slowly. "Have fun on your date."

"Thanks. And good luck to you and your friends."

"Thanks!" Penny grabbed her bike from the driveway and started riding toward town hall.

Is it possible to feel better about something, she wondered, *but also worse about it at the same time?*

★

Penny recognized the skateboard and one of the bikes locked up in front of town hall. Daniella and Lainie must be waiting inside. They still had ten minutes before their appointment, which meant there was a little time for Penny to stop into a restroom and make sure she wasn't about to burst out of her dress.

She slid her bike next to Daniella's, closed up the lock, and started toward the entrance.

Where there was a boy waiting.

And the boy was Dex.

Penny drew in a breath, not sure if she was seeing clearly.

"Hey," Dex said.

"Hey," Penny replied.

"I just got a text from Jamie. She said you were on your way here, and I should come talk to you ASAP."

Penny wanted to slap Jamie. Or hug her. Maybe both.

"ASAP is right. How did you get here so fast?"

Dex smiled. "My place is right around the corner. I never got a chance to invite you over."

He paused, staring at Penny. She stared back. What was she supposed to do next? Then Penny thought about Daniella in New York City, making new friends and composing her first original music. Lainie, figuring out how to coexist with, and then actually like, a girl she'd started off hating. Penny realized she'd also stepped out of her comfort zone lately. Doing so well at her job, and of course . . . Grumpy Gus. This meeting wouldn't even be happening if Penny hadn't had the guts to talk to him.

"Come here," Penny said, taking Dex by the hand, leading him away from the building entrance and toward the flagpole. "Can I explain a few things?"

"Please," he said.

"My parents have been fighting all summer," she told him. "My dad might be having an affair, and I'm worried they're going to get divorced.

I'm not telling you that so you'll feel sorry for me. It's because . . . I've never had a boyfriend before, and every minute we were together, I couldn't believe anyone would like me. Especially someone as amazing as you. It felt like, any minute you'd realize you'd made a mistake and find someone beautiful. Like Jamie. Or I mean, not Jamie because now I know Jamie's not into guys, but that kind of person."

Dex dropped his head back and looked up at the flags fluttering above them.

"Penny," he said. "*You* are beautiful. But that's not why I like you. We just . . . click. Everything feels easy and fun when we're hanging out, and I never want to it to stop."

Penny narrowed her eyes. "Back up a second," she said. "You think I'm beautiful?"

Dex did something Penny didn't know was Dex-like. He blushed and let his bangs fall over his face like he was trying to hide. "Yes."

"You're crazy," she blurted out.

"Maybe. But not about that," he said, shrugging. "Can we try this again?"

This question filled Penny with a sweet kind of sadness, her heart in her throat.

"But the summer's going to be over soon. What's the point?"

Dex reached out and touched her arm. "Every day we have together is the point. Plus, we don't live that far apart. We could meet up on weekends."

It felt too good, too maybe-amazing, to be possible.

"Long distance relationships never work . . ." she muttered, echoing a line from something she'd heard or read somewhere.

Suddenly Dex was putting a hand on either side of Penny's face, drawing it closer to his. Then he kissed her. Quickly, but deeply.

He pulled away and raised his eyebrows at Penny as if to say, *Is this okay?*

She answered him by kissing him back. It didn't feel at all like the pillow she'd been practicing on since she was eleven. This felt like . . . a silent conversation. Questions, and answers, then questions again. His lips were warm and soft, and Penny could feel that he was smiling as they continued to kiss. She felt pulses of electricity in her limbs and fingers and toes.

After a minute, they broke away from each other and exchanged a raw, disbelieving look. Then they both laughed.

"I'm sorry it took me so long to do that," Dex said. "Maybe if I had, you would have known for sure how I felt. But I was waiting for the perfect spot and the right moment."

Penny glanced around at the bike rack, the town hall building, the flagpole.

"Good choice, Dex," she teased.

He grinned. "I think so."

Penny grinned back. *Is it rude to kiss him again right now?*

Then the front door of the building squeaked open. It was Lainie.

"Are you guys *done*?" she asked. "They're calling us into the meeting!"

⋛ 35 ⋚

WHEN THE MAYOR SAT DOWN AND ASKED THEM what she could do for "you girls," both Penny and Lainie looked at Daniella. In the past, they let Carly speak for all of them in any situation. *Am I that person now?* Daniella thought.

"Thanks so much for meeting with us, Mayor Donato," she began.

"Please, call me Mayor Toni," the mayor insisted. "Gus said it was important, and he never thinks anything is important, so now the curiosity is killing me."

Daniella nodded. She opened her purse and pulled out a handful of photos she'd printed out at the drugstore that morning—found the one they'd all taken at the jetty the year before, on Labor Day.

"This is us with our friend Carly," she said, sliding the photo toward Mayor Toni. "She was my cousin, actually. And she died last January."

Mayor Toni glanced down at the photo, a shadow crossing her face. "I'm so sorry to hear that."

Daniella gripped her bag a little tighter in her lap. "Carly loved

308

Ocean Park Heights, and she spent every summer here. So Lainie had this amazing idea to buy one of the new memorial benches for Carly, and she started planning a really special ceremony. It took a while to raise the money, but a lot of people chipped in. Lainie's grandmother is Dulcie from the bakery and they put out a collection jar. My parents own the Sea Spray and lots of customers donated. Anderson's collected, too. But by the time we finally had enough, all the benches were claimed."

"Ah . . ." Mayor Toni said sadly.

"We were really upset and disappointed. But then we noticed that there isn't a bench across from the jetty. Right here."

Daniella slid another photo across the desk.

"Which seems kind of funny," she continued. "Because the jetty was a special place to us. To Carly. We'd go out there every Labor Day morning and watch the sunrise."

"Every year?" the mayor asked, impressed.

"Yeah, it's part of this Bucket List thing we always do."

Daniella took the shell purse out of her bag, then the Bucket List out of the shell purse. She held it up so Mayor Toni could see it.

The mayor looked impressed. "I see a lot of check marks there."

Daniella smiled, feeling oddly proud. "Carly wrote this year's list before she died, and I found it. We started off the summer doing the list for her." She paused, glancing at her friends. "I think somewhere along the way, we were doing it for us."

Mayor Toni got a faraway look in her eye, then picked up the two photos from her desk. She looked from one to the other, back and forth. Then she put them down and placed her hands flat on the desk surface.

"I'm going to give you some good news, and some bad news. The good news is that I think there should be a bench at this spot, and it should be a memorial for your friend."

The girls glanced at one another, wide-eyed. *We did it!*

"Now the bad news," Mayor Toni said. "The benches we just installed were ordered a while ago. They take a long time to arrive."

"How long, exactly?" Penny asked.

"Six weeks, give or take. Can you have your memorial in the fall?"

Daniella felt the excitement sliding away from her. She wanted to yell, *Hell no.* But that would be rude. She cleared her throat.

"The fall is kind of . . . well . . . Lainie lives, like, four hours away. And . . ."

Mayor Toni shrugged. "Driving four hours isn't too bad. For a special occasion."

"Summer is our time here, together," Penny said, coming to Daniella's rescue. "It was our time with Carly. We were Summer Sisters."

Lainie finally spoke. "We *are* Summer Sisters."

Slowly, the mayor broke into a grin. "Exactly," she said.

"Huh?" Daniella said, before she could stop herself.

Mayor Toni picked up the phone and dialed a number. "Hi, Marcus. Can you come into my office right now?"

She hung up, then looked expectantly at the door. Which then opened.

"Mr. Berry," Lainie said, as if surprised.

"Marcus," Mayor Toni said. "We're going to add an extra bench across from the jetty. It needs to be here as soon as possible. Call all over the East Coast and see who has one ready. I don't care how far away it is. We'll send someone in a town van to pick it up. Heck, I'll do it myself if nobody else is available."

"All right, then!" Mr. Berry looked at the girls, confused or impressed—maybe both—then left.

"I love doing that," the mayor said, laughing. "Hey, do you know who helped me get elected?"

She spun her chair around, grabbed a framed photo from the credenza behind her desk, and propped it up for the girls to see. In the picture, a college-aged Mayor Toni posed on the beach with two other girls.

"*My* Summer Sisters."

⋛ 36 ⋜

LAINIE HAD SET HER ALARM FOR 6:30 A.M., BUT when her eyes fluttered open, it was still halfway dark outside her window. The clock read 5:42.

Once again, her brain had set its own alarm. The memorial was starting at 2:00 p.m. and the to-do list was miles long. Biscuits, breads, and cookies to bake. Fruit and cheese to cut up. Sasha said she would pick up all the drinks donated by the Sea Spray Café, then she and Nana were going to help Lainie with food prep.

She couldn't just lie in bed going over all these plans. Lainie got up and tiptoed into the living room, which was flickering with light and shadows from the television. She made out the slouched figure of her grandfather on the couch.

"Papa?" she whispered.

He turned. "Mija, you're up early."

"Not as early as you," Lainie said, then headed into the kitchen. "Do you need something to eat? Or drink?"

"Surprise me."

Lainie poured two glasses of orange juice and grabbed two buns from a bag of Dulcie's baked goods. Nana always brought home whatever hadn't sold that day. It was never much, but usually the right amount for the three of them. Lainie carried the food to the couch and handed her grandfather a glass. Then she sat down and raised her own to his.

"Cheers," Lainie said, hoping this would make Papa laugh.

It did.

Her grandfather had only been home a few days, but it was hard for Lainie to see him like this. Low-energy. Quiet. Serious and a little out of it. The doctors had told them he might act differently for a while, as if he'd had a personality change. Lainie knew he was sad about not being able to take out the boat anymore. Papa didn't belong on land all the time. He was probably part sea creature.

"I'm sorry you can't come to the memorial," Lainie said. "But Penny's going to take video of the whole thing and turn it into a little movie."

Papa smiled. "Once I'm cleared to start going out for walks, your bench is the first place I'll go."

Your bench. It was Carly's bench. Or really, everyone's bench. The whole world's. Whoever wanted to sit there. But secretly, Lainie did often think of it as hers.

"You know I can't mind my own business," Papa said. "I have a little surprise planned for you and Penny and Daniella. For later, after the memorial."

"What kind of surprise?" Lainie asked.

Papa smiled, a true smile she hadn't seen in a while. "The *surprise* kind."

"Ha-ha," she said as he booped her on the nose, just like he used to do when she was little.

Then they sat and ate in silence, watching an episode of an old TV sitcom.

When Lainie had finished eating, she stepped out onto the screened porch to double-check all the supplies that were being stored there. There were plates, napkins, paper cups, and crackers. Daniella's parents had also sent over a big plastic tub of cotton candy. Lainie could see the pink-and-blue colors through the translucent sides of the container. The memory of that last morning on the jetty was like a wave knocking her over. She hadn't thought about the cotton candy in months.

Lainie glanced up, out toward the water and the brightening sky above it. Then back at the cotton candy.

They matched almost perfectly.

You don't have time for any new ideas, Lainie told herself. *Don't even think what you're about to think.*

But she couldn't help it.

$\star$

The sky was now striped with wide, flat clouds, and a slight breeze kept cycling through. The kind that felt amazing on your face and arms when you needed it most.

For Lainie, the weather was perfect.

She pulled a wagon with the last load of food from the house, down the boardwalk and over to the bench. She'd balanced a big plastic container on top of the stack of boxes and bins and kept looking over her shoulder to make sure it wasn't about to tumble off. Lainie wasn't sure the goods inside it would survive the fall.

Then she turned the corner and there it was: Carly's bench. Mayor Toni had sent over some staff from the parks department to set up chairs on the sand and two tables on the edge of the boardwalk.

Sasha was standing at the bench, a paintbrush in her hand.

"What are you doing?" Lainie called as she drew closer.

"One spot doesn't look right," Sasha replied. "I was touching it up."

The bench was officially the most colorful one in Ocean Park Heights. When Lainie had asked Sasha if she'd decorate the bench for them, the first thing she'd done was burst into tears. Then she asked to see the Bucket List, along with Bucket Lists from past summers. She'd taken notes and given them back and told Lainie to trust her.

Now the bench was covered in pictures representing items on all those lists. The Dragon Coaster and the Delusion at FunLand. The Titanic ice cream sundae. Beach cruiser bikes and candy and Silly String. A microphone. Ocean waves. Papa's fishing boat.

Sasha had also asked about things that were especially *Carly*, so to one side of the memorial plaque on the bench's back, she'd painted a camera; on the other side, a sewing machine. When Lainie had first seen it the day before, she'd been speechless. Seeing it again today, right before the memorial, she found she still had no words.

"Sasha," she said. "This looks . . . I can't . . ."

"I know," Sasha said, taking a few steps back to survey her work. "I'm pretty happy with it."

"It's better than I could have imagined," Lainie said, hoping those words would be enough for the time being. "Thank you. Like, a million times over."

"You're welcome," Sasha said. "But also, thank *you*."

Lainie glanced at Sasha, to see if she was being sarcastic. It looked like she wasn't. "For what?" Lainie asked.

"This sounds weird, because these Bucket Lists were your and your friends' thing. But I'm glad you invited me to be part of it in some way. While I was painting this, I started to think OPH could feel like home."

When Sasha said the word *home*, Lainie felt that familiar flare of jealousy. She always would. But she also felt a bittersweet kind of happiness for Sasha.

"I hope you find your people here," Lainie said.

Sasha nodded. They were quiet for a few moments, the tide crashing in the distance. Finally, Sasha pointed to the wagon and said, "Can I help?"

They went to work unpacking the food, drinks, plates, and napkins. Lainie had drawn a little picture of how she wanted everything arranged on the tables. Sasha laughed at it, but then went ahead and followed Lainie's vision.

"What's in that white container?" Sasha asked Lainie as she was unloading the cart.

"You'll see," Lainie said, then tucked the container underneath the table.

✶

Later, as Mayor Toni gave a short welcome speech, a voice inside Lainie's head started whispering advice. *Remember this*, it said. *You made this happen and it's all perfect. Enjoy it now.*

So as she sat in her chair in the front row, Lainie started taking mental snapshots of every part of the memorial ceremony. Floating inside each moment, absorbing it, for as long as she could.

Mayor Toni talking about how the bench happened, and how proud she was to welcome such a beautiful and unique addition to the Ocean Park Heights boardwalk.

Daniella playing *Summer Without*, solo on her oboe, and it sounding just as gorgeous and powerful that way. Daniella looking gorgeous and powerful herself.

Penny getting up to read a poem by Emily Dickinson that made her think of Carly. Dex had squeezed her hand so tight when she got up from her chair. When she came back, he put his arm around her.

All the faces gathered on the beach. Nana, sitting with Sasha and Mr. Mason. Carly's parents and sister, all huddled close together, holding hands. Daniella's mom and dad. And in the back, next to the mayor, Grumpy Gus.

Then, after everyone had spoken, Dex pulling out a huge box of bubble bottles from under a table and passing them out to everyone.

Even when Lainie had to get up in front of everyone, she focused on the here and now. Not planning. Not worrying. Simply . . . present.

"Okay, all!" she called out, scanning the faces and the hands holding bubble wands and the waiting sky. "One . . . two . . . three!"

A *whoosh* sound from so many people blowing breaths at once. The bubbles rose quickly, some tiny and some huge, then got carried by the breeze away from the beach.

"We love you, Carly!" Penny shouted. Others echoed her, a chorus of voices rising into the air.

When the bubbles had all popped, Lainie turned to Daniella and Penny. They hugged silently, no words needed.

Then Lainie drew away and said, "Now we eat!"

Sasha and Nana had already set up most of the food, and people started gathering around it. Lainie pulled her mystery container out of hiding and placed it on a table. She turned to Penny, Daniella, Nana, and Sasha, who were all watching with curiosity.

"*Finally,*" Sasha said, rolling her eyes.

"I've been learning and baking all the Dulcie's recipes this summer," Lainie said. "You know, I wanted to preserve them so I could bake them anytime I wanted. But I didn't get a chance to make up anything of my own, until this morning."

Lainie popped the lid off the container.

It was filled with blue-and-pink sandwich cookies, each stuffed with blue or pink cream in the middle. Lainie pulled one out and held it up.

"I'm calling them Cotton Candy Sunrise Sandwiches," she said.

Penny reached out a hand. "Gimme."

"Oh God, Lainie," Daniella said. "They look amazing!"

Lainie held up the container so everyone could grab one and tried to take in what came next.

"I can't believe you just came up with these," Daniella exclaimed after the first bite.

"This is all I'm eating from now on," Penny mumbled through a full mouthful.

"Mija," Nana added. "These are excellent, even if you did use a little too much sugar."

"Thanks," Lainie replied. "I was thinking I could work on them a little more when I get home. Then maybe I could start my own little business. Making and selling these somehow, and if it's okay with you, a few of the Dulcie's recipes."

Nana reached out and stroked Lainie's forehead with her thumb. "If you don't do that, I will be very, very angry with you."

"Pardon me." A man in a baseball cap was suddenly standing next to Nana. It took Lainie a moment, but she recognized him as one of Papa's friends.

"Jimmy!" Nana said to him. "How are you?"

"I'm good, Dulcie. How's Arturo doing?"

"Better," Nana said. "Not one hundred percent, but better."

"He was well enough to hire me for a private boat trip," Jimmy said, slapping his hands together expectantly and looking at Lainie.

Lainie frowned, confused, then remembered Papa's sneaky comment about a *surprise*. "A boat trip for who?" she asked, even though she had an instant hunch about the answer.

Jimmy grinned. "You and your friends. I do whale watches. We can go any evening you want, but the whales are extremely active this week. The sooner, the better."

Lainie and Nana exchanged a smile. "Would you give me one minute?" she said to Jimmy. "I'll be right back."

Lainie rushed over to Penny and Daniella. As promised, she was back in a minute—less, even—and addressed Jimmy.

"Question for you," she began. "Can we go, like, now?"

⸘ 37 ⸘

DANIELLA HUNG HER BARE FEET OVER THE SIDE OF the boat, her toes skimming the surface of the water. She loved thinking about how, with even that slight touch, she was connected to everything underneath the surface.

Then she tipped her head back and closed her eyes. *Carly should be here*, a voice inside her said. That familiar voice she could never escape. Now, for the first time, she had an answer for it.

Yes, she should. But it's going to be okay.

"Hey," Penny said as she sat down next to Daniella, kicking Daniella's feet with hers. "Jimmy just got off the radio with some other boats. He says there's a pod a few minutes away."

"Fingers crossed," Daniella said.

Lainie sat down on the other side of Daniella and handed her another Cotton Candy Sunrise Sandwich. Daniella took a bite, then passed it to Penny.

"Do you think we'll actually see a breach?" Lainie asked. "I was trying to remember how many times we've tried in the past."

"At least five or six," Penny said. "Remember how pissed off Carly would get, that we couldn't make it happen? I still don't understand why it was so important to her."

"I think I finally figured it out," Daniella said. "Remember how we learned that whales breach because they're trying to get rid of parasites that are making their skin itchy? But most people think they're jumping for joy?"

"Yeah," Lainie said. "It's kind of funny."

"I think for Carly, that was a lot like how everyone saw her as this incredibly strong, happy, perfect person. But I learned from Aunt Tina that she had trouble with stress and anxiety and not feeling good enough. Like anyone else, I guess."

They stared out at the horizon, letting that settle. Penny handed the remains of the cookie back to Lainie, who finished it off.

"You know, even if we strike out again," Lainie began, "I can't think of a better way to say goodbye to Ocean Park Heights. I wouldn't want to be here with anyone else."

Daniella frowned. "What do you mean, *say goodbye*?"

"Well, even if I come visit next year, it won't be the same."

"Why would you only *visit*?" Daniella asked.

Lainie opened her mouth to say something but seemed to be stuck for words.

"Oh my God, Dee, don't torture her like that!" Penny said, swatting Daniella on the shoulder. "Tell her!"

"Tell me what?"

Daniella finally let out the smile she'd been holding in. "My parents want me to invite you to come stay with us next summer, for as long as you want. I still have the trundle bed in my room and it's been lonely without Carly. Even if I do the music academy again and I'm not here the whole time, they're happy to host you. Maybe Mr. Mason would even hire you at Dulcie's."

Lainie's jaw dropped. "That. Would. Be. Incredible."

She gave Daniella the biggest sideways-hug Daniella had ever received.

"I mean, thank you," Lainie said. "And thank your parents. I'll definitely take you up on that, although I'm not sure how long I'd stay."

"You wouldn't come for the whole summer?" Penny asked.

Lainie shrugged. "Maybe. Maybe not. If I really can start a baking business back home, who knows what next year will be like. You guys might be busy, too, you know."

"True," Daniella said, then thought, *Now we know how much can change in a year.* Time was speeding up and warping. Everything about their lives was morphing faster in a month than it had in a year back when they were younger.

"Hey, girls!" Jimmy shouted from the top deck. "We're coming up on the pod! Get ready!"

Daniella, Penny, and Lainie stood up and slowly moved to the seating area at the stern of the boat. Penny took out her phone, preparing to shoot video.

Daniella glanced at the sky and crossed her fingers.

★

An hour later, the boat was motoring back to Ocean Park Heights.

Daniella curled up in her bench seat and let the wind whip up the beginning of tears in her eyes. She couldn't believe they'd failed. Again.

"Where's the list?" Penny asked her.

"Where do you think?" Daniella said, patting the shell purse she'd had strung over one shoulder since they'd climbed on board.

"Hand it over."

"Why? We're not done with it yet."

"Daniella," Lainie said, moving closer to her on the bench. "We are. We saw a lot of beautiful whale fins and tails and even some noses. It was great. But we're not trying again."

Daniella caught Lainie and Penny exchanging a loaded look.

"So you guys are outvoting me on this?" she asked.

"Yes," Penny replied. "Hand it over so we can sign our names."

"No! Don't you want to do this for Carly?"

"We *tried*, for Carly," Lainie said. "Don't you think that's enough? I think all that matters now is that we keep doing Bucket Lists every year, and we keep doing them together."

"The Bucket List was Carly's thing," Daniella murmured.

"You know that's not true," Penny said. "Not anymore."

Penny got up and went to talk to Jimmy. He let her take the wheel for a minute as he went belowdecks. Penny turned to Daniella and Lainie and pointed at the wheel, waving and grinning.

"Hey!" she shouted. "Should I floor it?"

"Nooo!" Daniella screeched.

"Don't you dare!" Lainie added.

They were all still laughing when Jimmy came back above deck and handed something to Penny.

"Here," Penny said when she came back to their seats. She slapped a yellow legal pad down in front of them. "The purple pen, please."

Daniella reached into the shell purse and handed over the pen. She and Lainie watched as Penny wrote in big letters across the top:

SUMMER SISTERS BUCKET LIST
10th Grade

Next summer. Daniella had almost forgotten there would be one. But it was out there, waiting for them underneath a layer of fall, winter, and spring. Waiting for them to arrive and shape it into something. Molding new patches around the *forever* parts.

"I have an idea," Penny said. "How about, *See an arena concert without any parents.*"

Daniella couldn't help but smile. She'd always wanted to do that. Maybe go up to the Meadowlands to see one of her favorite pop artists.

"I like that, Penny," Lainie said.

"Me too," Daniella agreed. "Put it down."

Penny scribbled in that first item. "What else?"

They were quiet for a bit, each lost in their own brainstorm, bobbing up and down with the motion of the boat. The ocean, reminding them that they were truly standing still.

"Oh my God!" Daniella said. "I just thought of a great one."

Penny handed her the paper and pen. Daniella took it.

And she started writing.

﹥ Acknowledgments ﹤

DANIELLA, LAINIE, PENNY, AND CARLY CAME INTO
my life at the height of the Covid-19 pandemic. At a time when, in our
real world, we were all struggling to stay connected and grow in a new
normal, I was writing about young people who were . . . all struggling
to stay connected and grow in a new normal. In different ways, but also
not really. I'm grateful to the Summer Sisters for helping me explore
that space when I needed it most.

My editor at Hyperion, Kieran Viola, has cultivated this story since
it was the shadow of a seed of an idea. I owe much to her deep understanding of these characters, their individual journeys . . . and the
particularly timeless joys of beach-town summers.

Jamie Weiss Chilton has been in my corner for thirteen years, and
I can't ask for a better agent/cheerleader/advocate/friend. We live on
opposite coasts but in my mind, we meet for a fancy afternoon coffee
every week.

Thank you to Terry Smith, whose experiences and insights as a music educator helped shape the Future Forward Music Academy. Giant shout-out to all those Facebook people who chimed in with "teenage summer" writing playlist suggestions and the juicy details behind them.

Big love to my family and my circle of fellow Glorious Oddballs for supporting me in whatever way I needed on any particular day. Especially my daughter Clea, who helped me brainstorm a key story line while we were on a summer road trip, to visit one of her long-distance "sisters from another mister," no less.

And finally, because I really need to park this somewhere, thank you to that claw machine game at the Fantasy Island arcade in Beach Haven, New Jersey. I never, ever win stuff. When the Squishmallow puppy I wanted dropped down the prize chute, I knew everything was going to be okay.